JET III

VENGEANCE

Russell Blake

First Edition

ISBN: 978-1484814932

Published by

Reprobatio Limited

AUTHOR'S NOTE

JET III – Vengeance is a work of fiction, and any resemblance of characters in it to real people or organizations is strictly coincidental. As far as I know, the Mossad and CIA are honest, hardworking organizations above reproach – however, that doesn't make for a very compelling action/adventure thriller, so I've taken some literary liberties and imagined organizations that are riddled with corruption.

The entire *JET* series is an over-the-top romp with an unstoppable female protagonist. If you're looking for reality, or *Sophie's Choice*, this ain't it. If you're looking for a pure adrenaline-filled thrill ride that's unapologetically larger than life, you've come to the right place.

Yemen is the poorest country in the region, plagued by ongoing civil wars and tribal strife, and many of the areas outside of the capital of Sana'a are dangerous to the point of being a death sentence for those foolhardy enough to venture there. That said, it is also a country of remarkable beauty, a study in contradictions. I have chosen to focus more on the ugly than the sublime, however, as again, a portrayal of the postcard spots doesn't make for much of a thriller.

The situation in the Middle East is, and has always been, complex, as has America's relationship with many of the players. Iran was a bastion of U.S. support until the Shah's government fell from favor with the population it governed, and then a fundamentalist regime took over and it became the enemy. Iraq was for decades an ally, throughout Saddam Hussein's rule; then one day it wasn't, and he was the devil. Saudi Arabia is counted as an ally, and yet is also the largest terrorist financier in the world. And so on. It's complicated. I have tried to simplify some things that are essentially complex. Hopefully you'll allow that literary conceit.

PROLOGUE

Two weeks before, Alatfain Valley, Yemen

The battered gold-tone Toyota Land Cruiser ripped down the dirt road, throwing up a cloud of yellow dust as it approached the desolate hamlet, which was deserted except for a Mercedes sedan – the lavish vehicle incongruous amid the wind-torn walls and half-collapsed structures of what had once been a hopeful little village, long abandoned to the encroaching desert.

The SUV rolled to a stop near the car and the rear doors flew open. Two men stepped out holding assault rifles. The front passenger door swung wide and a figure in a navy-blue pinstripe suit, carrying a briefcase, climbed from the cab and moved towards the nearest building, his black eel-skin valise gleaming in the harsh sunlight.

The gunmen surveyed their surroundings with suspicious eyes, though there was nothing to see but the dizzy haze of the ravaged land, distorted by the heat waves rising from the sand. A few miles in the distance, a ridge of hills shimmered with the same washed-out palette as the rest of the landscape.

The sand and dust permeated everything eventually. Even in the rarified atmosphere of the SUV, with filters for the filters, the fulvous essence of the desert seeped in, coating everything with a desiccated film.

The suited man seemed unfazed by the brutal heat, appearing for all the world to be a successful banker or businessman on his way to the office rather than an interloper in the inhospitable landscape. He stepped gingerly over the bloated corpse of a dead dog, ignoring the swarming congregation of black flies. Glancing around, he strode into the building past his bodyguards, whose postures conveyed agitation at this solitary rendezvous, their weapons sweeping the horizon.

"That's far enough. Tell your men to stay back. Only you approach." The sandpaper voice was abrupt, the accent harsh and foreign. Russian was obviously not the man's forte.

"Of course. They are merely here to ensure we aren't interrupted. I have no doubts about you, or I wouldn't be here," the suited man assured – his insincere half-grin tugging at his wormy lips. His Russian was fluid, languorous, musical, with the cadence of a native speaker. He made a gesture, and the gunmen took positions in the shade just inside the clay brick entrance, one of them eyeing the aperture overhead where the roof had collapsed, the victim of an errant mortar round.

"You have brought what was agreed?" the robed man demanded, his *thawb* gathered around him as he sat cross-legged on the dirt floor. Armed with machine guns, three guards clad in the distinctive dress of the local tribesmen stood in the shadows at the far end of the room.

"Yes. A token of our intent. Enough so that you can verify our claims. And to save you some trouble, I also brought you some footage of the effects on a *volunteer.*" The corners of the suited man's mouth twitched with the beginnings of a smile.

"Very well. Show me." The seated man gestured for the suited man to approach.

As he reached into his suit pocket, the guards bristled, watching him as he slowly extracted a cell phone and held it out. The seated man rose and stood facing him, eyes fixed hawk-like on the screen.

A date and time indicator ticked away in the bottom right corner, indicating that the footage had been captured three days prior. Static gave way to the drab gray of a room with raw concrete walls, where a young man sat on a bunk behind bars, sipping a bowl of soup, obviously unaware that he was being filmed. The lighting changed subtly as the images jumped ahead an hour. The prisoner was pacing his cell, wiping perspiration from his face, his ragged shirt drenched with sweat stains, screaming in a panicked voice for his captors to help him. The time indicator jumped ahead another two hours: the man was now lying on his bunk, shaking and moaning, his body racked by tremors. Two more hours and he was convulsing, his face distorted by agony. Two hours further and his nose, mouth, and ears were seeping blood; his pants were soaked with it, a trail of crimson vomit on his shirtfront as he lay gurgling on the floor in a pool of his own making.

The robed man's eyes flickered from the screen to the suited man's steady gaze, then back to the image. One hour later: The corpse's skin was discolored, bluish-black, already bloating from the pressure of internal gasses.

The final frame was of something barely recognizable as human: the epidermis split open, rotting as the flesh liquefied, horrifying to witness even on the tiny screen. The digital counter froze. Total elapsed time: a little over eight hours.

"And this can be introduced how?" the robed man finally inquired, his face betraying nothing.

"It was engineered for airborne delivery. Anyone breathing it will suffer the same fate as the man on the video."

"Is it contagious?"

"No."

The robed man grunted, and then returned to his spot on the floor. "Can you make it contagious? So infection can occur without direct inhalation required?"

The suited man appeared to consider the question, as if it hadn't been a topic of hot debate with his superiors. Eventually, he nodded. "Anything can be done for a price. But it would be very time-consuming, and it isn't simple."

"It never is."

"One of the concerns is that taken beyond its weaponized form and made contagious, we couldn't allow it into anyone's hands until there was a one-hundred-percent effective antidote or vaccine. Otherwise this would be more than simply a bio-weapon. It would mean the end of human life."

"Hmmm. Well, we don't want that, do we? Just the end of *some* human life." He motioned for the suited man to sit across from him on a blanket and cushions that had been placed on the ground for the purpose, and shifted on his own cushion. The suited man sat, as though this sort of meeting was a common one for him.

"I have a sample with me, which should be enough to try on a handful of subjects, so you're assured of its effectiveness. But I warn you, the bodies must be disposed of. Cremated, so there are no trails to follow. And you absolutely cannot release it in any way. Even a hint that this has made its way into the world will shut down all discussion with my group and bring about the harshest of consequences. That is not negotiable." The Russian's tone had softened.

The robed man's eyes narrowed to slits in the gloom; an ugly look had taken residence on his face. "You dare to come into my world and threaten me?" he growled.

"Of course not. I am merely passing on the message, as instructed."

After a tense moment, the robed man nodded his understanding, and the other slid the briefcase towards him, scraping a trail in the yellow dust.

"There is no way to reverse-engineer this agent, and it will only remain active for seventy-two more hours. The production version will be effective for one week. Handle it with supreme care – the slightest deviation from the accompanying instructions will result in disaster," the Russian said.

"I will make the transfer to your account. Twenty million euros, correct?"

"Yes. As agreed. Once we have that, I will need to understand how large a batch you will be ordering, and will get some estimates on the cost of making it contagious. How large a population do you need the agent to…neutralize?"

The robed man's eyes rolled towards the ceiling as he considered the question. He frowned. "As many as possible. Thousands. Millions, if it can be done."

The suited man's expression didn't change. "I see. That will be expensive. Especially if we are able to make it contagious."

"I expect that it will be – very expensive. Do not worry about costs. Leave that to me. Just go back and convey my requirements."

The suited man rose. "We have concluded for now. Remember, no traces of your verification tests, or this contract will be terminated before it begins." He tossed the phone containing the footage to the seated man and turned without another word, his hand-crafted Scarpe di Bianco shoes rustling on the dirt as he made his way back to his waiting gunmen at the building's entry.

A whippet-thin bodyguard with an ivory-colored headdress approached the briefcase, waiting until the robed man nodded before shouldering his weapon and stooping down to pick it up.

"Providence has smiled upon us," he said in a reverential tone, cradling the valise carefully in his gnarled hands.

"Indeed it has — we are close to achieving our goal now. Closer than ever before. The infidels will soon pay an unimaginably high price for their arrogant imperialistic ways. But come — we are done here. Prepare to leave," the robed man ordered, steepling his fingers as he regarded the case.

Outside, the Land Cruiser started with a roar and returned down the track, dust billowing from behind as it disappeared into the blurred beige horizon.

From a strategic position on the far hills, a figure shifted binoculars back to the hamlet, waiting for the Mercedes to depart. Steel-gray eyes peered through the lenses, and a rivulet of sweat trickled through the powdery crust on the man's face, leaving a dark streak as it worked its way towards the arid ground. He was invisible, he knew, as long as he didn't make any sudden movements, the rocks he was nestled behind cloaking his position.

He lifted his satellite phone to his ear, pressed the transmit button, and murmured into it, all the while watching the rendezvous site.

A flash from below caught his attention. He swung his glasses towards the glint and, for a brief second, saw a gunman looking in his direction through binoculars of his own; then watched in horror as the man dropped his glasses to his chest and called out to the guards in the building, pointing up at his position.

Shit.

He was blown.

There was no point in waiting for the inevitable. The screaming man pulled a phone from his robe and made a call, then barked instructions as four guards clamored out of the structure to join him.

He had seen enough. Moving stealthily, he ducked back behind the cover of the boulders and then crawled down to a ravine. Once out of sight of the buildings, he bolted for a small cave on the other side of the hill where he'd made camp the day before.

He lost his footing on an area of loose gravel and went down hard, wrenching his ankle and slamming against the ground. His binoculars hit the rocks with a clatter and one of the lenses shattered. The impact stopped him, but he shook it off. Every second counted now; there was no time for hesitation.

From across the expanse, he heard motors start. One would be the Mercedes, but he wasn't worried about the sleek sedan. It was the others that had been concealed around the back of the village that were trouble —

but an even larger concern for him was the phone call the gunman had made.

He hurriedly limped to his ATV, pulled off the camouflage netting, and climbed onto the parched seat and cranked the starter. The engine sputtered to life with a puff of blue smoke, and within seconds he was flying down the back side of the hill towards a gap, where the trail he had taken led to a dry river bed that would deliver him back to relative civilization.

A hazy cloud followed him as he roared up the ravine, his ATV's tires gripping the sandy terrain tenaciously as he goosed the throttle, mind racing over his escape options even as he climbed in altitude. The dry air stung his eyes, grit borne on the wind an ever-present hazard; he squinted, ignoring the discomfort as he raced from his pursuers.

He slowed once he came to the riverbed and cocked his head, listening.

It sounded like at least two ATVs coming after him.

The options weren't good. He could try to outrun them but had no advantage other than a slim head start, so it would likely come down to whose gas tank contained the most juice. He knew he had a half tank, but if one of the pursuers had more, he was toast.

That left him with the option of finding an area of high ground and ambushing them.

The strap of his Kalashnikov bit into his shoulder, as if urging him to allow it to solve the problem. That choice held a lot more appeal than running through the desert mountains in the hopes his pursuers would run dry first.

The rumbling sound of approaching motors decided it for him. If he didn't ambush them, he was a dead man.

Twisting the handlebars, he gunned the gas and shot for a rise several hundred yards away. With any luck he could reach it before they came into view, and then it would be child's play to pick them off, even with the questionably accurate AK-47.

He rolled to a stop next to an outcropping of brown rock, killed the engine, and dropped to a crouch before moving away from his vehicle. No point in telegraphing his position if they caught a glimpse of it. The tan paint job made that unlikely, but his luck wasn't running strong and he didn't want to chance it.

The strident protests of the ATVs' motors grew louder. He gripped his rifle, wedging it between two smaller stones for stability. The pursuit was a minor disaster, but one he could recover from.

As the first rider rounded the trail's dogleg bend, he sighted, waiting for the second to come into range before opening fire. The ATV slowed, as if sensing a trap, and then the other flew into view, skidding on the fine gravel as the pilot struggled to maintain control.

The Kalashnikov kicked, pounding against his shoulder as he squeezed off three rounds at the emerging ATV. The shots sounded like grenades detonating in the hills. He watched the rider drop to the ground, his chest pummeled by two of the three bullets, his vehicle skidding askance before crashing into a ledge.

The second rider twisted the throttle and tore for a nearby boulder. Slugs slammed into the sand around the dodging ATV but none found home, and the rider made it to a position of safety behind the huge rock. He cursed to himself as the gunman disappeared from view – he could expect return fire any moment.

As expected, a sharp crack erupted from the boulder almost immediately and a chip of stone sundered from the rock beside him.

Great. Just what he needed. Out of all the possible adversaries he could have drawn, he had to get one that could actually shoot reasonably well. As if confirming his thought, another boom echoed in the canyon and a round slapped into the hill immediately behind him. Too close for comfort.

He fired back, peppering the sides of the boulder with lead, then rolled behind a larger outcropping that would provide better cover.

Barring a miracle, they were at a standoff. Neither man would be able to move without exposing himself to the other.

The sun beat down with relentless fury as they exchanged shots, neither doing any damage. He glanced at his watch after another ineffective volley, wondering how much more time he had. If the man on the sat phone had called in reinforcements, it was all over. And there was little doubt in his mind that he'd done so.

The hot breeze became stagnant as he ran options in his head, and then in the distance he heard a faint roar – a rumbling that seemed to shake the ground. He dared a peek to the north and his heart sank as the sky darkened with an ominous brown, the cloud impenetrable as it moved directly at his position. This was the dreaded *ghobar*– a sandstorm that could be deadly if you were caught in the open.

Experience of the region's storms had taught him that he would only have a few minutes to prepare. He fired off another three shots to keep his pursuer occupied, then unwound his headdress and wrapped it across his nose and mouth. He was completely exposed except for the scant cover of the rocks, which would do little to cushion the force of nature's ugly wrath headed his way. His only real hope was to keep his face pressed as close to the rocks as possible while he waited for it to pass. The struggle against his adversary would have to take a back seat until the *ghobar* passed.

The air pressure plummeted, and then with a *whoosh* the sky overhead darkened as the raging cloud of sand pummeled him at full force. He clenched his eyes tight and focused on keeping the worst of it out of his ears and nose with his head cloth, but could barely draw breath. The barrage of airborne confusion tore at his flesh like fishhooks, and the few areas of exposed skin felt like they were being sandblasted away – which wasn't far from the truth.

It was all he could do to hold onto his rifle and ride out the relentless battering. The wind noise escalated to a deafening howl as the storm blew by him with locomotive force. It seemed impossible that anything could live through this.

Eventually, the sting of the sand lightened in intensity, and he could breathe a little easier – the worst had passed, leaving him shaking and worn, but alive.

When the roaring in his ears diminished to a tolerable level and the thrashing had subsided, he opened his eyes, squinting against the return of the sun's blistering rays.

A shadow crossed his line of vision, and the blurred form of a robed native loomed over him as he fumbled to bring his rifle up; but he was too late. The curved blade of a dagger slashed across his throat, spraying a rubicund shower of blood into the wind as the tail of the sandstorm dragged his life with it, his existence terminated in a sweltering no man's land at the ass end of the planet by a grinning killer with soulless black eyes and leathery skin the color of jerky.

CHAPTER 1

Present day, Montevideo, Uruguay

Jet's running shoes pounded against the ragged pavement as she bolted towards the narrow alley mouth. Puddles of stagnant water glimmered as the morning haze burned off, a breeze from the nearby ocean carrying with it the salty promise of a balmy summer day. She accelerated in a burst of speed and ran two steps up the vertical expanse of wall, using the momentum to push herself off and pivot in mid-air before grabbing the roof edge of the building across from it, her fingers gripping the lip with iron determination as she pulled herself up onto the flat rooftop.

After sizing up the area with a glance, she tore across the tar-papered surface towards the far side of the building and threw herself into space, seeming to hang in the air before landing on the next roof and rolling to dampen the shock of her impact.

She leapt to her feet and raced to the long-abandoned multi-story office buildings that rose above her, feeling with her hands for a window ledge. She climbed, pushing herself higher with her toes as her fingers found holds, her shoulder and arm muscles straining as she scaled the sheer building side. At the top, she swung her legs onto the third-floor roof and then risked a look back. Two figures were tearing across the roof towards her. They would be on her within five seconds, maybe ten, depending on whether they could climb the wall as quickly as she had.

Jet sprinted for the far roof edge and peered down, where the nearest building was a story lower, across at least a fifteen-foot gap over another alley. She brushed perspiration out of her eyes, backed up, and then ran full speed at the expanse, hurtling out and down through the heavy air, again tucking and rolling as she hit the roof.

Five long strides and she threw her body over the building side, clutching a drainpipe and using it to scissor her legs sideways to one of the window apertures, the glass long gone from vandalism and the effects of the elements. With a final push, she drove her legs through and landed on the debris-strewn concrete floor, pausing in the rubble to get her bearings.

Two thumps sounded from above. They were getting closer – gaining on her.

She spotted a stairwell and bolted to it, latching onto the iron railing with steel hands and throwing her torso into space, spinning in mid-air and catching the rail of the floor below. She pushed herself off and repeated the maneuver until she was on the ground level.

Her gambit had gained her a few critical seconds.

She heard the distinctive sound of soles slamming against the floor above at a dead run, and took a few deep, calming breaths before she darted through the doorway and out onto the street.

A once-bustling common was deserted, eerily silent except for the sigh of the wind and her measured inhalations as she approached an outdoor stairway leading up to the second and third levels of an empty parking complex, all gray concrete and exposed steel beams marred by graffiti and neglect.

She raced for the stairs and jumped, grasping the rim of the molded concrete handrail and pulling her body up; then took four running steps and dived for the third-floor stairs, catching the edge with sure fingers before swinging her lower body onto the landing.

Jet didn't wait to see how far behind her they were.

Her legs burned from effort as she tore across the cavernous interior, barely pausing at the concrete half-wall before she vaulted over it, right leg extended in front of her like a ballerina. Her feet landed on the rough-textured rim that served as the exterior of the structure; then, with a sidelong look, she clamped a hand on the top and swung in the air, suspended by one arm before allowing momentum to carry her down one story onto the second-floor wall.

She alighted with catlike grace, then slipped to the unforgiving cement of the second level and made for a gap twenty feet away.

With a labored grunt, a body struck the ground behind her, deciding her next move, which was headfirst out into empty space before landing on the dirt and tumbling, scarcely pausing as she rose, and then running down the long block towards a closed construction site – an older building that was being renovated at a snail's pace by workers who arrived late and left early.

There was nobody there at this hour, so she clambered over the chain link fence and darted through the open entry without looking back.

Gazing up at the narrow atrium, she spotted open air four stories above. The fence outside clattered, signaling that she was out of time, and she padded to the far end of the space on silent feet, where an elevator shaft loomed dark.

Jet dropped down into the cavity at the bottom of the shaft. She stretched her arms, wedging them against the sides, then did the same with her legs, alternating as she chimneyed up the confined area, supporting herself with opposing appendages as she rose, ascending the four stories in fifteen seconds. Her sweating arm reached for the top of the shaft and she gripped a steel girder, then hoisted herself higher into a cavity that led to the roof.

With a push, she was out in the open again, running across the gravel-covered slab to the building's edge. Another section stretched two stories beneath her; she made a snap decision and threw her body over the lip.

Her feet dropped onto a window sill a story below. She pushed off and performed a backward somersault before landing in a crouch, her arms helping to absorb the jarring impact.

She forced herself to keep moving, clambering spider-like across the narrow rooftop to the side, where she flung her legs out and sailed towards the perimeter wall a story below. She landed precisely on the flat wall top, sprang off with another flip, and hit the sidewalk running.

Jet looked over her shoulder at her pursuers, then bolted for the far side of the deserted street to an embankment separating the desolate industrial area from a busy thoroughfare, filled with commuters beginning their long slog into the office. Traffic noise of the early rush hour rose to greet her as she approached. She leapt off the tip of the embankment, arms extended, caught the edge of the off-ramp twenty feet across from her, and hung, suspended a story above a dirt patch below the structure. Then she dropped effortlessly and rolled before running at the wall and propelling herself with two massive steps up its side, pushing off, and executing a back flip.

Whistles and applause from eight hoodie-clad young men and women greeted her performance. A second later, another body flew through space, catching the lip as she had, and dropped to the ground, followed closely by a second.

Jet watched their final flips with a grin, then extended her hand and high-fived the first pursuer, a twenty-something-year-old youth with a lopsided smirk and close-cropped hair.

"I guess we can agree that the old lady still has a few chops, no?" Jet asked with a smile.

"That was some crazy shit. Really. Props to you," the second runner panted, nodding his approval.

"Nice to know that I'm not completely over the hill. Now what about our bet?" Jet asked.

The taller runner stepped forward, fishing around in his baggy pants before pulling out a thin wad of currency. He peeled off a two-hundred-peso note, roughly equivalent to ten dollars, and grudgingly handed it to her. "I'd say you earned that fair and square. I ain't never seen anything like it," he admitted. "How long you been at this?"

Her eyes sparkled as she took the money from him and waved it under his nose. "How old are you? I've probably been free running and training parkour since before you could walk – or fall over, even."

The group laughed again, then two of the younger boys ran at the wall in tandem and executed back flips, landing side by side in unison. A young girl, sixteen, took a run at a low wall and vaulted it, somersaulting and landing on her feet as the admiring youths looked on.

A crawling rap song with a gangsta beat blared from a boom box by the gathering's backpacks, and money changed hands among the clique as the morning's wagering on the outcome of the race came to a conclusion. The girl snatched a hundred pesos from the shorter of the racing pair and blew him a kiss. He pretended to swoon, then did another flip off the wall as he held his hands over his heart. One of the other young men broke into an impromptu break dancing display, ending with a virtuoso gymnastic performance that culminated with a single-armed handstand, his tautly muscled legs jutting straight above him as he held the seemingly impossible pose.

"All right. I have to get going. Catch you all later," Jet said with a wave, and then turned and made her way past the hulking buildings towards Montevideo's business district. She had been in Uruguay for three months after fleeing Thailand and had settled into a comfortable routine, free running three mornings a week, doing her calmer five-mile conventional run the remaining four. She increased her pace to a fast jog and burned the three miles to her rented townhouse, uneasy as she ran, a vague sense of being watched tingling the nape of her neck.

She stopped abruptly a quarter mile from her house and, under the pretense of tightening her shoelaces, scanned her surroundings for threats. A sparse scatter of pedestrians ambled on their way to coffee or work, the city having yet to completely awaken. Her senses on alert, she methodically scrutinized each area but saw nothing sinister; only the unremarkable coming and going of the residents.

Shaking off the lingering feeling, she stood and strolled the rest of the way home, stopping at a bakery to get several fresh croissants and a cup of coffee, which she carried down the tree-lined streets. As she rounded a corner and stepped off the curb to cross the street, a car screeched as it slammed on its brakes, having cheerfully ignored the stop sign mounted at the intersection. The woman driver shot Jet a dirty look as she prattled away on her cell phone, oblivious to the world outside the windshield. Jet bristled, then decided to let it go. She didn't need trouble, and had gone out of her way to blend in with the locals. It wouldn't do to get into an altercation over right-of-way and driving etiquette.

Jet felt for the reassuring shape of her front door key suspended from a chain around her neck as she approached the entry of her two-story brick townhouse. She opened the wrought iron gate that protected her postage-stamp lawn and was stepping onto the short entry path when a hand gripped her arm. She twisted free, adrenaline spiking as she prepared to engage, her right arm coming up to her chest level in a defensive posture that could quickly transform into an offensive strike. She whirled to confront her assailant and found herself facing an ancient woman with white hair and wild bloodshot eyes, her pupils the faded color of afternoon sky, unfocused and yet strangely intent. One claw-like hand gestured, begging for change. Jet studied the leathery lines that life had etched on her face, memorializing an unknowably harsh existence of love lost and promises broken and opportunity long departed for distant shores. Dropping her defensive posture, she extracted a few loose coins from her pocket and dropped them into the crone's withered palm.

"*Gracias. Muchas gracias,*" the woman rasped gratefully, pocketing the money as she reached for Jet's arm once again.

Jet nodded, and with gentle pressure on the panhandler's grubby shoulders, steered her away, then carefully pulled the creaky gate shut behind her as she moved to the door.

She glanced at her watch, confirming that she wasn't running late, and then eased her way through the entry while calling out to let everyone know she was home.

Across the cobblestoned street, under a sagging tree near the corner, a tall man with a goatee and shaggy hair the color of wet sand scrutinized her from the cover of his newspaper, then rose from the black lacquered bench where he'd been reclining and made for the café down the block, anxious for another cup of coffee and some bread to feed the bustling pigeons as he watched and waited, patiently biding his time.

CHAPTER 2

"Mama," Hannah cried out with glee, launching herself down the hall towards Jet as fast as her cherubic little two-and-a-half-year-old legs would carry her.

"Hello, sweetheart. Mommy loves you," Jet said, dropping to one knee and holding both arms out in welcome. Hannah barreled into her and gave her a hug – a morning ritual since they had moved into the townhouse.

"*Buenos dias, Señora Elyse,*" Magdalena, her housekeeper, said from the end of the living room, where she was dusting a coffee table.

Jet had used her newly minted Thai identity to take up residence in Uruguay, and everyone knew her as Elyse Nguyen. Nobody tried to use her last name, preferring the easier to pronounce and remember Elyse, which was fine by Jet. She'd had so many identities in her life that it didn't really matter to her what people called her.

"Good morning, Magdalena. Is she behaving herself today?" Jet asked in fluent Spanish.

"Yes, of course. She's an angel. As always," Magdalena assured her, a warm smile lighting her face.

"I don't know about that, but I'm glad to hear she's having one of her good days." Jet stood and took Hannah's hand and led her to the kitchen, where she set the bag of croissants down on the counter and washed her hands, examining the calluses, an inevitable by-product of her parkour ritual, for tears. After confirming that all was well, Jet moved to the dining room table and helped Hannah into her child seat. She carefully broke off a portion of the croissant, tore it into small bites, and set it on her plate. Hannah waited patiently for her mother to finish, her eyebrow cocked, tiny fingers fiddling restlessly. Once Jet had sat and nodded to her, she picked up a morsel and dug in.

"There's a croissant for you, Magdalena. Fresh."

"Very good. Thank you. I'll get to it when I'm done in here," Magdalena responded from the living room.

Jet had met Magdalena on her third day in town while looking for long-term rentals in Montevideo. She'd chosen Montevideo, the capital of Uruguay, a hundred and twenty miles north of Buenos Aires, across the huge bay at the mouth of the Rio Plata, because it was civilized and obscure. It also had the most advanced banking system in South America; the country had long been known as "the Switzerland of South America" and deserved its reputation. The infrastructure was relatively modern; it was safe and clean; and best of all, it was one of the farthest points on the planet from her old stomping grounds in the Middle East.

After the disaster in Thailand, she'd fled the country and decided on South America rather than anywhere closer to Asia. There were too many bad memories associated with Matt's death, and she wanted a change of scenery. After a day on the web scanning for possible destinations she'd decided on Montevideo – the descriptions were glowing, and she didn't know anyone within two thousand miles. Perfect for her purposes.

The fifty million dollars in diamonds Matt had entrusted to her care were safely ensconced in a nearby safe deposit box at the largest bank in Uruguay, and she'd been able to access her account with the ten million dollars from her Thailand adventure by wiring chunks to her local bank a few blocks away. She still had a million and a half in the operational account Matt had given her, but she hesitated to use it, preferring to save it for emergencies.

Magdalena had been recommended to her by the real estate agent who had helped her find a home, and she'd been a godsend from the first day. She'd agreed to move in and now lived downstairs in the en-suite servants' quarters – a typical amenity for homes of that era in Uruguay. Her children grown and living their own lives, Magdalena had seemed grateful for the chance to help with a toddler – Jet suspected that it brought back fond memories from her past – and she was wonderful with Hannah, who adored her.

"I want to take Hannah to the mall today. She's growing so fast, it's time for new shoes," Jet called to Magdalena while munching on her croissant. Jet poked a finger into Hannah's plump side, and she squealed with delight.

"Do I need to come with you?"

"Whatever you want. Do you have a lot to do here?"

"Well, if you don't mind, I think I'll stay. I've been meaning to do something about the back yard, and it's not going to fix itself. Are you sure you don't need me for anything with Hannah?"

"I have it covered. I'm pretty sure I can handle a trip to the mall without help," Jet assured her, finishing the croissant with a flourish and waggling her eyebrows at Hannah.

"Very well, then. I'll get to it as soon as I finish with the living room. Do you want breakfast?" Magdalena asked.

"No, the croissants are enough. Although I see no reason not to have another cup of coffee. I got some at the bakery, but it's never the same as home-made…"

"Nothing ever is. I made a fresh pot. I'll pour you a cup."

"No, no. Do what you need to do. I'll get my own."

Hannah was making a complete mess of her area, which was expected. She hadn't yet mastered getting most of the food into her mouth, and she would barely tolerate Jet feeding her – already, she had an independent streak that defined most of her interactions, although she was less reluctant with Magdalena.

The townhouse was a find: centrally located and huge, with three bedrooms upstairs, servants' quarters downstairs, and a sprawling layout. The rent was pricey by Uruguay standards, but about half of what a similar place would have cost in most European cities – and Jet had to keep reminding herself that money was no longer a concern.

That had taken her a little psychological adjustment. She had never been materialistic and tended to be frugal, given the choice. It was part of her efficiency drive, which colored everything she did – efficiency in motion, in action, and in living. But she was a rich woman now, by any measure, although the entire thing seemed surrealistic. The numbers involved were so vast to her they defied belief.

Still, her training had taught her to never own anything. Rent, don't buy, was her rule, especially when she might have to disappear from whatever life she'd assumed at a moment's notice.

And so it was that she rented her home and took taxis everywhere rather than braving the traffic with her own vehicle. At some point she would get a car, but in a city like Montevideo it was hardly necessary, and she couldn't see the point to adding another responsibility to her load.

Jet checked her watch. It would be an hour before the stores opened, so she had plenty of time to rinse off and get to the mall. She had made a play-date with several of the other mothers she had met at the botanical gardens, and their thrice weekly get-togethers were a high point of Hannah's week.

"Magdalena, could you watch Hannah while I take a shower? I'll be about twenty minutes or so."

"Of course. I'll be right in."

"Thanks," Jet called out, moving to the kitchen to get her cup of coffee.

When Magdalena materialized in the dining room, Jet went upstairs and stripped off her wet exercise clothes, noting a few scraped areas from the morning's contest. Parkour was her favorite part of her exercise routine, and she was glad she'd been able to resume the sport when she moved. There were plenty of half-finished buildings or vacant commercial areas in which to free run – Uruguay had been affected by the financial downturn just like everywhere else. She'd been pushing herself as she rediscovered all the moves and muscles she'd developed over years of practice, and had been pleasantly surprised that the locals had a small but enthusiastic group that shared her passion.

The discipline was part gymnastics, part sheer athleticism, and part daredevil, and she supposed that she was getting a little past her prime, judging by the average age of the kids she'd met running her favorite courses. Even at twenty-eight, after a run like this morning's she felt ancient, in spite of her bravado in the moment.

Naked, she twisted the worn bronze handles and waited for the creaky pipes to deliver warm water and considered her reflection in the full-length mirror. Not so bad for an over-the-hill mom, she supposed – seven percent body fat, six-pack abs, and a gymnast's build – a testament to her training and her daily ritual of several hours of grueling workout, rain or shine.

The routine, as she thought of it, was a tie to her past, but one she was unwilling to cut. Her fitness had saved her more than once, and it would be a cold day when she lapsed and got lazy.

Steam rose from behind the shower curtain, and she adjusted the flow to something approaching comfortable and then stepped under the spray.

It was all so hard to believe. Here she was, in a country she'd never visited, wealthy beyond her wildest fantasies, with a daughter she'd thought dead at the beginning of the year...and her biggest concerns were shoe shopping and visiting with the local soccer moms.

Life was strange.

Jet scrubbed herself vigorously with soap and then lathered her short hair with a floral shampoo Magdalena had bought, and then rinsed herself off before stepping, dripping, onto the bath mat.

She considered her reflection again as she ran a brush through her hair, now dyed dark brown, growing out from the severe short cut she'd had in Thailand.

The thought of Thailand stopped her.

It seemed so long ago, and yet it had only been ninety days since she'd been standing, watching the smoke from Matt's ruined beach house curl lazily into the sky.

An eternity, and yet the blink of an eye.

So much had changed. She was a completely different person. Domesticated, at peace, Hannah her priority now that she didn't have to run any more.

Unlike Matt. Who had believed his time of hiding was over as well, but discovered by paying the ultimate price that the past never stays buried. He had obviously misjudged the lengths to which the CIA group he'd been battling would go to see him dead. A critical mistake – and one that Jet would never make.

He had sounded so happy on their last couple of phone calls. Living on the beach in paradise, calm, his exile in the wilds of Myanmar's jungles finally over.

If only things had turned out differently…

She finished brushing her hair and with it, her ruminations. No good would come from reliving the ugly events of her past. What was done was done, and nothing would bring the dead back.

Perhaps it was best that they stayed buried.

Now was her time to be with Hannah, in the moment, enjoying her childhood and celebrating the experience of motherhood. Waxing nostalgic over those that had passed on went nowhere good.

Better to focus on the future.

Because for Jet, and Hannah, the future had never looked brighter.

CHAPTER 3

Hannah wasn't happy. Her face was scrunched up in a frown and she was pouting. The shoes she wanted, shiny patent-leather flats, had been nixed by Jet in favor of more sensible athletic shoes with Velcro straps for easy changing. But Hannah wasn't a creature of practicality, and when she'd seen the other shoes she'd been adamant – the tennis shoes were fine, but the patent-leather flats were a necessity.

Jet wasn't in the mood to let a toddler dictate terms; she didn't want her to get used to getting everything she wanted. There were boundaries, and sometimes the world failed to deliver on one's desires. That was an important lesson if Jet was going to avoid raising a spoiled monster – which was a danger, given her impulse to lavish her daughter with everything she could think of. Memories of her past always intruded: her own childhood playing out, the death of her parents, the lack of nurturing thereafter, her foster father, the difficult times in orphanages…

If she could give her daughter everything, why not? It wasn't like she had to pinch pennies.

The answer was obvious to her. Hannah was already spoiled rotten, attended to by her own servant; the pint-sized mistress of the house. Letting her run the show was not on the table. She'd wear the shoes Jet had selected and be happy about it.

The clerk rang up the purchase and Jet paid cash, then took the oversized plastic bag with the shoe box in it and moved towards the entrance.

Hannah dragged her feet as they departed the store, the air-conditioned cool washing over them once outside the storefront, and Jet felt the increasing resistance of a stalling Hannah against her hand as they walked away. Sensing trouble, she stopped and got down on one knee, bringing her face to eye-level with her daughter, whose head looked ready to explode with fury at not getting her way.

"Sweetie, you just got new shoes. You have a play-date later. You're out at the mall, having fun. Maybe we'll find a toy you don't have yet. Don't be upset because you can't have those shoes. They're not what we were looking for today. We got what we needed," Jet said reasonably, watching for a sign of surrender.

"Hannah want."

"Yes, I know. But not today. Today we got the other pair."

Her face scrunched up as if Jet had misunderstood her demand.

"Hannah...*want*..."

"Well, maybe some other time, but not tod–"

Hannah let loose with a shriek that rivaled a bullhorn for volume, reminding Jet of nothing so much as a locomotive locking its wheels after the emergency brake was engaged. Her face turned red...no, almost purple, and she screamed to wake the dead.

Horrified, Jet looked around at the near empty mall, where a handful of early shoppers had stopped to see who was torturing their child. Hannah screamed again, an enraged screech that signaled a completely out-of-control toddler, and a pair of older women gave her a disapproving glare.

"You stop screaming, now, Hannah, or so help me..." Jet warned.

Hannah greeted her order with the loudest and rawest of her exclamations yet, an angry and abused sound that spoke to endless suffering, and stamped her feet on the floor to underscore her displeasure at having her wishes questioned.

The first time this had happened, Jet hadn't known what to do or how to react, but she'd quickly come up with an effective coping technique.

With a lightning motion, she hoisted the plastic bag containing the new shoes and scooped Hannah up, clamping her hand over her mouth and hurrying to the nearest exit. The trick was to eliminate Hannah's ability to disrupt. Once robbed of that power, she would invariably settle down. These sorts of tantrums only lasted a few minutes, and like hurricanes were violent and destructive but of short duration.

Hannah struggled, further enraged at the ease with which her mother could physically bend her to her will, but it was no use. As stubborn as the little girl was, Jet had experience and superior strength on her side, and no small reserves of resolve herself. In this battle there would only be one winner. Jet thought of the technique as "crushing her spirit." Hannah just needed to be reminded who was boss when she forgot.

Howling into Jet's hand, Hannah continued her tantrum until they were outside the mall, standing on the sidewalk, at which point Jet set her down and let her wear herself out. After a few more minutes of howling while her mother watched impassively, she tired and slowed from a banshee wail to sniffling, tears streaking her cheeks.

"Are you done now? Or do you want to keep behaving like a baby?" Jet calmly asked. There was nothing Hannah hated more than being called a baby.

Hannah kept crying, but the wind was out of her sails. Jet waited patiently for her to get hold of herself, ignoring the looks of curious pedestrians. Nothing existed in the universe except for Jet and Hannah, and they would make peace, one way or another.

Eventually Hannah nodded and swiped at her face with her arm, brushing the tears away, the incident already passing, any memory of the shoes now fuzzy, as can be the case only with small children. Jet watched her struggling to regain her composure and felt her heart lurch. She was so decent and good, even after throwing a tantrum. In the end, she was simply too young to manage her emotions.

"Are we finished? Everything better?" Jet asked, and Hannah nodded.

"Yes, Mama."

"Good. Then let's get a taxi and take you home so we can get ready to go play. How does that sound? Are you up for some playtime?"

Hannah's smile radiated happiness at the idea. Jet reached into her purse and pulled out a tissue.

"Blow."

Jet held the tissue out and Hannah obligingly blew her nose into it.

"All right. Let's get this show on the road."

Hannah grabbed Jet's hand and pulled her towards the waiting cab line, pointing lest they be delayed from playtime any more than absolutely necessary, and Jet grinned to herself. If only she could return to a time where life was that simple.

When they arrived at the taxi queue, a driver disengaged from the group of men loitering near the entrance and motioned to his car. He held the door open for them and then jogged around the front to the driver's side before wedging himself behind the wheel and inquiring where they wanted to go. Jet gave him the address and he repeated it emphatically as he started the car, and then honked as he swung into traffic with hardly a glance at the oncoming vehicles.

They watched the city fly by, Hannah on Jet's lap so she could see, and Jet wondered again at what a miracle this whole experience had been. She had gone from being a lone wolf, struggling to get through each day with no more meaning to her existence than surviving another twenty-four hours, to being the caretaker of a little bundle of complexity for whom every moment brought new wonders.

A bus roared beside them and the cabbie honked again, making an obscene gesture at the offending conveyance before cutting the bus off and accelerating past it.

Hannah gave Jet a look. Even at her tender age she had picked up that some gestures were insulting, and when she moved her arm and clenched her fingers, trying to get them to form the same shape, Jet shook her head. That was all she needed – Hannah showing her playground friends the latest obscenity she'd learned while shopping with Mommy. Jet saw the internal struggle play across her angelic features, torn between obeying and the impish delight of forbidden fruit, and then Mom's proximity decided it and she dropped her arm.

Another small battle won.

Jet relaxed and smiled.

She'd take it.

CHAPTER 4

A gentle wind blew off the bay, rustling the tree tops with a fresh snap of chill on the unusually warm day. Seasons were reversed in the Southern hemisphere, and summer was the region's winter, with temperatures averaging fifty degrees Fahrenheit in September. But today the cold had been broken by an unseasonable warm front that had spiked the temperature all the way into the sixties – signaling that perhaps the worst of the cold was behind them for another year.

Jet and Hannah walked hand in hand down the park path to where her friends were waiting, ready to destroy their clothes and get filthy in the blink of an eye. All part of the process, Jet had discovered, and at Hannah's age there was scarcely any difference between the boys and the girls. Both genders seemed to delight in rolling around in the grass, clenching moist dirt, rubbing it all over each other, and generally undoing an hour of washing and preparation within moments of arriving.

Jet saw Miriam and Daphne, two of the mothers she had befriended, sitting on one of the benches, chatting while their children, Paolo, Maricela, and Fortuna gamboled in the shade on the grass in front of them, chasing each other and squealing in playful excitement. Maricela was the oldest at three and a half, and her brother Paolo and her best friend in the world, Fortuna, were both two and a half. Fortunately for everyone, Paolo hadn't gotten to the age yet where he didn't want to play with girls, and he was happy to have company to cavort with, especially after weeks of being restricted to being indoors during the coldest months.

Hannah's eyes lit up when she saw her friends and, with a glance at her mother, released Jet's hand and ran to join them, her toy-stuffed pink Hello Kitty backpack clutched tightly.

"Ah, there you are. How are you, my dear?" Miriam greeted Jet as she approached, and both women rose and kissed her on the cheek, as was the local custom.

"Good. We went shopping this morning and Hannah turned into Satan's spawn for a while, but everything's fine now."

Miriam and Daphne exchanged knowing glances.

"Shopping has that effect sometimes. Try it with two of them, each wanting to buy everything in the store," Miriam said, and Daphne nodded.

"We've all been there. Isn't it nice how they always choose the most public place to go crazy? It's like they save it just for the occasion," Daphne agreed.

"Speak for yourself. When you have a boy, trust me, they don't save it. They have endless reserves," Miriam countered, and they all laughed.

The children had abandoned the toys they had been playing with in favor of the new arrivals in Hannah's bag, causing a minor riot as everyone grabbed for the same toy at once.

As the hour wore on, Jet couldn't help but feel a tingle of anxiety again – the same sensation of being watched as earlier, only more intense. Behind her darkened sunglasses her eyes scanned the park, trying to be subtle, but she didn't see anything unusual. Couples strolling together or lying on the grass, involved in their own dramas. The occasional pensioner walking by himself, or pairs of older women taking their constitutional. Nothing stuck out, and yet she couldn't shake the unsettling feeling.

This was the first day she'd felt this way since moving to Montevideo. Which didn't necessarily mean there was a threat. The hyper-awareness wasn't like some sort of crystal ball that accurately predicted the future...but something had set it off, and she'd spent far too much time in the field to dismiss it out of hand.

The women chatted about the rising cost of everything, about the worsening conditions in nearby Argentina, about the alarming increase in drug use among the youth of both countries.

They stopped talking as a young man, no older than eighteen, walked by, his gait unsteady and his movements jittery.

"You see that? It's everywhere. That's *paco*. It's a huge problem in the poor areas," Daphne explained.

"*Paco?*" Jet had never heard of it.

"Yes. That's what they call it. It's a combination of cocaine residue and kerosene, or sometimes rat poison. Sometimes it's even mixed with glue and crushed glass. You smoke it. It's incredibly addictive and only costs a few pesos per hit. I saw a TV special on it last week," Daphne said.

Jet listened politely, but her gut was now blaring a warning. And it wasn't because of some junked-up punk roaming the park looking for an unattended purse to steal. She checked the time and decided that she'd had enough – they had been playing just short of an hour, and she wanted to get out of there.

"Honey? Come on. Playtime's over," Jet called to Hannah, who was chasing Paolo around in circles as he waved a plastic toy plane over his head. Hannah pretended not to hear, and Jet called to her again, pointing to her watch and rising to her feet.

The other mothers joined her in corralling their offspring, and after some grousing and squabbling, the toys were returned to their rightful owners and everyone was ready to leave, their attitudes glum at the day's high point coming to a close.

Jet kissed both women again and they parted, Jet moving down the southern path leading back to the boulevard, the other two going north to the opposite end of the massive park, for lunch in a nearby district with a host of pricey restaurants.

She took Hannah's hand and picked up the pace, still uneasy, but Hannah was dragging again.

"Sweetheart, I need you to walk faster. Now. This isn't a game."

Hannah looked at her uncomprehendingly, but increased her speed – only not enough to satisfy Jet.

"Honey, I'm going to pick you up and carry you a little, okay?"

Hannah bristled. She hated being carried. *Like a baby*. She dug her heels in and stopped, forcing Jet to stop too. Jet's eyes swept their surroundings as she spoke.

"This is not the time. I need to carry you. No arguments."

Jet's tone was serious enough to warn Hannah off another display of temper, and she meekly nodded agreement. Jet lifted her and began moving hastily towards the park entrance.

Something on the periphery of her vision caught her attention, and she turned her head just as a pair of schoolboys in their early teens almost bowled her over as they ran to catch up with their friends. Her free hand had automatically dropped into her purse, where she had the butterfly knife she'd acquired on her second day in country. She was still waiting for her residency application to be finalized, at which time she could buy a gun, but in the meantime she'd had to content herself with only the knife for self-

26

defense. It wasn't much, but it was better than nothing – and in her hands it was as deadly as a revolver.

They were almost to the park exit and nothing had happened. Perhaps she had gotten her signals crossed. There was no sign of any threats, and the boulevard was only fifty yards ahead.

A tall man in an overcoat turned off an adjoining path ahead and made his way towards her, and her hand felt for the knife again, a bad feeling surging through her veins upon seeing him. He was staring at her, but that was hardly unusual. Even with Hannah in tow she was a remarkably attractive woman, and men noticed. But his demeanor, the way he carried himself, hinted at something more ominous than a walk on a nice day.

Her fingers tightened around the knife handle as she held his gaze, and then he looked away, reaching into his pocket as he did so. She had to make an instantaneous decision – flip out the blade and stab him preemptively, or wait to see if he was going to attack. Hannah's presence won the round, and she hesitated for a split second, the knife ready in her grip.

He raised a cell phone to his ear and answered it, speaking softly in Spanish as he brushed by her, offering another admiring glance as he passed. She exhaled with relief, then a chill ran up her spine as she looked over her shoulder: two men on the path behind her, walking with focused deliberation, both of them focusing their attention on her.

She reached the entry and darted to the right. Another glance at the men convinced her to risk crossing the street in the midst of automobiles hurtling past her like possessed juggernauts. Dodging between honking cars, she chose her openings carefully and made it to the other side. As she mounted the curb she peered back to where the two men were emerging from the park, joined by four others as one of the followers pointed at her.

She didn't wait to see what happened next. Searching the vicinity, she spotted a cluster of office buildings that were closed for construction – a common sight in many of the better areas of Montevideo, where speculators snapped up prime properties to remodel them into high-rent candidates. If she could get to the buildings she could find somewhere to hide Hannah, and then deal with whoever this was.

That they were following her wasn't in question – she had seen more than enough. But how she handled the situation over the next thirty seconds would be determined by her daughter more than anything. She had no idea who this was, but she was now operating on pure instinct, her brain calculating escape vectors even as it searched out the best environment in which to take on her pursuers.

Jet broke into a run and raced for the buildings. Horns clamored noisily from behind her, where the men were discovering first-hand how difficult it was to cross a Uruguayan street against traffic. She estimated she had gained another fifteen to twenty seconds – which could be just enough.

"Sweetheart, listen to me. You remember us playing hide-and-seek? We're going to play that right now, and I need you to promise me that no matter what happens, you won't make a sound until I come back for you. Do you understand?"

Hannah didn't respond, but Jet couldn't blame her. Her mother had just torn across a busy thoroughfare and was running as fast as her legs would carry her.

"I need you to promise me, Hannah. Now."

"Okay, Mama. Okay," she whispered timidly, her eyes wide as they came to the half-demolished structures. No workers were in evidence, and the site hadn't been fenced in. Jet bolted through the nearest opening and across to an attached low-rise building before glancing around and taking the concrete stairs at the far end two at a time to the second level.

A series of doorways greeted her, and she moved into the third one, finding herself facing a series of vacant offices, the plaster hanging from the walls, everything of value stripped out of them. At the far end she spotted a hole in a wall where someone had begun demolition. It looked like it would be just large enough.

She ran over and took a quick look inside, then lowered Hannah to the floor and stared deep into her eyes.

"You're going to hide in here. Don't make a sound. No matter what happens, stay here, and I'll come get you."

Hannah's eyes were wide as saucers, but she nodded silent assent, and then Jet prodded her into the opening. "Push yourself all the way to the back. I'll be back in no time. Oh, and plug your ears. Even if you get scared, don't scream, don't make a sound, and don't come out. Do you understand?"

"Y...yes, Mama."

Jet heard scraping from below. They were in the first building. She was out of time. She held a finger to her lips and handed Hannah her backpack, then turned and eyed her surroundings. With a final look at her daughter's frightened face staring out of the shadows, she pulled her purse strap over her head, securing it so that she wouldn't lose it, and focused on her predicament.

Six men. Four buildings. One Jet.

She liked her odds.

CHAPTER 5

Debris crunched beneath the men's feet as they spread out, silenced pistols drawn, any pretense of stealth discarded. The woman had seen them, so this was endgame. They had their instructions. She was to be terminated with extreme prejudice.

The leader of the group made a curt gesture, a hand signal with two fingers indicating where the men should look first. One trotted to the stairwell and ascended silently, while the rest spread out. They moved with practiced fluidity, a unit, each member with his role.

A crash came from a building two over from the one they were in, and the leader motioned with his head, taking the lead. The group crept through the courtyard that connected the three-story edifices, and then they heard another clank in the largest. The leader exchanged a look with his second-in-command – a short, stocky goon in his mid-thirties with hard features and simian eyes. The smaller man nodded and tapped two of the men on the arm, then moved to the side of the doorway. On his nod, the first of the gunmen ran through the opening in a crouch, weapon sweeping the room, and then the others followed. They slowed, their ears straining for any further sounds, but there was nothing but the moan of the breeze through the glassless window frames.

An empty soda can stirred on the far side of the space, nudged by the draft, and the leader made another series of hand gestures. The men fanned out, two moving towards the stairwell as the rest searched the ground floor.

The leader wasn't happy with this new twist. They'd had her dead to rights, but he'd made the decision not to execute her in the park, preferring something less public. But the situation had quickly turned, and now they were in an urban labyrinth, their advantage gone.

He'd read the dossier on her. It was impressive.

Then again, so was his.

This wrinkle presented additional difficulty, but it wouldn't change the outcome. It was just a matter of time until either she, or the child, made a sound, and then they would have her.

He swung through the first opening on the right, leading with his silenced Beretta barrel, quickly sizing up the room in the shadowy gloom before moving to the next one. The men were all seasoned professionals, good at what they did, and even if this woman had similar field experience she would be no match against all of them.

He heard footsteps from above, coming from both sides of the building, and he grinned to himself. Six against one in broad daylight – and she was likely unarmed. This would be over in no time.

ॐॐ

A sound jarred one of the upstairs gunmen as he wound his way along the maze of offices and he froze, swiveling his upper body to face whatever was making the noise. It was coming from the end of the hall, in a particularly dark area. The noise came again, spurring him forward. He cautiously placed one booted foot in front of the other, clutching his silenced pistol in a military two-handed grip as he edged towards the sound.

At the end of the hall, he turned a corner and saw the source of the clamor – a tarp, hanging from one of the walls by the window, flapping in the breeze. His shoulders relaxed and he lowered the weapon, chuckling to himself at being spooked by construction debris.

He barely registered the movement as a figure swung at him from above, hanging upside down. He was raising his weapon when a five-foot long piece of rusting rebar stabbed through his chest, impaling him as it drove clean through his back. His face froze in shock from the blinding spike of pain as the woman dropped from the ceiling's exposed pipes with a somersault and drove the palm of her hand into his nose, ramming the cartilage and bone into his brain, instantly ending his life.

Jet stood in front of the gunman as he slumped to the floor, watching him without pity, then stooped and retrieved his pistol. She did a cursory search of his jacket and pants, but all he had was his weapon – no ID, no money, nothing.

The second gunman turned the corner, having heard the commotion, and she squeezed off two shots, obliterating his face and driving him backwards. He dropped hard against a pile of rubble, his weapon clattering against the debris.

Jet ran to him and scooped up his gun, dropping it into her purse as she spun and sprinted back the way she'd come. Other than the sound of the men from downstairs ascending the stairs, the building returned to uneasy silence.

The leader spotted the second man's corpse and threw himself flat against the wall, waiting for any sign of their quarry. He listened intently, but heard nothing. Pointing to the area the fallen gunman had been approaching when he'd been killed, he directed the two men with him to separate and take alternate routes, sealing off any chance for the woman to escape.

The tarp's flapping caught his attention and he stopped, evaluating likely sources of the sound. When it flapped again he resumed inching forward towards the bend in the hall, his heartbeat pounding in his ears.

A pigeon flapped in panic from a room on his right and he swiveled, firing at the sound. He watched as the gray bird soared out the window and scowled. This was rookie behavior. The unexpected death of one of his team had spooked him. That wasn't good.

Returning his focus to the hall, he edged to the bend and peered around the corner. He saw his second man slumped in a pool of his own blood, skewered, the rebar still protruding from his chest, his face a bloody smudge. The tarp shifted again, making the noise that had first caught his attention.

One of his men appeared from the office at the end of the hall, and then another's gun came around the corner, followed by his crouching form. Their eyes locked and the entrant lowered his weapon, and then caught sight of his fallen comrade.

The leader held up one finger and made a circular motion. The two gunmen shook their heads. There was nobody on the floor – it was empty.

He took soft steps to the window and whipped his weapon out as he leaned to see if anyone was outside, but all he saw was sheer wall and a two-story drop. Above, another window loomed empty, but there was no obvious way to reach it.

Two of his five men were down, killed by the woman, who was now in possession of both their guns – and who had disappeared where no escape was possible. He turned to his men and pointed up, and then his head exploded as a slug tore through it, Jet firing as she swung through the window, a rope around her waist, one arm holding the loose end while the other pumped the pistol trigger.

The two remaining shooters dived for cover, one rolling towards a doorway as he let loose a volley of muffled shots. Ricochets ripped chunks of plaster from the wall as Jet hit the ground, letting go of the rope and reaching into her purse as she continued firing with her right hand. She heard a grunt from the doorway where the second gunman had thrown himself, blood trailing from where a round had hit his leg as he'd hurtled through the opening. Another shot rang out as a bullet missed her head by a few millimeters, and she returned her attention to the shooter behind the rubble. Raising the second gun in her left hand, she fired both weapons as she ran headfirst towards him, then dodged into an office fifteen feet away from him.

Rounds slammed into the wall near the doorjamb as she searched frantically for an escape option, and then she saw it – the floor of the room had partially collapsed, leaving a gaping hole.

The gunman stopped shooting from his position behind the rubble, conserving ammunition. He waited a moment, then two, but detected no movement. Rising cautiously, he trained his pistol on the doorway as he crept to the office where his partner had taken cover and was now moaning softly.

He entered to find the man's leg soaked with blood, a puddle spreading beneath him. He understood in an instant that the round must have severed the femoral artery, and rushed to the man's side. His face was pale and drawn, and he had his hand over the wound in a futile effort to stop the bleeding. Seeing his companion, the wounded man shifted his fingers and blood spurted in a rhythmic surge.

The gunman put his Beretta on the floor, unfastened his belt, and cinched it around the wounded shooter's upper thigh, pulling it tight. The crimson tide slowed to a trickle, but it didn't look like he was going to make it. Too much of his essence had leaked out on the anonymous concrete slab already.

The gunman retrieved his pistol and rose, then slid to the door, weapon at the ready, anticipating a hail of bullets, but to his surprise he was alone. The tarp flapped again down the hall, but he ignored it – he knew where the woman had gone, and there was no way out he could think of.

A mound of refuse lay on the floor near the doorway to the room she'd disappeared into, the odor of rotting food lingering in the still atmosphere. He edged to the side of the opening and stood completely still, trying to detect which side of the room she was on.

It sounded empty.

Impossible as it seemed, she wasn't inside.

Surveying the garbage, he bent down and picked up an empty glass soda bottle and tossed it through the gap, and then rolled into the doorway as it crashed against the floor, splintering in an explosion of shards.

There was no movement, no shooting.

He stood and saw the collapsed floor at the far end of the room, and realized that the woman must have dropped down to the ground floor while he had been tending to his partner. That meant that she could be anywhere now. Sixty seconds was a lifetime in a trained operative's hands.

He was edging towards the gap in the floor when he heard the smallest of scrapes from behind him. Without thinking he whirled and fired, registering too late that it was his wounded partner who had somehow rallied enough strength to drag himself to imagined safety. Two slugs shredded his head and chest, and a look of resigned surprise froze on his face as he rolled onto his back, sightless eyes staring into space.

How had this turned so upside down so quickly? A routine hit, for which six men was complete overkill, had transformed in seconds to a bloodbath where a team of elite commandos had been slaughtered like lambs. It was impossible; and yet here he was, in a dark room, a dead man at his feet, bodies strewn through the hall, and no sign of the target.

He faced a difficult choice: drop down through the opening to the floor below, following her, or descend the stairs and try to pick up her scent. He debated, then went for the stairs.

As he crept towards the stairwell, the disturbing sensation that they had gone from the hunters to the prey took hold, and he had to remind himself that there was one man in the other building, which still made it two against one – under normal circumstances, a guaranteed kill. He tapped his ear bud, violating the order to maintain radio silence, and listened for a response from the other gunman.

The tiny device crackled, and then he heard a whisper. "What's going on? Where are you?" a voice asked.

He paused a few feet from the stairwell. "We were hit. Everyone's dead except me."

"Dead? Everyone? *Shit...*"

"Yeah. Shit is right."

"How?"

The one word trembled in the silence. How indeed.

"She got behind us. Somehow got one of the guns. It all happened so fast..."

"Where are you?"

"Second floor of the building we went into. She's on the ground floor now."

"That...that means she could be near me."

"Affirmative. Keep your eyes open."

"I'll do that. You coming down?"

"Yes. I'll be by this building's main entrance within twenty seconds."

"All right. I'll make my way over."

There wasn't much more to say. The stairwell was almost completely dark, the lights burned out or broken, the building electricity shut off. He peered up at the third-floor landing and then stepped down the first few stairs, moving as quietly as possible.

A shadow dropped from the rail above, and he whipped around, but not fast enough. The razor-sharp blade of the butterfly knife sliced into his abdomen, the point jutting up, through his stomach wall into his heart, driven with startling power by a hand with an iron grip. He dropped his gun and stared at the apparition before him in shock – it was the woman, a look of complete calm on her face, hardly winded by the impossible leap from the third floor.

Consciousness quickly faded and he collapsed, tumbling backwards down the stairs, his last image that of Jet, standing on the steps, her hand clutching a blood-smeared knife as she watched him fall into nothingness.

Jet moved down the stairs to the dead man and wiped the blade off on his jacket before flipping it closed and sliding it into the back pocket of her jeans. She unzipped her purse, pulled the silenced gun free, and cocked her head, wary of any further danger. By her count there was still one man left.

On the ground floor. Somewhere close.

She heard something from the first building, like something falling or being dropped, and thanked providence that these men had been so over-confident, which had translated into carelessness. And now the remaining gunman was blundering around, making her job easier.

She ejected the magazine and counted the remaining bullets, then slid it back with a soft click.

Four more rounds. Which would likely be three more than she would need.

CHAPTER 6

A terrified scream echoed off the building walls, freezing Jet in her tracks, the shrill reverberation like nails on a blackboard.

She would know that sound anywhere.

Hannah.

Her operational instincts battled her maternal ones, and in a blink, maternal won. She took the stairs three at a time and was on the ground floor within seconds, ready to hurl herself into the breach and do whatever it took to save her daughter. Then self-preservation slammed her with the force of a wrecking ball, and she slowed.

She wouldn't be of much help to Hannah dead.

With a measured determination, she stopped herself from bolting recklessly into an unknown situation – probably an ambush.

But Hannah was in danger.

As was she. And the only one that could save them both was Jet. Not a terrified woman who acted without thinking and blundered into a trap.

Regaining control, the icy calm that characterized her operational persona returned as she calculated the best approach. Hannah was one building over from the main one through which they'd entered, on the second floor. Rushing headlong to her aid was precisely what the remaining gunman was hoping for – that was the whole point, of course; to destabilize her and get her making emotional decisions rather than logical ones.

But they had Hannah.

Who needed her to be calm and effective more than at any point in her life. Everything Jet cared about hung in the balance. She couldn't afford the luxury of making a misstep.

৵৽

The second floor offices of the building where she'd left Hannah were still, no further screams disrupting the quiet.

A hand clutched at the window sill, and then the ugly blunt cylindrical shape of a silencer slid into view, followed by Jet's face, then her body. She had scaled the exterior wall, approaching from the least-expected direction, hopefully flanking whoever was lying in wait.

Every nerve in her body twitched as she crouched by the window, waiting for something – anything – to give the gunman away.

She waited a minute, then another. Nothing. The breeze from the window tickled the back of her neck, and in spite of the cool temperature, a bead of sweat worked its way from her hairline to her taut jaw. She wiped it away with the back of her hand, eyes never leaving the far doorway.

Still nothing.

Patience waged war with the need to do something, and eventually, action won out.

She padded to the office door and stood just outside, trying to pick up any trace of whoever was waiting to kill her.

Odd. She didn't detect anyone.

She knelt and reached into her purse, then felt around with and extracted her makeup compact. Flipping it open with one hand as she clutched the pistol with the other, she used the tiny mirror to take in the room, angling it slowly to ensure she was seeing everything. Satisfied, she snapped it shut and slid it into her pocket.

She rose and turned the corner, entering the room, weapon leading more out of habit than necessity, and moved to the recess where Hannah had been hiding.

Empty.

Jet fought down a surge of panic and mentally ran through her options. They had her; or Hannah had run away, her toddler's nerves finally overruling her promise to stay put.

Neither situation was good – the latter only slightly more promising.

She retraced her steps and then moved to the stairwell, hesitating before she descended, listening.

In the long ground floor hall, she spotted a body at the far end, near the exit leading to the buildings she'd just come from. When she reached it she saw the sixth gunman, a single bullet hole in the back of his neck, execution-style.

Jet did a mental count. All six were dead. Unless she'd missed a seventh who had joined them after they'd crossed the street, all were accounted for.

Which didn't solve the mystery of where her daughter was; or for that matter, who had shot the final gunman – and why.

She toed his weapon away from where it lay by his outstretched arm and picked it up – a Heckler & Koch USP, also 9mm, with a more compact silencer. She popped the magazine out. Full. Fifteen more rounds at her disposal.

Chambering a round, she slid the Beretta back into her purse, switching to the USP, and edged away from the corpse. The building sounded empty. That left four more to search, assuming that Hannah was still in the complex.

Edging forward on catlike feet, she moved to the exit doorway, peering out before stepping into the sunshine and trotting to the building on the left, opting to try the areas she hadn't been in yet rather than returning to where she knew five men lay dead.

As she searched room-to-room, her thoughts whirled with the ramifications of the shooters having come after her in Uruguay, battling for prominence in her mind with the hysterical fear for Hannah's safety. The only positive, if there was one, was that they were after her, not her child, except as a tool to get to her. That meant that the likelihood that they had killed Hannah was extremely low. She served no purpose dead.

The thought brought slim consolation.

She was halfway through the top floor of the third building when she heard a scrape from outside, in the courtyard. Almost imperceptible, but there.

She whirled and inched to the nearest window, then dropped to one knee and looked over. *There.* At the fourth building. A glimpse of a man's back clad in a dark blue overcoat, carrying a bundle. A bundle with a small pink arm dangling from it.

Hannah.

And then he was gone.

Jet calculated the drop and the rate at which she could descend, but dismissed climbing down the wall – she'd be exposed the entire time, and there was no guarantee she would find good holds. She debated jumping, but she knew that there was no way to do a dead fall from the third story. A two-story jump with sidelong momentum she could just pull off, but not three from a stop. That was a guarantee of disaster.

She made for the stairs and was on the ground floor within ten seconds, now unconcerned about the sound of her shoes slamming against the bare concrete in the confined space. At the base she sprinted at full speed across the cavernous open room and then slowed when she reached one of the exit doors.

Holding the pistol with both hands, she looked over at the building into which the man had disappeared, and seeing nothing, ran to it, pressing herself against the concrete wall by the entrance, wary of any motion inside.

She waited a few beats, then peered in.

The building was entirely gutted, only a few structural support columns holding up the ceiling. Black oily water pooled on the floor near pipes sticking up from the slab, and Jet saw that she was alone.

Instinct told her to move, to run, to get to the far side, to where the man with Hannah must have gone. But caution told her to check the second story, to be methodical, to not take any chances – a bullet to the brain being her reward if she made a rash call.

She inched to the stairwell and then froze as a man's voice called out to her.

"Jet. Stop where you are and put down the gun."

She blinked. She knew that voice. It had been years, but she knew it.

What the hell was going on?

"Jet. Now. We don't have much time."

CHAPTER 7

"I'm going to kneel down and place the gun on the ground. Nothing tricky," she said, then did so. "There. I'm unarmed."

"The purse too."

Damn. She had hoped he wouldn't think of that.

"All right."

She lifted the strap over her head, then placed it next to the gun.

"Now what?" she asked, squinting at the darkness.

A blur of motion ran at her. Pink-clad motion on small, unsteady legs.

"Mama, Mama…"

She knelt and gathered Hannah in her arms, hugging her tight, eyes welling with tears of relief as she held her.

"Are you all right, sweetheart? Are you hurt?"

Hannah shook her head.

"But scared, huh?"

She nodded, crying. "Wait…long time."

Jet hugged her more. "I know. You were good. You were more than good. The best."

The man stepped from the shadows and took several steps towards her, his gun by his side, pointing at the floor.

"The gunman in the other building…" Jet started.

He nodded. "That was me."

"What are you doing here? How did you find me?"

"I'll explain everything, but right now we have to get going. The backup team will be here when those guys miss their radio check."

"Backup team," she repeated.

"Three more men. They aren't screwing around."

41

"You're here to help? Why? Who are they?" she demanded.

"Jet. There's no time. Promise not to shoot me now. You understand I could have killed you ten times over in the last few seconds. Pick up your things, and let's get out of here. I'm serious. We're on borrowed time."

She did as instructed. "Where to?"

"Follow me. Out this way."

They ran to the exit on the far end of the room, and he held up a hand, pausing as he looked outside.

"They'll be looking for a woman with a child. Let me take Hannah. That's the best cover you can hope for. And they probably have a description, so take off your jacket and tie it around your waist," he instructed.

Jet kneeled down and fixed Hannah with a calm, serious gaze. "Sweetie, you need to hold the man's hand while we leave here, okay? Can you do that for me?"

"He…He scary."

Jet nodded. "I think we're all a little scared right now. But he's a friend. Please do as I ask, Hannah."

She considered the request, then agreed. "Okay."

Hannah wobbled over and took the man's hand.

"Last time I saw you, the front of your apartment was blowing all over the sidewalk in Yemen," Jet said. "You're supposed to be dead."

He looked back at her. "There's a lot of that going around, I guess. Reports of my demise were somewhat exaggerated."

"How did you find me?"

"Later. Now come on. Follow maybe twenty yards behind me until we get to my car," he said, and then strode through the door, Hannah holding his hand, as though nothing was amiss.

They skirted the outer perimeter of the construction and then followed the large boulevard one block before making a right onto a smaller street. He approached a Peugeot sedan and hit the keyless remote, and the lights blinked once. Surveying the area as he turned, he opened the back door and motioned to Hannah to get in. She hesitated.

"No. Need Mama."

Hannah had been cautioned to never get into a strange car without her mother.

The man rolled his eyes, and with a final glance up both directions of the street, he signaled to Jet, who made her way at a moderate pace before sliding into the back with Hannah, pulling the door shut after her.

He started the engine, and then with a glance at his side mirror, revved the motor and slammed the transmission into gear.

"Buckle up and hang on to her. We've got company," he warned, and then stomped on the gas, cutting off a truck as he swung into traffic and roared towards the nearest intersection.

"How could they find us?" Jet asked, gripping the seat back and holding Hannah to her with her free arm.

"We took too long. They must have had watchers around the site. One of the hit team probably called them and reported their position. These guys are pro."

"Not that pro. I left five of them back there."

"Six of them. Not to be technical."

"The sixth was yours, so I'm not counting him."

He twisted the wheel and they careened onto a larger street, three lanes of traffic in each direction. "Hang on." Horns blared as he cut in and out of the already fast-moving stream of cars, occasionally cutting into oncoming traffic to get by slower vehicles.

"I see you've gotten the hang of the local driving customs. How long have you been in town?" Jet asked.

He peered at her in the rearview mirror, a look of studied concentration on his face. "Not very long. Three days."

She looked back and saw a black BMW sedan mirroring their moves, carrying three men, including the driver. "They're gaining," she said.

"It ain't over till it's over."

He wrenched the little car hard left, tires screeching in protest, and veered crazily down a narrow alley, knocking garbage cans skyward as he regained control and floored it. She watched as the BMW appeared at the alley mouth and roared towards them, the Peugeot's four-cylinder engine no match for the Bavarian brawn of the German sedan.

"Honey, hold on to the seat back and close your eyes, okay?"

Hannah looked up at her and nodded, and then threw her arms around the passenger seat, eyelids clamped tightly shut.

Jet reached into her purse and extracted the H&K, then rolled her window down.

"Hold this thing steady for a few seconds, will you?" she shouted, the engine and wind noise deafening in the small cab.

"You got it. Make them count."

She leaned out the window with the pistol and squeezed off five shots. Two missed, but one punched a small hole in the windshield directly in front of the driver's head; she saw a splash of red spackle the windows, then the car slammed into a building on the right side of the alley, leaving a trail of sparks as it scraped along before flipping over, end to end, and sliding to a stop upside down, wheels spinning in the air.

"Problem solved," she announced, slipping the weapon back into her purse.

"Nicely done. You haven't lost your touch."

"Thanks. Now would you mind telling me what you're doing in Uruguay, alive, with a hit team in tow?"

"Sure. But let's get someplace quiet first. You can't go back to your townhouse, I'm afraid. They'll be watching it. Have you got a kit stashed somewhere?" he asked.

"Of course. At two different banks. But what's this all about? Who are 'they'?"

He ignored the questions. "What about ID? I think it's safe to assume that your current ID is blown," he cautioned.

"Damn. It's a legit one. Cost me a small fortune."

"Luck of the draw. Do you have any others?"

"Yes. Three more. But only one other for Hannah. Which reminds me. How did you know her name?"

"Her name?"

"Back at the building. Before I told you what it was, you used her name. You said 'Hannah.'"

He sighed as he pulled out of the alley onto another medium-sized street, eyes darting to the mirrors to ensure there were no more followers. "I suppose I did." He didn't say anything more.

"You need to tell me what the hell is going on, Rain."

"I know. But right now, I think our time would be better served if you told me where your banks are located. We need to get your kit and as much cash as you can carry."

"I'm familiar with the drill. But some information would be nice."

"Okay. I'll start at the beginning."

"Any time."

"I obviously didn't die in Yemen. That was a ruse to get me out of a situation that had gotten too hot."

"You faked it?" Jet asked.

"I didn't have to. I knew that the cell was planning to take me out, so all I had to do was pretend not to notice their clumsy incursion into the apartment. Christ, I mean, it was like drunk blind kids planted the bomb. Anyway, I let it detonate – it was set up to go when I hit the light switch, which was a piece of cake to rig to remote-trigger using a cell phone – and poof, no more Rain."

"Nice. And it seems somewhat familiar."

"It should. Your death gave David the idea."

She hesitated. "You know about David and my death?"

"I know everything. I know about Trinidad, and the Russian, and even about Hannah."

Jet digested that. "But how?"

"David. I spoke to him for the last time the day you both blew up the Russian's boat. The day…the day he died. In the morning. He told me about what you were getting ready to do, and wanted me to have as much information as possible, in case…in case things didn't go well."

"Why would he trust you with that? He would never tell anyone."

"Yes, he was a secretive type, wasn't he? I suppose that goes with the territory."

"So why?"

"Because…we were close. Closer than you can imagine."

"David wasn't close to anyone. Believe me, I know."

"I'm sure you do. But there are some things that, for all your knowledge, you were left out of. You couldn't know, because David was very, very good at keeping secrets." He swiveled and glanced down at where Hannah was still hugging the car seat, eyes scrunched shut, as instructed, then reached out with his right hand and stroked her hair. "She's a heartbreaker, isn't she?"

"What secrets are you talking about? What's going on here?"

He pulled onto another street, slowing as they approached a red light, and when they rolled to a stop he turned in his seat to face Jet. "There's a lot you don't know."

"So start talking, and not in riddles."

He nodded, seeming to have come to a decision. "David was more than my control officer, and probably the most gifted schemer the intelligence industry has ever known. Besides being a genius, he was also the closest person in the world to me."

Jet didn't speak, holding her breath.

"David was my brother."

CHAPTER 8

One week before, Moscow, Russian Federation

The sun struggled to burn through the scattered clouds that lingered over Moscow's sprawl as the Sunday morning lurched into gear. A black stretch Mercedes limousine pulled onto the larger thoroughfare from the quiet neighborhood near the Bolshoi theater, two SUV guard vehicles following it, and rolled past the roundabout without slowing. An old Lada sedan was crashed into the massive trunk of a centuries-old oak, its unlucky driver hanging half out of the vehicle, face down on the hood from where he had flown through the windshield. The eyebrows of the limo passenger – a young blond man with typically Slavic high cheekbones and piercing blue-gray eyes – didn't even rise at the sight of the carnage.

"Drunks," his companion, a severe-looking woman in her early fifties, spat.

"Yes. It's always like this after a long Saturday night."

"The people are weak. They have no direction. So they drink and kill themselves. Losers," she pronounced dismissively. She reached over and stroked the young man's cheek with the back of her hand. "Thank God you know better than to go down that road. The road of the insect; of the slave. It's been the national curse as long as there's been a Russia, this weakness. A nation of drunks and degenerates, with no hope."

"Not all, Mother. Not all."

"There are two kinds of Russians, my son. The serfs – peasants who toil away, blunting the horror of their life with drugs and alcohol – and the leaders. Never forget that almost everyone you meet in your life will fall into the first category, no matter what their station. If a man is willing to turn over control of his life to a drug, whether it's alcohol, nicotine, or worse, he isn't fit to be a leader. A leader must be above the temptations of the flesh. He must be better than that."

He let her continue her monologue. He'd heard it almost every day since he was a small boy. There was nothing new there, but she seemed to enjoy repeating her philosophy as if it were some sort of mantra, and he saw no harm in it. Although sometimes he wanted to tell her to shut up, stop with the Nietzsche-inspired superman rant, he never dared. She deserved respect, and commanded it in everyone around her, her unrelenting demand for excellence one of her defining qualities. She had been a prima ballerina with the Kirov Ballet before she had gotten pregnant, and had achieved more in her aborted career within a few short years than most did in a lifetime. And she had guided him, advised him through difficult times, which had resulted in him reaching an unlikely summit in his business even at his tender age, when most of his friends were just starting out in their chosen fields.

The limo pulled up to his company headquarters, and he waited as the two SUVs emptied of the heavily armed bodyguards before signaling his driver that he was ready to exit the vehicle. The man murmured into an ear bud, and a suited older gentlemen emerged from the impressive entry of the towering glass building and opened his door for him.

"Nice to see you this morning, Mr. Grigenko," the older man greeted.

"Is everything ready?" Grigenko asked, curtly ignoring the welcome as he stepped onto the sidewalk, the armed men creating a gauntlet leading to the front doors.

"Of course. As you ordered."

"Very well. Mother, come. Let's see what progress I've made since the last time you watched." Grigenko extended a hand, and she took it as she slid her still-elegant, graceful dancer's legs out and emerged into the sunlight, her oversized black hat and sunglasses giving her the aura of a diva – which in some respects, she was.

"I'm sure it will be quite impressive, my son. I expect nothing but the best from you."

They walked together to the entrance, and another man waited by the massive tempered glass and chrome doors as they entered, the panels sliding open and closed with a whisper. The ultra-modern lobby was decorated with Scandinavian minimalism, and several colorful original abstract oil paintings provided welcome color in the monochromatic space. Grigenko's hand-tailored British oxfords were nearly silent on the high-gloss Italian marble slabs, his mother's Christian Louboutin pointed-toe pumps snicking alongside him – fitting accompaniment for a master of the universe entering his earthly kingdom.

Sergei Grigenko owned the entire thirty-story edifice, but his offices occupied only the top three floors. He entered the private elevator that would whisk them up to the penthouse level and waited as the older man punched one of the buttons on the control panel. The doors slid shut and they ascended at dizzying speed in the Japanese-crafted contrivance. Time was at a premium in his world, and Grigenko had ordered the fastest elevator made for his private realm – every time he took the trip, a small smile of satisfaction tugged at the corners of his brutally handsome mouth.

When the stainless steel door opened, they stepped into a lavishly appointed lobby, with security men stationed at each door on the floor. At the far end, a small graying Asian man stood wearing a white *judo-gi* – the classic judo training pants and jacket, held in place by the black *obi* belt – and a black headband tied around his balding pate.

Grigenko and his mother approached, trailed by the older man, and Grigenko executed a small bow, which was returned by the Asian.

"Yamaguchi-sensei. Nice to see you again," Grigenko said, his tone conveying respect.

"Nice to be seen. I have everything prepared. We begin in five minutes, yes?" Yamaguchi's Russian was rough but serviceable, his native Japanese softening some of the harder consonants.

"That will be fine. Just fine," Grigenko said, then gestured for his mother to go into the gymnasium he'd had custom built and take a seat.

He emerged from the dressing room a few minutes later, wearing his *judo-gi* and a black belt of his own. His bare feet padded on the imported wood floor to where Yamaguchi stood with another young man, Asian as well. Grigenko sized up his opponent and then bowed to both men, who returned his bow, and then Yamaguchi stepped forward.

"You have mastered many of the martial arts, Sergei. Karate. Judo. Jiu-Jitsu, taekwondo. Systema. Bartitsu. Krav Maga. At your request, the time has come to put your skills to the test against a new adversary every week. In this, your first match, you will be taking on one of Malaysia's most adept fighters, who has also achieved a mastery of his craft. For this match, there are no rules. There is simply one goal – to win. Do what you can, and must, to emerge victorious. Unlike a traditional match, I will limit the sparring to three rounds of three minutes duration. You may use whatever disciplines you like. Are there any questions?"

Both men studied each other, and then Grigenko gave a curt shake of his head. His Asian adversary eyed him with a flat look, but as they turned to walk to their respective spots Grigenko could have sworn he saw the twitch of a smile play across his face before it settled into the serious expression he'd maintained since Grigenko had entered.

They taped their hands and donned four-ounce fingerless gloves, and then put in dental guards in preparation for the fight.

Grigenko and his adversary did a five-minute warm-up of stretches and then took off their tops. The Asian had colorful tattoos crisscrossing his powerful torso, whereas Grigenko's body was unmarred, the steroid-augmented bulk of his sculpted musculature bulging in the natural light from the far floor-to-ceiling windows. Yamaguchi brought them together to where a large rectangular mat was adhered to the floor, and had them bow to each other before he dropped a red cloth onto the white surface.

The Asian came straight at Grigenko with a blinding flurry of kicks and blows, which Grigenko parried while levying his own barrage of kicks and strikes. Grigenko took the first thirty seconds to size up his opponent and understand his favored techniques – all martial arts fighting eventually came down to stand-up techniques, clinching, and ground approaches. Grigenko was adept at all three and could adapt at will, and he knew that one of the best ways to win a fight quickly was to draw his adversary into whatever style of fighting he seemed least comfortable with. He had just about decided that the Asian was a combination stand-up and clincher, when he tried to flip Grigenko onto the ground – a maneuver Grigenko was only just able to slip out of, breaking the clinch hold and delivering a set of strikes that would have had most adversaries on the ground, out cold.

The Asian seemed scarcely winded by the exertion, taking carefully measured breaths, his speed lightning fast. Grigenko noted that he favored Muay Thai strikes, bouncing in the distinctive way, less rigid than taekwondo or karate. He allowed the Asian to get closer to him and willingly took several brutal blows to the chest and stomach, and then sweep-kicked him as he fought for a finish hold, flipping over and gripping the Asian's neck with his legs before dropping him to the mat.

The Asian broke the hold at the last second and twisted free, and Grigenko threw his legs into the air and flipped back up onto his feet, continuing the momentum with an unconventional back flip that terminated with three devastating strikes, the last one to his opponent's shin.

The crack of the Asian's tibia and fibula was as audible as a gunshot, and he screamed in agony as he went down, the bone edges jutting out of his skin in a compound fracture with a spray of blood. Grigenko spun and leveled a powerful kick at the falling man's head, snapping it back at a sickening angle, and his torso went limp with a shudder on the bloody mat as Yamaguchi ran to break the fight off.

Grigenko's chest heaved as he bounced on the balls of his feet, adrenaline coursing through his system, a crazed look in his eyes, and then he seemed to return to reality and register the Asian's inert form, Yamaguchi crouched over him with an expression of alarm. He paced back and forth as the old man tried to revive him, and then walked away, pulling off his gloves as he moved to his mother and the older gentleman who had accompanied them in the elevator.

"Take care of this. Get him out of here, either to a hospital or to a ditch in the countryside. Pay whatever needs to be paid," he ordered, then caught a look at his mother's eyes, gleaming bright with excitement at the image of her son's bare-chested form, beads of sweat running down his iron pecs, shaved smooth – the powerful victor in an all-or-nothing test of skill and prowess.

She leaned into him and murmured in his ear, her hand on his shoulder, her musky perfume blending with his scent as her lips caressed his cheek. "You are twice the man your father was."

Grigenko said nothing, only nodded, and then without looking back at Yamaguchi or his fallen adversary, strode back to the dressing room, the buzzing of combat awareness slowly receding in his ears as he crossed the polished wooden floor, ready to shower off and join his mother for a late breakfast at her favorite club.

CHAPTER 9

"He was your brother? David didn't have a brother," Jet said, shaking her head.

"I was illegitimate. His father's bastard son. But we were brothers."

They rode in silence for a few blocks, Jet's mind processing the news. "But the team. The Mossad would never allow family members to work it. That was one of the conditions. You had to be alone in the world, with no connections or relationships..."

"Correct. Nobody knew. I had my mother's last name. As far as anyone was concerned, we weren't related. It was our little secret. Until now."

"That means..."

"I'm Hannah's uncle. Uncle Alan. She's got some of my flesh and blood in her – my only living relative now. My mom passed away years ago, and so did our dad, so that leaves Hannah."

"I...when did you know about her?"

"Not until David told me, the day he was killed. Like so much in his life, he played that one close to his chest."

"Which brings us to how you found me."

"In a second. Where am I going? Which bank? Can you give me some guidance here?"

She thought about which was closer, then gave him the bank name and an address. "Next big street, take a left towards downtown, then I'll direct you."

They drove on, lost in their thoughts, Hannah now sitting on Jet's lap gazing vacantly out the window at the passing scenery.

"How did you find me, Rain?"

"Alan."

"Okay. How?"

"It's complicated. I'm on a mission right now, but I've been working on tracking you down, and one thing led to another."

"That's not an answer."

"I followed the money."

"What does that mean?"

"You've been accessing one of the operational accounts David set up years ago – which now has around ten million dollars in it. Once I saw activity on it, it was child's play to track you here – I followed the wire transfers to Uruguay, and then hacked the local bank. All I had to do was wait for you to show up at the ATM you've been using. You went there two days ago. Bingo."

"How did you get the account information? Nobody had that…"

"One person did. David. He emailed me an entire dossier that last day, just in case. Made me promise I wouldn't open it unless…unless something happened. When I saw the headlines and he never got in touch again, I figured it out."

"And Hannah's background was in there?"

"Yes. He included everything I would need to know. I had the address in Nebraska, your bank account, the whole works. I even flew to Omaha, but by the time I got there, Hannah was nowhere to be found. The trail had gone cold. So I waited. I returned to Yemen, and waited."

"Alan. What were you doing in Yemen? And why fake your death?"

"I'd gotten wind of a particularly nasty new terrorist group that was working out of Yemen and Syria – sort of an adjunct to Al Qaeda, but even more anti-American, with the usual seasoning of an all-encompassing hatred of Israel. The cell I'd infiltrated had established a relationship with this new group, but I couldn't get any sort of definitive data on it. I think my interest triggered some alarms, because my cell began getting suspicious. It was time to pull out."

"So David knew all along that the Yemen explosion was theater."

Alan nodded. "With an important twist. It gave us the opportunity to end my involvement in Yemen so I could pursue this new group. David was in charge. When he disappeared, I got in contact with the director. David didn't trust anyone else in the organization, so neither did I. Anyway, I briefed him on where we were on this new mission, and he decided to keep me working in the field, on my own, reporting directly to him."

"Okay, so you're working directly for the director. What does that have to do with me?"

They made the left onto the boulevard where Jet indicated and crawled their way downtown, the lunchtime traffic an angry snarl.

"It looks like there may be some overlap I haven't completely figured out."

"What does that mean?"

"That one of the groups that's come up as probably involved with this new terrorist organization, is a familiar name. Grigenko."

Jet leaned back in her seat. "Impossible. He's dead. I watched him die on the runway in Nice."

"I believe you. But we're talking different Grigenkos here. I'm talking about Sergei, his son."

"I didn't know Grigenko had a son..." Jet's mind raced over the ramifications.

"Yes, and like dad, he's a real piece of work. If anything, worse than pops. He's only twenty-five, but he's already into a host of ugly sidelines – Russian mob, murder for hire, arms dealing, drug running, you name it. He inherited all of his father's money and has taken over his petroleum interests, but his real love seems to lie in the illegal. That was how he made a name for himself until the untimely death of Grigenko senior, and rather than stepping out of the underworld once he'd inherited several billion, he's used the money to expand his criminal syndicate and wage war against his adversaries. Quite successfully, I might add."

"Nothing like a few billion to help solidify your position."

Alan nodded. "The lucky sperm club. But he's not happy resting on his laurels. Among other things, he's now moved into some seriously nasty shit. Bio-weapons. Nuclear material. Bad, bad news."

"Chip off the old block."

"Indeed."

She pointed. "Next street, make a right, and the bank will be up on the right, three blocks."

"A different one than you've been using for the ATM, huh?"

"Yes. The ATM was just a convenience, closer to home."

"I see. Mind if I ask where you got ten million dollars in that account?"

"We both have long stories to tell, don't we?" she hinted cryptically, then shifted Hannah to her other leg. "But none of this explains what you're doing in Uruguay."

"Watching out for Hannah," he said simply.

"From what?"

"Everything. It was my promise to David. He made me swear that if anything happened to him, I would stand in for him and ensure that no harm came to either of you."

"Well, that's very sentimental, but I can't help but notice that you showed up, and then a hit squad was close behind."

"I know. That's troubling. I don't understand it myself. It's an extraordinary coincidence that I'm investigating Grigenko, and then when I finally find you, his goons appear. You know the odds of that being random chance..."

"Effectively zero. Pull over here," she instructed. "So what's your theory? How did they find me?"

He shook his head. "They just showed up on the scene, so they couldn't have known about you for very long. It could be that there's another loose end we aren't accounting for. I haven't had a lot of time to develop a hypothesis..."

"All right. Wait here and I'll be back in ten minutes. I need to get into the box. I'm taking Hannah with me. No offense," she swung the door wide, preparing to step out.

"None taken."

"Come on, sweetie. Let's go." Jet hoisted Hannah off her lap and set her standing on the car floor, then slid past her and got out, extending her hand for her daughter to follow. Hannah grabbed it and pulled herself out of the car using her mother's arm.

"Do they have any problems with your going inside the bank packing a silenced pistol?"

"Not that I know of. Guess we'll find out," she said, and then slammed the door shut, her thoughts in turmoil as she walked the thirty yards to the bank entrance. Everything had happened so suddenly. Only hours ago her only care in the world had been Hannah going berserk over not getting her way, and now she had a Russian hit squad gunning for her – and her idyllic existence in Uruguay had been abruptly terminated.

There was no way she would be able to remain in Montevideo. If they had tracked her here, her only option was to disappear again. Although the Russians' ability to locate her was disconcerting – she needed to close the loop on that and figure out how they had done so, or she would never be safe anywhere.

Worse yet, Hannah would never be safe. Jet's past had come back to haunt her, again, and now threatened not only her safety but that of her daughter. She snuck a look at Hannah trotting alongside her, the trauma of the events in the office buildings already fading.

Jet entered the bank and approached the manager, who quickly escorted her to the safe deposit vault, where the palm scanner verified her identity. She went to her large box and emptied the contents onto the table, Hannah her sole accompaniment.

A backpack. Three passports: her Thai diplomatic ID, her Belgian identity as an investigative reporter, and the fake Mexican one she had gotten made in California before she and Hannah had slipped over the border. Next was Hannah's Mexican passport and Thai ID. Several credit cards. A hundred thousand dollars in cash. And a small pouch on a leather cord.

Her heart lurched as she picked it up, fingers tracing lightly across the rough seam, and then she pulled the cord over her head and nestled the little bag between her breasts, out of sight, hidden by her sweater. A bittersweet memory of Matt flitted through her awareness, but she dismissed it. No point in getting sentimental over what might have been. The clock was running, and she needed a clear head.

She packed all the items into the backpack and then returned the empty box to its slot and signaled to Hannah to join her. Mother and daughter left the vault, and Jet stopped and thanked the manager again before she exited onto the sidewalks crowded with business people and office workers hurrying to lunch. They allowed themselves to be carried along by the throng in the direction of the car, and then Jet froze, gripping Hannah's hand tightly as she stared at the green sports coupe parked where Alan's Peugeot had been.

There was no sign of him.

Alan was gone.

CHAPTER 10

Jet waited on the street with Hannah for a few minutes, thinking that Alan might have had to move the car, but then when it became apparent that he wasn't coming back, she began thinking through her next move. With or without him, she had a problem, and it wasn't going to get better as time went by.

"Mama, Hannah hungry."

Of course she was. It was way past her normal meal time, and Jet knew that if she didn't get food into her soon and then find someplace for her to nap, she would go berserk. That was just how Hannah was. She needed to be very regimented with her food and sleep, or her head would start to spin around.

"All right, sweetie. Let's get you fed, shall we?" Jet asked, and Hannah nodded, but she was already starting to pout. Jet had maybe five minutes before she had a full meltdown on her hands.

She looked around for a restaurant and saw a crowded diner at the end of the block. They pushed their way in and had to wait a few minutes until a couple vacated a booth by the back. The waitress was quick to clean it, and soon they were considering the menu, Hannah becoming increasingly agitated as her hunger took hold.

"Oh, boy. Look at these choices. Wow. Spaghetti. Grilled cheese sandwich. Noodles with butter. Macaroni and cheese," Jet read.

Hannah's eyes lit up on the mention of the last choice, and she started banging the table with enthusiasm. "Macaroni! Macaroni!"

They ordered, and Jet kept her occupied with some bread and butter, which Hannah gratefully took small pieces of and stuffed into her mouth, and when their entrées arrived, she fumbled with her spoon until Jet helped her. Jet's fish was only so-so, but she wasn't in any mood to complain, and she ate it mechanically, mulling over her options.

The townhouse was off-limits – it was the first place they would be looking for her. And being hunted with Hannah was going to pose some serious problems. It was hard enough to evade a professional assassination team without having to worry about the care and feeding of a toddler. She needed to find someplace safe where she could regroup and craft some sort of a response – and right now she had no plan and only a vague idea of what she was up against.

She paid the bill and Hannah yawned noisily, alerting Jet to the next item on the day's agenda – it was natural that her child would be exhausted after all the excitement. Jet rose and took her hand.

"Honey, we're in for a treat. We're going to stay in a hotel for a little while, just like when we were in Mexico!"

Hannah regarded her doubtfully, and then shrugged. She was tired, and when she hit the wall like this she didn't really care what they did as long as she got to sleep.

They exited the restaurant and were meandering down the block when two loud honks from a few feet away startled them.

"Hey. Come on. Get in," Alan called.

The blue Peugeot was double-parked by the bank, occupying one of the four precious lanes of the downtown street. They ran to it and Jet opened the back door. Hannah threw herself in headfirst, and then climbed onto the rear seat. Jet quickly followed her, and when the door closed Alan pulled away, waving apologetically at the cars behind him.

"Where did you go? I thought we'd lost you."

"It would be nice if you had a cell phone or something."

"I do. A burner. I suppose I should have given you the number," she conceded.

"A cop came along and was pretty interested in the scrapes on the front fenders from the garbage cans. It took me fifty dollars' worth of pesos to make him go away, and I didn't think it was a smart idea to wait around, in case someone had reported the shooting in the alley. Sorry. It took a while to circle around in the traffic, and by the time I made it back, you were nowhere to be found."

"We need to get Hannah to sleep. Any ideas?"

"Can she sleep in the car?"

"I suppose so." Jet turned to her daughter. "Can you go nappies in the car?"

Hannah thought it over, and then nodded, her eyes drooping.

"Okay, we'll find someplace quiet to park and then you can get some shut-eye." He glanced at Jet in the mirror. "How long does she sleep for?"

"An hour usually does the trick, although left to her own devices she'll stay down for two."

"Let's get out of downtown and find someplace quiet. You know the neighborhoods better than I do. Where to?"

"There's an area over by the botanical gardens that's usually deserted. Keep going this way. I'll direct you."

"Did you get everything?" he asked.

"Yes, mission accomplished, although we're going to need to get some clothes pretty soon. At least a couple of outfits apiece."

They found a tranquil street ten minutes later and he parked, leaving the windows down a crack as Hannah snuggled on the seat, using her backpack as a pillow. Jet moved to the passenger seat so Hannah could have the back seat to herself, and she was out in two minutes. Jet knew from past experience that you could set off a bomb next to Hannah and she wouldn't wake up, so she was confident that a quiet, much-needed discussion with Alan wouldn't disrupt her nap.

Jet watched her daughter slumbering, sleeping the untroubled rest of the innocent, and then leaned towards Alan. "How bad is this going to get, Alan?" she whispered.

"I'm not going to lie to you. It's very bad. You can't stay here anymore, and we need to find you someplace safe to start over," he whispered back.

"Until they come for me again."

He shook his head. "There are no guarantees in life, but I would hope that you can go deep enough so that—"

She cut him off. "That didn't work this time, did it? How much more off the beaten path can you get than frigging Uruguay? Come on. Had you even heard of it before you came here?"

"Fair point. If we knew how they tracked you, it would make life a lot easier."

"Agreed. But we don't. So where does that leave us?"

"All you can do is hide and start over."

She shook her head. "I've been thinking about this. I don't think it's that easy. They won't stop trying to find me if they've gotten this far. Which means I'll always be in danger. And so will Hannah."

RUSSELL BLAKE

He had nothing to say to that.

"I need to know everything, Alan. What's this all about?"

"It was a complete surprise to me when they showed up. I was watching you, waiting for a chance to approach you, when I spotted them. I wasn't sure you were being tailed, but after a couple of days I was positive. I took photos with my phone when I first suspected you were the target and checked them against the Mossad's data base. One of them came up as a match. The leader. Ivan Slasky. A known Russian mob enforcer, ex-Spetsnaz, for the last two years part of the entourage of our favorite young entrepreneur – Sergei Grigenko. When the response came back and I saw the last name, I knew the shit had hit the fan. That was yesterday evening. I was going to warn you today, but they got to you first."

"And you're targeting Grigenko as part of your terrorist mission?"

"Yes. He's a nasty piece of work, but there are plenty of those. What makes him special is he seems willing to go down the nuclear and bio-weapon road, whereas most won't touch that. Too risky. Too much heat. But Grigenko seems emboldened now that he's a billionaire. It seems like the money transformed an ugly piece of human garbage into a monster."

She twisted and looked at Hannah again, who was deeply asleep, then leaned forward. "I'm going to have to go after Grigenko. That's the only way we'll be safe. Same as with his father. I'm not going to live every moment looking over my shoulder, wondering whether today is the day Hannah doesn't come home because his men got to her," she said, her voice low, angry.

"I think that's a terrible idea. He's got unlimited power and money, and as far as I can tell, he never leaves Moscow. So that would mean tackling him on his home turf, with some of the best security in the world."

"You know my history. I've done much harder and I'm still standing."

"I know. So have I. But eventually your luck runs out."

"I don't think you understand. I'm not asking you for advice or permission. I'm telling you what I'm going to do. I didn't ask for this, but I'll finish it. I'm not afraid of whatever he can throw at me, or worried about it." She sat back and stared at the Peugeot. "He's as good as dead."

"What about Hannah? You have a kid now. Whose safety is partially my responsibility. I promised my brother..."

"I appreciate the sentiment, Alan, but you can't stand guard over her twenty-four hours a day, and neither can I. We lose that battle if we try to

60

fight it. I need someone to look after her while I do this. I'm thinking my housekeeper. She adores her, and it shouldn't be for very long."

"They'll be looking for Hannah, you know. And once you disappear, they'll be trying to find anyone who might know about you. Which means your housekeeper will be a target, too."

"Yeah, but I pay her cash, under the table, so there are no records. And she's not from Montevideo. I think she's from San Carlos; about seventy miles east of here. Nobody here knows her – she doesn't talk to the neighbors. The house on one side of us has been empty since we moved in, and she detests the cleaning woman who works in the other and won't give her the time of day. I don't think I've ever seen her interact with anyone since she's been living with us – she keeps to herself. I'll ask her to go somewhere where she doesn't know anyone and take Hannah. I can give her enough money that she'll never have to work again, so I can make a pretty compelling argument. And if something goes wrong...I can leave enough so neither Hannah nor Magdalena will ever want for anything. I'll get a will drafted."

"Which brings me to the ten million dollars in that account. I'm sure there's a story behind it," Alan commented.

"There is indeed."

She weighed how much to tell him, and gave him a sanitized and highly abridged version of the adventure with Matt and the diamonds.

"Wow. So you're rich."

"Yup. Which will solve a lot of logistical problems. Money may not buy happiness, but it can sure as hell buy a lot of firepower. I can afford to spend the kind of money a country would to take Grigenko out. He picked the wrong enemy with me."

"I'll say. But it won't be easy."

"Nothing ever is. The question is, will you help me, or do I do this alone?"

"What are the chances I can talk you out of it?"

"Zero."

"That's what I thought. Okay. I'm in. What are you thinking?"

She leaned her head back and studied the wisps of clouds outside, and considered his question. What indeed was she thinking?

"I'll need everything you can get on Grigenko. Habits, girlfriends, home and business blueprints, travel routine, the works. We do this exactly like we were planning a mission, with no shortcuts. If we do it right, we can be in and out before anyone knows he's dead. And that'll be the end of the story."

"Timing?"

"No time like the present."

"And Hannah?"

"Glad you mentioned that." She looked at her watch. "I need to talk to someone."

"They're probably monitoring the house phone line. And yours, if it's registered in your name."

"It isn't. But I'm going to chuck it anyway and get a new one. Can't be too careful."

She pushed the door open, watching her daughter, who shifted but didn't wake up.

"Can you watch Hannah for an hour while she naps? Shouldn't take much longer than that. I'll be back before you know it. She sleeps like a rock, so it's not rough duty."

"Not a problem…but I have to warn you. I have no experience with kids."

She smiled. "Join the club. Don't worry. She won't break. Just don't get her angry."

"Like her mom, huh?"

Jet looked at the tree-lined street and nodded.

"Exactly."

CHAPTER 11

Magdalena dropped the plate she was cleaning when Jet suddenly appeared out of nowhere in the hall.

"Oh my…I'm sorry. You surprised me. I didn't hear you come in…" the woman said, flustered, surveying the fragments with a frown.

"Don't worry about that. I'll clean it up. Magdalena, I have a problem I need your help with. Come over here and sit with me. We need to talk."

"A problem? Is Hannah all right?" she asked, alarmed.

"Yes, she's fine. But I'm going to have to ask you to do something very important for me, and you need to follow my instructions to the letter, with no variation. Do you understand?" Jet asked, holding the older woman's gaze.

"Of course. What's the problem, and what do you need me to do?"

Jet told her a story, about an angry, jealous ex-boyfriend, violent, a criminal, who had suddenly appeared with his bully boys and had placed both Hannah and her in danger.

"I need you to move up the coast – I'm thinking Maldonado. I'll meet you there and bring Hannah. You need to leave now. Leave everything here, but take your paperwork so there's no trace of anything but your clothes. Here's a cell phone I just bought. I'll call you when I get there and we'll rendezvous." Jet handed her the phone.

"*Señora* Elyse, I'd do anything for Hannah, but there's no work for me in Maldonado, and I don't know anybody there, and, well…"

"I understand. In return for helping me, I'll give you enough money that you'll never need to work again." She named a figure in pesos, and Magdalena's eyes widened.

"Are you…are you serious?"

"Absolutely. But I need you to agree to rent a nice apartment there, and take care of Hannah like she's your own child. That's our bargain. If I leave my flesh and blood with you, I'm leaving the most valuable thing in the world in your care. There's no way I would do that if I could think of another way, but there isn't one. The money isn't a problem. I'll bring it with me. For right now, I have this." She set a bundle of hundred dollar bills on the table, and Magdalena looked at it as if it were a poisonous snake. "Ten thousand American dollars. That should take care of an apartment and anything else you need for the foreseeable future. Go get your things, and don't worry about your clothes. I need you to walk out the back door as if you were going to the market, no suitcase, just your purse, and then disappear. Do you understand? Take a taxi or a bus to Maldonado, get a place within the next twenty-four hours, and then I'll come to you with Hannah. But Magdalena? You cannot tell *anyone* about this, or the money. It has to be secret. This man is very dangerous, and if you talk, he'll hear about it, and then you, and Hannah, will be in extreme danger. He's killed before…"

Magdalena shook her head.

"No, I won't tell a soul. Nobody can know – I'd be robbed if anyone suspected I had that kind of money. Fortunately my kids live here, and my friends live in San Carlos – there isn't a lot of work in Maldonado outside of the resort and hotel industry, so older people avoid it because the hotels won't hire them. If I get an apartment close to the resort area it's very safe, and I won't run into anyone I know. How long do you think I'll need to stay there?"

"Plan on it being for a long while. I don't think this will take more than a few weeks to fix, but if it does, I don't want to have to worry."

"And you are completely serious…?" Magdalena still had a sense of disbelief. It was like Santa Claus landing on her roof and telling her that all of her financial problems had been solved.

"Completely. No matter how this turns out, you'll get the money."

"I'll take care of her like she's my own daughter, *Señora* Elyse. I raised three children by myself, so I have some experience at it."

"I know, Magdalena, I wouldn't have asked you if I didn't trust you completely. Now go get your stuff. I'll wait here."

Magdalena was back in three minutes, dressed for shopping.

"Remember. I'll call you. Within the next twenty-four hours or so," Jet said, and Magdalena nodded and held up the phone.

They said their goodbyes, and then Magdalena left via the back door, pulling a small shopping cart. Jet watched the street, conscious of possible surveillance, as Magdalena trundled down the sidewalk and rounded a corner. Detecting no followers, Jet went upstairs and hurriedly packed her backpack with clothes for Hannah and a few items for herself, and then donned the baseball cap and sunglasses she'd arrived with, the oversized blue soccer shirt she'd bought a few minutes prior, and loose black cargo pants, giving her the look of a slacker teen from a distance.

She slipped out the bedroom window and stood on the sill, feeling for holds on the brick façade. Her hand found a good grip and she dug in, then pulled herself up. Her toes found another ridge, and then another, and within a few seconds she was hoisting herself onto the flat roof. She leapt to her feet, and after glancing at the neighboring roof, took a running jump, landing easily, and repeated the process until she had traversed the block and was one home away from the far side street. Peeking over the edge to confirm that she wasn't being watched, she lowered herself onto a second-story window sill and swung out into open air, catching a tree branch at the last second before dropping in a controlled fall onto the lawn. With a final look back, Jet disappeared into the neighbor's yard, then slipped over the wall and landed on her feet, an apparently bored youth shuffling down the street on a typically dull day.

❧❧

When Jet reappeared at the car Alan didn't recognize her, and had to do a double take. "That's quite a transformation. You look like a boy."

"That's the idea. It helps that kids these days look like bag people."

"Did you get your situation taken care of?"

"Yes. We're going to go for a drive tomorrow, up the coast. How's Hannah?"

"Still asleep. Hasn't budged since you left."

"Good. She needs the rest after a day like today."

"That's what I figured."

Jet tenderly roused Hannah, who was still punchy from her sleep, then took her to a café on the corner for a potty break before returning and slipping into the back seat again.

"The ten million is compromised, but I need to go to another bank and arrange for a transfer from a different account, and then find an attorney to draft a will and set up a trust to pay out to Magdalena so she has a steady annual income," Jet announced. "Once this is over I'll bounce the ten all over the world and sanitize it. But for today, I need an attorney."

"Think you'll be able to find someone competent on short notice?" he asked.

She studied her watch. "Shouldn't be a problem. I'll ask the bank manager."

He started the engine. "Back downtown?"

"You guessed it."

The errand wound up taking two hours. She was introduced to an attorney, Enrique Gomez, a block from the bank, and he assured her he could have the documents drafted and an account set up for the trust by the following day. They agreed to meet again at eleven the following morning, and then she would transfer the funds. Magdalena would contact him to arrange for monthly deposits to the branch in Maldonado, where she could make withdrawals without restrictions. The bank would pay a reasonable rate on the entire deposit, so the interest alone would fund a comfortable lifestyle for her in perpetuity, ensuring that the trust would outlive Magdalena before running dry.

The next item on the agenda was to find someplace to stay the night. Jet suggested one of the hotels on the eastern side of town, near the beach, where there would be plenty of tourists, so they would easily blend in. They found a boutique inn, and Alan booked a two-bed suite for them under one of his aliases, paying cash. Jet marched Hannah up to the room, where she immediately set about exploring the wondrous new environment as Jet unpacked the backpack and took stock of their meager possessions.

"So this is it, huh?" Alan asked, looking around.

"For tonight, anyway. Tomorrow's a whole new day."

"Could be worse."

"I think we've both seen worse," she agreed.

"How long do you think it will take to get to Maldonado tomorrow?"

"I've never been there, but I'm thinking worst case, couple of hours," she guessed.

"Have you given any thought to what happens once Hannah is settled there?"

She watched her daughter playing in the corner and dropped the tiny shirt she was folding. "No, Alan, I haven't. I'm barely keeping up with things right now. I figure I'll cross that bridge later."

"We should talk about it."

"I know. But give me a little breathing room. This is a big change. Actually, a lot of big changes in just a few hours."

Alan let it go. Perhaps now wasn't the best time to broach the topic. Jet was obviously preoccupied with the ramifications of having to leave her daughter with Magdalena. He could relate – even though she was highly trusted, the fact was Magdalena was not her mother, and after spending years without her daughter, Jet was torn between her maternal instinct to keep Hannah close, and the logical choice – to move her to safety while she dealt with their predicament.

"No problem. All I'm asking is that you think about it. We're going to need to take some big steps over the next few days, and I want to make sure we're on the same page," Alan said.

Her tone softened. "Noted. I just need a little time."

He understood.

Although the truth was, time had run out.

CHAPTER 12

Voskresensk, Russian Federation

Doctor Ivan Radovich stood in the dank green hall, smoking a cheap Russian cigarette, the pungent aroma of the black tobacco hovering over him like a toxic cloud. The Soviet-era air-conditioning did little to mitigate the stench, but on a day like today, when it was raining outside, there was no chance that he would be climbing the two flights of stairs to the ground level, where he'd have to deal with the security men stationed there. Better to pollute the lower levels and put up with griping from his small staff than risk being seen out in the open – not that anyone would be watching. The old industrial complex on the outer edge of Voskresensk was just another in a seemingly endless string of eyesores left over from the Cold War, and the residents had long ago learned not to question anything too closely – especially the comings and goings of men rumored to be organized criminals, part of the Russian Mafia that was the de facto governor of the nation.

"Come now, why the long face, my friend?" Vladimir, his boss, approached from down the hall, puffing away on his own cigarette – imported, of course, Ivan noted. The man was a sponge for all things American and had never said no to anything, as evidenced by his waddle and his cane, in spite of his being a few years Ivan's junior.

"I'm not making any progress on developing a vaccine. There's insufficient time to do it right, and I won't rush it. This is far too dangerous."

"I understand. We're all aware of the stakes. But it's also an imperfect world, and the truth is that what the man upstairs wants, he gets. After all, he's paying the bills."

Always with the intimidation. Old habits died hard, Ivan mused. "This will take at least a year, minimum. And even then, there are no guarantees. I think you need to tell him the truth rather than allowing him to believe there's going to be a breakthrough. Not on this one. Not this time."

Vladimir took a drag on his Marlboro and inhaled the smoke deep into his lungs. "We have two weeks."

Ivan spat on the floor. "Impossible."

"I know. I'm just trying to figure out how to tell him without...without triggering his notorious temper. We all have a lot riding on this, my friend. I, for one, don't want to have to disappoint him."

"Maybe if you'd just told him from the beginning that what he was contemplating was out of the question, then we could have put this behind us by now and been spending our time on more productive pursuits. Like creating enough of the toxin to fulfill the order. We simply do not have the equipment or the time to make it contagious."

"But I thought we agreed it wasn't that hard."

"Well, it isn't difficult to make it contagious if you don't care about wiping out all life on the planet. That would be a piece of cake. It's the part where you develop a foolproof vaccine or antidote that's the niggling detail. A year is nothing. There's no guarantee that we could even get it done that soon. The truth is that nobody should ever be trying to weaponize an agent like this that has no antidote. This is a doomsday scenario waiting to happen. And Vladimir, I'm telling you, I want no part of it."

"All right. Don't worry. He's not insane. Just greedy. As are we all." Vladimir finished his smoke and crushed it under the sole of his shoe. Even from a few feet away Ivan could smell the telltale odor of vodka emanating from Vladimir after a long lunch. "I'll let him know that it'll be everything we can do to stabilize enough to affect, what...ten thousand people?"

"Maybe as many as twenty, depending upon the ventilation system. Ideally it would be released in a contained area to assure maximum exposure."

"Yes, yes. We've had this discussion before. The more concentrated the area, the better the result."

"If they're thinking, for instance, in a subway station, that could work, but it would have diminishing effectiveness over time. First ten to fifteen minutes of exposure, you'll be at near a hundred percent. But after half an hour, allowing for decay and disbursement, that will drop to more like sixty percent. Don't get me wrong; it'll still be devastating. But by the second hour, it will have done what it's going to do. Ideally you'd have a scenario where the largest number of people inhale it within the first ten minutes." Ivan studied his smoldering cigarette and took a final puff before dropping it into a pool of murky water by the wall. "The trick is to modify it just enough so that we don't reduce its efficacy too much, but so that it can never be traced back here."

"Understood. I'll relay that." Vladimir hesitated. "Is there anything else?"

"We can have enough stabilized within ten days on the outside. But making it contagious is off the table. At least while I'm running this show."

Vladimir nodded. "I'll go pass on the news. Just keep focused. In the end, these ragheads will be happy to get whatever we give them, so don't give the contagion part too much thought. They asked, we did some research, end of story. Not in the cards." He sighed. "It's a shame we couldn't get into one of the old labs. G-6 is only an hour from here."

Ivan studied the man's face, wondering if he was joking. "Vladimir. Besides the fact that the army guards those installations with orders to shoot any intruders without asking questions, you don't want to open that can of worms. There's shit in there that should never have been attempted. We both know that. Even this little horror is child's play compared to some of the other stuff in those bunkers."

"Of course. Thank goodness for all of our fortunes we were able to make this one vial of agent go missing. But I suppose it's too much to wish for a repeat performance."

"Those were the old days. They've tightened up everything now. This is enough, with some tinkering, to make us all richer than we have any right to be. Enough for ten lifetimes. So let's just be glad we've got something marketable, stabilize it so it can be field-deployed, and call it a day. We'll all want to be long gone when this hits the news."

"I'm thinking Dubrovnik. I hear that you can live like a king there. Indulge any appetites you can imagine," Vladimir mused, then shook his head. "This will all be over soon, and years of work will have paid off. We'll all collect big fat paychecks and be done."

Ivan remembered the last decade – the constant fits and starts, the illusory progress, and the devastating disappointments before he'd finally been able to modify the agent so that it was controllable outside of a lab, with a short enough lifespan that it wouldn't wipe out whole nations. As part of the top secret and hotly denied post-Soviet biological weapons program, both Vladimir and he had been guaranteed positions and prosperity for life. But then, like so much in the brave new modern Russian world, things had changed, and their career positions had been abruptly terminated, their skills no longer required. It had only been because of Vladimir's contacts with the underworld that they had found a niche – setting up meth labs – and then later, had been the go-to resource when a vial had gone missing from one of the forbidden laboratories.

Vladimir had convinced his patron that it was worth the effort to convert the precious agent into something that could be sold. Nobody needed to voice the question of who would be buying agents of death like this one. There was always a ready market for certain items, and their role wasn't to question the political or ethical motivations of the groups who were willing to pay top dollar for the most specialized of weapons. Weapons that would inspire terror – of the beast waiting to be unleashed; of what the morrow would bring.

Vladimir patted Ivan on the shoulder – a habit Ivan had grown to loathe over the thirty years they'd known each other – and then he trundled off back down the hall, his considerable bulk seeming to take some of the light in the dank space with him as he left, like a fleshy dark star.

Ivan thought about their discussion with unease. He'd known Vladimir too long to imagine that everything was going to be fine from here. If there was one thing he understood, it was that he couldn't trust the man. Vladimir had been a manager when Ivan had been one of the scientific staff, and like all managers he knew just enough to assume an air of smug superiority without having to fuss with all the annoying details that came with actually knowing what he was talking about. In the old days, his greatest strength had been that he had never heard an order that he would question. That had been the primary job requirement; but then communism had collapsed under its own weight, leaving him a yes man without anyone to suck up to.

Ivan, on the other hand, had always been aloof – an academic forced into distasteful work by ugly circumstance. Ultimately, it had been a job, and at that point in his life, with a marriage on the rocks and slim prospects, a job had looked like a lifesaver. And after a time, he got to the point where he didn't question what he was doing with his beakers and tubes and vials. It was all theoretical. The world left him alone, and he got to play chemist in the comforting gloom of the top secret labs where he was one of the acknowledged masters.

But nothing stayed constant, and a man still needed to make a living, especially in these difficult times. The prospect that one of his creations would finally make it out into the world was both exciting and horrifying to him – the abstract made concrete. Though it wasn't like he was going to do the deed himself; what he was doing wasn't really any different than what he had been doing for the government, when the dust had settled. Someone else was going to take his work and kill, in the name of God, or country, or ideology. Ivan had been too long in this world to make much distinction among them anymore. The truth was that man had been killing his fellow man for eons, and would continue to do so until there were no more walking the earth. Why one in particular wanted to exterminate some others wasn't of that much interest, and if he didn't provide his agent, then the buyer would simply go elsewhere and find a different route to achieve the same ends. The only difference for Ivan in this case was that he benefitted financially – a selfish but meaningful distinction to him.

In any other scenario he continued to scrape by, eking out his miserable livelihood, and the buyer rewarded someone else with his money.

The outcome didn't change.

At heart, it was a simple decision.

Morality and ethics were always easier to debate on a full stomach.

CHAPTER 13

Washington D.C., United States of America

The dark sedan pulled to the rear entrance of a private club in Georgetown so exclusive that it didn't have a name. No discreet brass plaque announced its presence to an uncaring world, no whispered invitations to its hallowed chambers were bandied about as a form of status. The club had been in the same location for over a century, and yet nobody had ever heard of it except for a small cadre of the select. Powerful figures from the political, banking, and corporate fields needed neutral ground where they could safely discuss whatever was necessary, without prying eyes or anyone noting who was sitting with whom.

A tall man in a black suit got out of the passenger seat and walked to the rear car door, glancing in both directions down the empty alley before opening it and holding it for the occupant. A stooped gray-haired figure emerged, his aura emanating authority despite his frail physique and advanced years.

The rear entrance of the club swung wide, as if by magic, the discreetly mounted cameras having captured the latest arrival – the last expected that night. The black-suited man helped the older one up the three stairs and then turned, his job done until he received a cell phone call to come and pick up his charge later – perhaps much later, depending upon the evening's agenda.

A dignified figure in a tuxedo, ebony skin gleaming in the light from the overhead chandelier, welcomed the old man with a smile and an offer of a libation, which was waved off.

"No drinks for me tonight, Gerald. Where are the rest of them?" he asked.

Gerald nodded courteously and gestured towards a heavy hand-carved door at the far end of the wood-paneled hall. They walked past the scowling admirals and dignitaries whose oil-painted countenances watched over the corridor with silent disapproval. Gerald rapped twice on the door, then held it open.

The older man stepped into the room, greeted by seven sets of eyes from the large oval conference table, and took a seat near the door.

"I don't have much time tonight, so let's get right to it. Where are we?" he demanded, his voice soft but tinged with steel.

"Everything's on track. The President has the ability to commandeer virtually every aspect of the nation's defense, finances, and law enforcement, for anything resembling a national emergency – a deliberately ambiguous term. This effectively transfers power over the country from the Congress to the President. That national emergency hits, and he has complete authority to do whatever he wants," the speaker said, reading from a small notebook, his easily recognizable profile thinner in person than on his near-daily television appearances.

"Are we still convinced that this will work? We can't afford any missteps," the older man cautioned.

"There are never any guarantees, but when the stakes are large enough, it certainly seems worth the risks," said a younger man in his mid-forties, quiet pragmatism conveyed with every carefully chosen word.

"Gentlemen, I appreciate the work that has gone into assembling all the necessary pieces to put this into motion. This is the final stumbling block to solving several problems in one fell swoop. We can get complete control over the region, so the Chinese are at our ultimate mercy to get the oil they so desperately need from Africa, and it will solve our currency problem. I won't belabor why this regime must go, but suffice it to say it's not for any of the reasons we're piping to the media every day. Still, make no mistake, this is going to require considerable art to pull off. There can be no mistakes. I don't want to see any exposés on YouTube a week after it all goes down. No WikiLeaks. Am I making myself clear?" the older man asked, leaning forward and gesturing to one of the others to pass him a bottle of water. "There can be no trail to follow, no memos to leak."

"I don't think there's anyone in here who isn't aware of the importance of this operation," said a heavy-set balding man with a florid face and a southern drawl from the other side of the table, as he slid a bottle from the collected stack just behind his chair to within reach of the older man.

"Then let's get down to business. I want a complete update on where we are, who is responsible for the various pieces, and how polished our response will be. Remember that when this happens, it's going to happen all at once, and we'll need to seem both disorganized and surprised, but also competent, all within a short period. We'll obviously have the support of our allies – the British will jump in on our side immediately, as will Canada and Australia – but we can expect the French to be more skeptical, as will be the Russians and the Chinese."

The men spent the next two hours running scenarios, double and triple checking their preparations, and taking action items to ensure that nothing fell through the cracks. By the time the meeting was over, the older man felt every one of his almost seventy years weighing heavy, but at the same time, he was exhilarated by how close they finally were. Soon the final step in a plan that had spanned decades would be taken, and then the world as they knew it would change forever – which was the history of the species. The largest quantum leaps weren't pretty or organized and invariably involved massive dislocations. The old ways would have to be discarded to respond to a new world threat, and within a generation nobody would remember a time before things had changed. They would only remember the day the earth stood still, and life as they'd known it stopped and a new one began.

As he made his way cautiously down the stairs to his car he groaned, his knees stiff from sitting for so long. The meetings were hard on him, but necessary if they were to prevail. These were exciting times, and the spoils would justifiably go to those who had the foresight to take bold measures.

It was the way of the world.

Always had been.

And the victors always got to write the history books. He was sure they would be kind to him. As his assistant held the car door open, he'd never been more sure in his life that he was standing at the threshold of a civilization-changing moment, which, if all went well, would solidify his group's final grip. From there, it was just a matter of time until they controlled everything of any value.

His driver looked at him in the rearview mirror with a raised eyebrow.

"Home, Sidney, home," he said, and then closed his eyes as his assistant took his position in the passenger seat and the heavy car purred from the curb, unremarkable to any watchers, just another anonymous government vehicle in a city of bureaucrats and power brokers eager to stay below the radar while they made moves behind the scenes that influenced untold millions.

The next week's preparations would be critical.

They had never been closer.

He swiveled his head and looked out the tinted window at the late straggling traffic on its way back from dinner. Like ants, the inhabitants had no idea what was directing events, and simply soldiered on as they always had, believing themselves to be masters of their destiny. Nothing could have been further from the truth, he knew.

Self-interest drove everything in life. His was no different.

Yes, it was time for a change. The masses had been allowed to muddle along quite enough. It was time to take them in a different direction – one that might mean a lot less freedom, but ultimately, a more controllable and safer future.

And certainly a more profitable one for him and his group.

The sedan swung onto a larger thoroughfare and made its way towards the freeway, the big engine pulling smoothly, his driver and assistant impassive, as always.

Soon.

It wouldn't be long now.

CHAPTER 14

Montevideo, Uruguay

Sunlight streamed through the hotel curtains as the morning rush hour began, the sound of trucks grinding their gears and revving their motors as deliverymen shouted to one another on the sidewalk outside blending with the dull roar of cars pulling down the street towards the waterfront boulevard that led to the town center.

Hannah shifted next to Jet and then flopped over, her arm circling her mother's waist as she burrowed into the covers to find a more comfortable sleeping position. Jet cracked an eye open and peered at her watch, and then reluctantly disengaged from Hannah and padded to the bathroom, noting that Alan's bed was empty. He must have beaten her to the punch on morning exercise, which was okay with her – every moment she got to spend with her daughter was infinitely more precious than any fitness concerns today.

Jet turned on the shower and paused to study herself in the mirror. She would need to change her appearance yet again, perhaps lightening her hair considerably, or go the opposite direction to near black, perhaps with some highlights. She didn't want to have to trim any off – it had just started growing back after the last short cut, and she wanted options down the road if she needed to switch her look again. Her emerald eyes gazed back at her as she scrutinized every aspect of her face, dropping to her body as she shrugged out of the T-shirt and shorts she'd donned for sleep.

Her workout routine and genetics had ensured that she had the physique of a swimmer, no extra fat anywhere – just solid, toned muscle sculpted by a lifetime of rigorous workouts driven by a requirement to be in peak condition at all times. In her old career, the difference between being fit or slacking could easily have meant the diffcrence between life and death, and the old habits died hard.

The pipes knocked as they changed temperature and she adjusted the stream to something just south of scalding, then stepped beneath the spray, allowing the water to pound her awake as she soaped off. A few minutes later she was clean, and she made a mental note to get Hannah scrubbed as soon as she woke up – there was no point in waking her any sooner than she had to.

She changed into the set of clothes she'd laid out the night before on top of the bathroom cabinet and inspected herself with approval before exiting the bathroom, morning ablutions complete. Hannah was still out like a light – not a surprise; she'd always been an astoundingly solid sleeper. Jet moved to her backpack and repacked her clothes and then heard the key in the lock. As Alan entered, soaked head to toe from his morning workout, she held a finger to her lips and gestured to the sleeping form on the bed by the window. Alan pointed to the bathroom – she nodded – and he grabbed his rucksack and carried it in with him, taking care to be as quiet as possible.

The bathroom door closed, and she remarked to herself again how different Alan was from David. Where David had sported wavy, longish, almost-black hair, Alan was medium brown edging towards blond, with a short, no-nonsense cut that was more utilitarian than fashionable. He was taller than his brother by at least a couple of inches – easily six foot two. And definitely more muscular, although with the same field-honed leanness that she had, which wasn't surprising. All the operational members of the team had shared the same physically demanding training, so it was no wonder they had carried that forward, even in Alan's case, when he'd been undercover for years.

For all the differences, though, she could also see the similarities between his features and David's, although Alan's were more symmetrical – she supposed she would have described him as more 'classically' handsome. David had been more interesting looking, with unusual features that were just a little out of balance, but combined had been startlingly attractive to her. Alan was easier to look at, although she remembered that the last time she'd seen him, in Yemen, his hair had been as black as hers. Perhaps that was his natural color – it was so hard to tell with operatives, who changed everything about themselves as often as most people changed underwear.

Hannah stirred on the bed and then opened her eyes, squinting at Jet with a baffled annoyance that was her unique way of greeting the world every morning, as though having to emerge from sleep was a personal slight designed to punish her for enjoying her slumber too much. She rolled over with a tiny moan and then sat up, staring expectantly at Jet.

"Good morning, sweetheart. You ready to take a bath and then have breakfast?" Jet asked.

Hannah nodded, still out of it.

"Just give it a few minutes and then Uncle Alan will be out of the bathroom and we're on."

"Uncle Alan?" Hannah pronounced it *Uncow Awan*, still grappling with the intricacies of pronunciation.

"That's what we're going to call him. He'll love it," she assured her.

Hannah gave her a juvenile look of "whatever" and looked around for something to amuse herself with, then announced she had to use the bathroom.

Jet knocked on the door and heard the shower shut off.

"Just a minute."

"We have a two-year-old who's made it clear that the time is now."

"Okay. Give me a second."

"That's about how long you have."

She heard frantic activity from behind the door and then he opened it, hair dripping down his face, a towel wrapped around his waist.

"It's all yours," he announced with a small bow and a hand gesture, causing Hannah to giggle at his bare chest and tousled hair before trotting into the bathroom. Jet gave him a neutral look and then followed her in.

"Girl time. Sorry. Be out in a few," she said, then closed the door behind her.

Alan listened to Jet coaching Hannah on the niceties of bathing and then moved to the dresser, where he donned his jeans and a long-sleeved tan button-up shirt. He studied his image in the half-height mirror and then rummaged through his bag for a brush, which he ran through his hair perfunctorily before stowing his hygiene kit. He decided that he looked reasonably presentable, and after a few more minor adjustments, put his things away and turned on the television, scanning the channels until he came to a local news broadcast.

The Russians' bodies had been found, and speculation about drug gangs moving into Montevideo was rampant in the three minutes devoted to the sensational carnage. There weren't any witnesses, but that created no shortage of locals to be interviewed and voice the opinion that the police needed to do more to crack down on the drug trade in the area.

He switched the channels and found another report, again long on speculation and short on facts. He was about to turn to another station when a representative of the police came on – footage from a press conference that morning. The somber officer gave the usual stern warnings and vowed that the perpetrators would be brought to justice, even as he cautioned that organized crime was a dangerous and violent world that brought with it the sort of sudden death that they'd seen the prior day.

So the authorities knew nothing. Alan breathed a sigh of relief and watched the remainder of the broadcast, which devoted itself to the economy, a half-hearted weather report, and a solid eight minutes of local sports. At least the station had its priorities right.

Jet emerged from the bathroom with Hannah behind her, and carefully packed her clothes into her Hello Kitty bag, along with the toys she'd been playing with at the playground.

"I guess we're ready. Any suggestions for breakfast? I'm starving," Jet announced with a smile, and while Hannah was amusing herself with her new shoes, leaned into Alan. "Anything on the news?"

"About what you would expect. No witnesses. No leads. No problem, at least so far."

"Well, that's a lucky break." She looked at her watch. "We have plenty of time before I need to be at the attorney's. Let's grab something at one of the bigger restaurants around here, and then I want to get Hannah some more clothes. That will kill some time, and she'll need them."

"I'm here to serve. Do you have any suggestions?"

"Sure. There are some places as we get closer to the town center that are very good."

"All right. You just tell me where to go, and I'm all over it. I'm ready."

"We'll need another few minutes. Hannah's hair takes a while to dry and brush tangle-free."

Half an hour later they were in the car, rolling along the waterfront.

"Look. There's a parking place, over by that van," Jet pointed – a lucky catch, only a few dozen yards from one of the restaurants she'd recommended. He signaled and tried to switch lanes, and was greeted by an annoyed horn burst from a taxi who had decided that he owned the right hand lane and wasn't going to allow anyone in. Jet exchanged glances with

Alan and shrugged – driving in South America was an acquired taste, she knew, as much about honor and machismo as about getting from point A to point B. Alan suffered the angry gesture from the taxi without emotion, and then pulled over and parked where Jet had indicated.

They got a table by the window in the busy restaurant, and a waitress came by and took their drink orders, dropping off two menus and taking a moment to smile at Hannah, who beamed back at the young woman with a movie star grin. When she returned with their coffee and orange juice Jet ordered for the table, and then they people-watched as the noisy crowd went about its innocent way, unaware that Uruguay's most wanted killers were sitting within spitting distance.

"You think you'll have any issues at the attorney's?" Alan asked, making conversation.

"No. Shouldn't think so. He seemed pretty competent yesterday, and this is a straightforward arrangement, at least as far as he described it. I would say we should be done by one, allowing for everything to take longer, just because."

"And then we head out?"

"The sooner, the better, I'd say. I seriously doubt we'll have any trouble leaving the city, but this sort of crime is unheard of here, so I don't know how the cops are going to respond."

"Let's hope that nobody called in an anonymous tip. It's been known to happen."

"I don't get the sense that these guys want me caught by the police any more than I want to be. I'd say they had a different fate picked out."

That stopped the conversation. They busied themselves with watching Hannah scrawl something resembling a bird on the paper placemat using a pencil Jet had found in her purse while they waited for breakfast, which was a long time coming due to the number of diners.

Alan gazed out at the water, and Jet studied his profile as the sun warmed it. He looked worried but relaxed. And something else: prepared. He had that same look of being ready for anything that Jet had. It had been a long time since she'd seen it – a long time since she'd been around anyone as adept as she was. The Americans she'd been with in Thailand were seasoned, but with a completely different level of skill than the members of her team – she had almost forgotten how hyper-competent they had been.

Although except for herself and Alan, not competent enough to stay alive.

Something to keep in mind if over-confidence reared its head.

All had been the very best. And all were dead.

Breakfast arrived and they devoured it, each lost in their own private reverie, wondering what would come next. The first salvo from the newest threat to present itself had been successfully rebuffed, but she didn't kid herself that it was over. History had shown that with the Russians, this sort of conflict was a cage fight, with only one combatant emerging alive.

Which is why she needed to get her daughter to safety and then bring the war to Grigenko.

If he wanted a fight, he'd come to the right place.

Watching Hannah push her food around her plate, she made the silent commitment to bury the Russian, hitting him before he had a chance to react. There was no way she was going to allow anyone to endanger her baby. He might have inherited a fortune, but all he'd managed to do was buy himself a death sentence.

As he would soon discover.

And then there would be hell to pay.

CHAPTER 15

Present day, Northern Yemen

"No. Please. I have done nothing. I swear. Nothing..."

The young man was filthy, wearing barely more than rags, and the two men who dragged him into the room were almost double his weight. His wrists and ankles were bound with cheap rope, stained from oil and grime from a prior life helping to bind a trailer to the rear bumper of a dilapidated truck.

"Shut up, dog. We know of your treachery. But fear not. Your failings as a human will still serve a noble purpose for the cause," the thinner of the two captors spat, then secured the prisoner's leg restraint to an old iron ring set in the concrete floor. The frantic captive continued to beg for mercy and insist on his innocence, but to no avail.

The two men moved to the steel door and walked out, making way for a third man to enter.

The new arrival held a polystyrene container and was dressed differently, in a twenty-year-old hazmat suit of Iranian manufacture left over from the Iraq/Iran war. When the prisoner saw him he renewed his efforts to twist free, all the while pleading for mercy. The figure in the suit regarded him through the glass of the mask, then shook his head and glanced up at the ceiling, where a small camera was mounted in the far corner, its light a steady green. He moved to the edge of the rough cot positioned next to a bucket and extracted a vial from the container and inspected it. Satisfied, he held it up so the camera could get a good shot of it, then moved to the door.

With a final look at the prisoner, he tossed the glass vial into the air and then slammed the door shut, bolting it from the outside. The fragile tube shattered on the ground near the prisoner, glass shards scattering as the horrified man screamed in vain.

In an adjacent room, a technician adjusted the lens of the camera remotely, zooming and panning to ensure a good shot of the broken vial on the floor, then returned to a wide-angle view. Hamid, the second-in-command, and one other man sat watching the feed on an old color television set on a weathered stand in the corner. Both leapt to their feet when their robed, bearded leader entered, and they clamored to get him a seat in front of the screen.

"It is done, sir," the technician said in a hushed voice.

"Very good. And you followed my instructions exactly?"

"Yes, sir. We have him captured on film, begging like a child. Good footage of the suit and the vial. It is all as you detailed."

"Excellent. So now we just have to wait for the full effect of the agent to be captured on video. I want at least two of these, for release a few days apart for maximum effect. I will film the statements that go with them at the same time. Later today. You have the required items?" the robed man asked, scowling at the technician.

"Of course. Everything is set up."

"And what about the website?"

Hamid stood and cleared his throat. "It will go live when the first of these examples is sent to the media. It is untraceable, and will be hosted on servers all over the world. We will only need it to stay live for a few hours. Once it goes viral, the web will do our work for us. It will be posted and reposted everywhere, and there will be no way to control its dissemination."

"And the first salvo?"

"We have already sent a warning and a demand. It will be ignored, of course, but it has started the clock. It is similar to our demand from a month ago, threatening dire consequences if the U.S. doesn't immediately cease all support for Israel. That got no attention. Perhaps this one with a specific threat will be taken more seriously?"

"I doubt it, but once we have the footage, that will change everything. The point to any terrorism is not to wreak maximum damage, but rather to create maximum fear in the population. That's where our brethren have strayed with their ludicrous suicide martyrdom efforts. After decades of young men and women blowing themselves up, everyone is desensitized to the effect, and it goes ignored even a few days after the act. It's a waste, and it forgets lessons that we have fought hard to learn. If you want an enemy to respect you, you need to scare the hell out of everyone, to the point where they are afraid to leave the house. Only then do you have leverage." The robed man nodded, finished with his monologue, pleased that his men were taking this seriously. They would follow his instructions to the letter, blindly, like good sheep, never questioning what they were doing or asking what the ultimate effect would be.

He stood, and with a final look at the prisoner on the flickering screen, moved back to the door. "You have battery back-ups and the generator fueled, in case we get hit with a blackout or a power surge?" he asked. The power in this remote area of Yemen was notoriously unreliable.

"Just as you ordered, sir."

"Very well, then. I will go prepare myself for filming the statements. This will be the most watched footage in the history of the world, so I want to ensure that everything is perfect," he said, absently stroking his luxuriant beard. "Good work, all of you. Have the next prisoner ready to go in once this one is dead. Leave the body in there to add to the effect of the subsequent release."

The technician and his two companions nodded together. Their leader, Saif al-Diin, a relatively new bright light in the struggle, would be a household name within a week, and would be remembered for all time as the man who had brought America, the great Satan, to its trembling knees. They were all honored to have been chosen to participate in his jihad. Unlike so many of the others, he was thinking globally, and had put into motion the required steps to rid the world of Israel once and for all, as well as purge the region of the arrogant Americans, who thought they could do what they liked in a land where they were interlopers. Soon they would discover the hard way that the price for angering the people whose rightful place was on the land the Americans coveted for its oil would be disastrously high – so high that they would lose interest in playing invader and meddling with his people's self-determination.

The door closed and everyone sat back down to watch the long show playing out on camera.

❧

"That's it, then. The funds should be in the account by the close of business today, and then all this, um, Magdalena needs to do is give our branch in Maldonado instructions on how she would like the money distributed every month. I will give you two copies of all the paperwork so that she has one and you do too, in case she has any questions." The attorney regarded her quietly. "See, I told you this would be relatively painless. Sorry it took so long. Sometimes even the simplest things take more time than one would hope."

"Yes, I know how that goes. Will you accompany me to the bank for the transfer, just so there's no confusion?" Jet requested.

"Of course. Let's go right now. I will have my secretary prepare your copies of the documents so that when we get back, everything will be in order."

"And the funds will be available on the first of every month?"

"Yes. Presuming it is not a bank holiday or a weekend. If so, then they will be released on the next business day."

"And the payout – fifteen hundred dollars monthly. That's more than adequate, right?"

"As I said yesterday, the average person here is living on a lot less. Just a little over nine thousand dollars annually. Plus, the way the interest is calculated, the amount will increase whenever rates move from their historical lows. The bank is getting a great deal. They pay four percent and lend at sixteen. Once things get better, she may see more like two thousand a month, which would be a very comfortable lifestyle in Maldonado, as long as she doesn't go crazy with her expenses."

Jet stood, anxious to get the final piece of the transaction done so they could hit the road. All of her errands were completed except for the final part at the bank, and she wanted to be out of Montevideo as soon as humanly possible.

They went downstairs and were greeted like visiting dignitaries by the bank manager, and after fifteen more minutes the transfer was done and the trust was funded. Jet's hope was that she would only have to be away from Hannah for a week or two, at which point Magdalena would have effectively won the lottery in exchange for disappearing from Montevideo and staying gone. Still, she was asking a lot of the woman, and with over sixty million dollars, Jet could afford to be generous.

"Now, to the matter of the will..."

"Obviously I hope that it won't be necessary to go down that road. But as you drafted it, my daughter will get a hundred percent of the money when she comes of age, as well as the contents of the various safe deposit boxes, correct?"

"Yes. And as you stipulated, a million dollars will be earmarked for your daughter's expenses and education, with me acting as the trustee to ensure funds are being used on her behalf. I'll run a quick copy for you, and then our business is concluded – although may I say that if you have any other needs, I stand ready to attend to them."

"Let's go sign the will. That should take care of everything, for now."

Back in the office, she affixed her signature to the required pages, and true to his word, the attorney made copies and gave her one, along with the two copies of the trust. They shook hands and he studied her, unsure what to make of such a wealthy young woman coming in off the street and handing him such an impressive piece of business, but when all was said and done, he was an attorney, so he knew better than to probe too deeply.

Jet exited the building and made a right, walked to the end of the block, and turned the corner. Alan and Hannah were sitting in the car, Hannah playing with one of her toys while Alan listened to the radio. She rapped on the window and Hannah's face lit up. Alan punched the stereo button and popped the electric door locks so Jet could get in.

"Everything go as planned?" he asked.

"No surprises, including the longer-than-anticipated wait. But we're done now."

"That's a relief. What's next on the agenda?"

"We get out of town. And I call Magdalena."

He started the engine. "Sounds like a plan. Which way?"

"Head to the waterfront and then when we hit Avenida Italia, head east, up the coast. It's pretty hard to miss," Jet said, and then extracted a cell phone from her purse and called Magdalena, who told her that she had rented a two-bedroom condo and would be awaiting their arrival.

When they crossed over the Carrasco Arroyo, Jet cautioned Alan to veer right, and soon they were making good speed on the wide highway. She was just getting ready to tell him that they were out of the worst of it when a sea of red lights greeted them, and traffic ground to a halt.

"What's this?" Alan asked.

"Accident?" she said doubtfully.

"I don't know. Could be a roadblock."

"Looking for what? A car full of killers in black, toting assault rifles?"

"The police have to appear to be doing something. The outrage over the killings is all over the radio. It's the biggest thing to happen here in a while, to hear the announcers," Alan said.

"Just look innocent and we should be fine."

"I'll try to remember that."

They pulled up to the checkpoint and coasted to a stop. Two truckloads of soldiers were standing in a rough line, weapons at the ready, looking prepared for a full-scale land assault at any moment. Up ahead four policemen were stopping every vehicle and pulling anything that they felt looked suspect over for a more in-depth inspection.

As they pulled up to the officers, Alan lowered his window. The policeman's face was stony, and he looked like he was under pressure, a tiny bead of sweat working its way down his neck even in the cool afternoon breeze. He fired off a series of rapid questions, each sounding increasingly accusatory, then stepped away from the car, hand on the butt of his gun, and pointed for Alan to pull the car over into another line where more soldiers were searching the vehicles.

As he complied, rolling slowly to where he had been instructed to go, his eyes met Jet's in the rearview mirror.

"Looks like we have a problem."

CHAPTER 16

Sergei Grigenko's fingers clenched reflexively as he studied the missile in the wooden crate, Russian army markings stenciled neatly on its sides in black. He didn't realize that the automatic habit was a giveaway to anyone negotiating with him – the nervous movement an indication that he wanted something, developed as a child while clasping for toys or a bottle to indicate desire. His hands spasmed again and the muscles in his jaw clenched.

"How many can you get, and how soon?"

"Up to twenty, with a few days' notice," replied Feodor, a furtive little man with oily strands of black hair brushed across his mostly bald pate. "They're new in the box, as you can see," he added with a smile.

"What about a volume discount?"

Feodor's eyes twinkled, the diminutive gnome bouncing on the balls of his feet, positively giddy with happiness at the question. "The price I quoted you *was* a volume discount. But if you wanted all twenty, I'm sure we could arrange for a further price drop...say, ten percent on the lot?"

"Sir. There's a phone call for you." One of Grigenko's bodyguards held up a cell phone. Grigenko didn't like to carry them – he had read extensively about possible connections with the radiation they emitted and cellular damage, so he limited his use to brief discussions and kept them away from his body to the extent possible.

"Not now," he hissed, angry at the interruption.

"It's important, sir," the now-hesitant guard insisted. "It's Grigori."

Grigenko sighed and then held up his index finger to Feodor, gesturing for him to give him some privacy for the call. The jolly arms dealer nodded and walked to the far end of the warehouse, his entourage of bodyguards accompanying him.

Grigenko snatched the phone and barked into it: "Where the hell are you? I haven't heard anything for almost twenty-four hours."

He listened intently, the color slowly draining from his face. "What do you mean, all dead? That's impossible," he said, then listened again. "All right. I'll deal with this disaster later. I'm busy right now. Get whatever resources you need flown in and get the job done. Am I clear? You knew about the failure of the prior attempt. These men were supposed to be better than that. You promised me." His voice had begun rising in volume, and the final phrase was almost a shout. "You promised me."

He threw the phone back to his bodyguard and fought to control his emotions, pacing as his mind raced. When he was caught unawares like this and didn't get his way, he had a tendency to be volatile – a by-product of the steroids he injected to increase his athletic prowess. But that would be unacceptable in the current setting, he knew. Fingers clenching and unclenching furiously, he took several deep breaths and forced himself to relax, then gestured to the arms dealer to return to the crate.

"I want all twenty. I also want twenty percent off the shipment," Grigenko stated flatly.

Feodor pretended to study the missile as his eyes darted to the side. He hadn't liked what he'd seen as he'd approached the young man again, and something about his tone froze the blood in his veins. He considered his response carefully before offering it.

"I'll need to check with the fellows I'm handling this for. In the end, it is their decision."

Grigenko's face flushed and he took a few steps towards Feodor, until his bulk was invading the small man's space.

"Listen to me, you cockroach. You either sell me what I want for the price I have offered, or you will be dead by sundown. Don't play games with me. I know your partners' cost basis is zero. I would suggest you consider carefully whether you'd rather make an enemy out of me, or figure out the right combination of words to use on your associates to convince them that this is a good deal. I am not in a mood to be trifled with today," he warned, and then reached down and clamped the smaller man's hand in his.

Feodor's bodyguards moved towards them but he shook his head, even as Grigenko squeezed until the pain was unbearable.

"If I exert just a little more pressure, I will shatter most of the metacarpal bones and you'll be unable to wipe your filthy gypsy ass ever again without help. I would gladly do it just for the insolence you've displayed, but out of respect for our ongoing business transactions, I won't. But listen, little man. You dance for me. Not the other way around. So say yes, go tell your partners that you had to sell the missiles for that price because otherwise I was going to chop you up and use you for fertilizer, and consider yourself fortunate that you are still breathing when the moon rises tonight. Am I clear?" Grigenko gave his hand a little more pressure and Feodor's breath caught in his throat, and then he released him, smiling, looking angelic as he waited for an answer.

"You miserable shit. You don't know who you are—" Feodor's response was cut off by Grigenko's hand clamping on his throat, cutting off the airway. Before anyone could reach them, he twisted Feodor's head with a sharp wrench. The snap of his neck was as audible as a gunshot, and Feodor's lifeless body dropped to the floor. Grigenko turned to Feodor's bodyguards.

"Put your guns away. Anyone that wants to now works for me – in spite of the fact you were unable to protect your boss. Anyone that doesn't put their weapons away will be dead within five seconds. Choose which you'd rather be," he said evenly. His security detail had drawn its weapons and had them trained on the arms dealer's men, who looked uncertain.

The leader of the group held up his pistol and then replaced it in his shoulder holster. The others followed. Grigenko allowed a smile to flash across his face.

"You. You're the leader, yes? Go back and tell this man's associates that he mishandled our negotiation. Suggest to them that they don't want to do the same. Tell them that I want an agreement to buy twenty of these missiles, delivery to occur by the end of the week. I will pay twenty percent less than their asking price. If they decline, they can expect the same fate as their toad here. If they do the deal, they will have eliminated a middleman and I will be able to take whatever they come up with in the future. That's the deal." Grigenko grinned. "Try to be convincing. As you might have guessed, I don't tolerate failure."

The man, fifteen years older than Grigenko and a hardened ex-Spetsnaz commando, simply nodded. He had never liked the arms dealer anyway.

Four years in his employ and he'd never gotten a raise. This young buck might be completely crazy, but perhaps he was more generous.

"I'll call when it's done."

Grigenko turned and walked the length of the warehouse, leaving his men to deal with the new additions. The pounding in his temples was easing, the pulse throbbing in his ears diminishing as he moved. *Perhaps I should have reconsidered killing Feodor.* Then another part of him dismissed the thought. All any of these people respected was power and strength. If he was feared and was utterly ruthless in his dealings, he would prosper. If he showed any sign of weakness, he would be eaten alive. That was just how the world worked, and he understood it well. His mother had drilled that into him since he was a small boy, and her counsel was sound. Never apologize, never allow another man to insult you, and periodically shock everyone around you with an act of brutality.

Grigenko didn't fear any retribution. Feodor's partners would drool at the chance to make a larger cut now that he was out of the picture, and Grigenko's reputation had preceded him, even though he was young. He had already made a name for himself in certain circles, and they would be happy to align themselves with a financially strong group like his. Grigenko's strong network of contacts for arms in Africa and the Middle East ensured that he could move whatever they wanted to sell. Feodor had been a parasite, glomming onto the profit in the middle and sucking what he could out of the transaction. Everyone would be better for his removal from the equation.

Grigenko stepped out of the building and rolled his head, trying to break the tension gripping him like a vise. The failure in Uruguay was a blow, but one he could recover from. He had read all the background information on the woman and understood that she was as deadly as a cobra, but he had been assured by Grigori that she would be dispatched. That had obviously been overly optimistic, but the game wasn't finished and he had infinite resources to throw at the problem. She was one woman. He was a force of nature.

But he would have to break the news to his mother, and he almost dreaded that more than anything else.

Mother wouldn't be happy.

And he hated making her unhappy.

A few minutes later his men exited the building and climbed into their SUVs. Ensconced in his Mercedes stretch limousine, he listened to Chopin nocturnes to soothe his frazzled nerves.

Perhaps he would wait a little before telling Mother.

That seemed wisest.

CHAPTER 17

The officers approached the car and ordered Alan to open the trunk, telling him they needed to go through the luggage. Jet caught his expression, frozen in friendly amusement, and rolled the window down to ask the police what was going on. One of the younger officers explained that they were looking for weapons or other evidence of criminal behavior, and she laughed, her eyes dancing.

"You mean like a two-year-old daughter? I'm pretty sure she's not a mafia kingpin. I can vouch for her," Jet teased, and the officer relaxed even as he tried to keep his face straight.

"We have our orders, *Señora*. We'll try to make this as fast as possible."

"Can I stretch my legs, then? While you're verifying that we don't have a bomb in the trunk?"

His eyes darted to his superior, and then he nodded. "Just stay by the car."

Hannah jumped out, already bored sitting in the back seat, and made engine noises as she played with her toy. Jet opened her purse and removed a tissue, then moved to Hannah and had her blow her nose before dropping it back into the bag.

After a cursory search of their luggage and finding nothing incriminating, the officers waved them back into the car and moved to the next in line. Jet herded Hannah into the back seat and Alan pulled cautiously forward, then merged back into traffic without saying a word. A minute went by before he glanced at her in the mirror.

"You have both guns in your purse?"

"I thought it might be prudent in case we were searched. You had yours in your bag, but I figured that nobody was going to go through my purse, especially if it was filled with kid-mucous-soaked towelettes. No male on the planet would sign up for that." She gave him a sweet smile.

"You're right about that."

Traffic was thin once they made it past the little suburb of Pinamar, and they meandered up the coast, stopping to pay tolls on their way east. When they hit the lake area of Laguna del Sauce, just south of Maldonado, Jet turned her cell phone back on and checked for a signal before calling Magdalena and getting directions to her new place.

Alan wound his way through town, and in another fifteen minutes they had parked outside of a relatively new condo complex in what appeared to be a clean, well-maintained section of the city. Magdalena came out to greet them and Hannah ran to her and hugged her – an auspicious sign to Jet, who was conflicted about having to leave her in a strange town with their housekeeper. But out of all her options, that was the safest one for Hannah, as well as the least disruptive. It might have been different if Jet had family or close friends, but she was alone in the world, and the truth was that Magdalena was probably the closest person to her.

They moved inside and did a tour of the condo. Jet nodded with approval. It had a security guard at the main entry and the interior was nice, and Hannah lost no time exploring her new surroundings with childlike curiosity.

Jet and Alan spent an hour with Magdalena. Jet explained the financial arrangements and the paperwork she had brought, while Alan did his best to keep Hannah entertained. But soon the excitement of the trip and the new situation had taken its toll on Hannah, and her eyes began drooping from fatigue, and Jet knew it was time to say goodbye.

"Sweetheart, come here. Mommy needs to go take care of some things, so you'll be staying with Magdalena for a little while. I want you to promise to listen to her just like it was me, and be good. Can you do that?" Jet had gotten down on one knee, as she usually did when she had something serious to discuss with her.

Hannah gazed at her with a look that broke her heart and nodded earnestly, unsure of what was being discussed, but eager to make her mother proud of her. They had talked about Jet's having to leave during the car trip, but now that the moment of truth was here, Jet was choking up at the sight of her beautiful daughter, whose company she'd been deprived of for so long, and now she had to spend yet more time apart from her.

Hannah threw her arms around Jet and hugged her tight, and then spoke the words that broke her mother's heart.

"I love Mama. Hannah be good. Promise."

Jet squeezed her, tears rolling down her face, and Alan and Magdalena busied themselves elsewhere, leaving them alone.

"I know you will, sweetie. I know you will. I love you. And I'll be back really soon."

They stayed like that for a long moment, and then Hannah pulled away and Jet blotted her eyes with her sleeve.

"Why Mama cry?" Hannah asked, uncertainty written across her face. As far as she was concerned this was only a short day or three without her mother, which was best.

"I just love you so much. I hate us being apart."

"I be good. Come back soon."

The simple sentence conveyed more than a thousand paragraphs.

Mother and daughter looked into each other's startlingly similar eyes, and an unspoken message flashed between them, their bond stronger than ever before.

Yes, she would indeed come back soon. And she would make those who had forced this upon her pay a very high price.

She would see to that.

❧❦

Back on the sidewalk Jet turned to face the condo balcony and waved to Magdalena and Hannah, who were standing behind the sliding glass door, watching her. They both waved back, and then Jet turned and forced herself to move forward, past the moment. The danger wasn't over, and she still needed a plan – and a clear head.

She turned to Alan.

"Are you okay?" he asked softly.

"I will be. I'm obviously not delighted about this."

"No, I wouldn't expect you to be."

"Tell you what. Let's go find someplace to spend the night, and then figure out our next steps. We can't just hang around in Uruguay."

"I know. I'm involved in an active mission. I have autonomy, but ultimately I'm chartered with figuring out what the terrorist group is planning, how Grigenko is involved...and I have to stop it. I didn't have any new leads for the last week, but I have to get back. I'm sorry, Jet, but that's a top priority. These turds are dangerous, and the information I was able to get from my contact before he went dark was that they were meeting with Grigenko's people to try to work a deal. We never found out what kind of deal, but I have a distinct feeling it's nothing good."

"Then maybe helping me take Grigenko out will actually work into your planning."

"Possibly, but I don't have any evidence that Grigenko is supplying these groups with anything. That's one of the problems I have."

"What about the terrorists? Who are they?"

"That's one of the other problems. This is a new organization. It's not associated with any of the usual suspects. We started hearing about it, or more specifically, about its leader, a year ago, and the more we discovered the worse it looked. Its rhetoric makes Hezbollah sound like moderates. I'm talking Al Qaeda times ten. Its charter is to bring the jihad to the enemy – and of course, the enemy is Israel and its hated ally, the United States."

"So just another group of angry crazies. How is that news?"

"They appear to be much more organized and far better funded. Before I had to get out of the Yemen situation, the rumor was that the new group was coordinating a large play that would change everything. Some of the members of my cell were impressed enough that they were considering joining them. That's rare, as you know."

"What are they called?"

"The Righteous Light."

"Didn't they come out with some announcement a while ago? I seem to remember reading the name."

"Yes, but nothing ever happened. It was just the usual vitriol."

"Then why is this time different?"

"Because of what was being rumored. That they were actively looking for either a nuke or biological warfare agents. Serious stuff."

"Al Qaeda has been trying to get its hands on those for years."

"Yes, but this group apparently has massive resources. The money that was being whispered about was mind-boggling. Billions."

"How is that possible? That kind of money can't move around easily. I know better than anyone that money leaves a trail."

"Apparently not as big a one as you'd think. The Mossad unraveled a network of financial entities that are suspected of being conduits: hedge funds that take huge positions in unregulated, over-the-counter derivatives. That market has no oversight, so it's a piece of cake to move half a billion, a billion, you name it, from one entity to another, using the derivatives as the mechanism."

"How does that work? I mean, with all the international regulations and 'know your customer' rules, how can that happen?"

"Because the really big money doesn't live by those rules. They've never stopped anything but small fry anyway. If you have five billion dollars you want to move from entity A to entity B, you have entity B, another hedge fund, write a boatload of derivatives and sell them to entity A – whatever instruments you want. Say, credit default swaps against the Russian ruble getting ten percent stronger over the next three months. Doesn't matter. The actual instrument is immaterial – it'll be an event that never happens. So now you, the law-abiding hedge fund in New York, transfer five billion dollars to the hedge fund that is writing those derivatives for you, and presto, nobody bats an eye. Five billion transferred on a bet that never pays off. It happens – sometimes you win, sometimes you lose. Maybe the bet is framed as a bet that the euro will suddenly strengthen and the European Union will begin getting its act together. The point is, it looks like a legitimate bet, so when the hedge fund loses, there's a convenient explanation. Meanwhile, hedge fund B, that wrote the derivatives it never expected to have to pay on, has the five billion. It distributes that as profit to its investors, who just happen to include a fund associated with the terrorist group."

"Really? That can happen?"

"Not only *can* it happen, it does, every day. We've tracked it. Many of the largest criminal syndicates use that mechanism all the time. Russian and Italian mobs, Chinese triads, Japanese *yakuza*, rogue nations. They all swim in the same pond. And there's no way to stop it other than by regulating derivatives, which will never happen because of the players involved and their political clout."

"So this Righteous Light could actually have the money to buy a nuke?"

"Easily."

They sat in silence as Alan pointed the car toward the row of high rise hotels in the distance near the marina in Punta del Este, Jet's mind processing furiously. As they neared a cluster of buildings, she pulled her sunglasses out of her purse and put them on.

"And Grigenko is involved in selling these animals this kind of weaponry?" she asked.

"We don't know for sure. But his name came up. More than once."

"What's the holdup, then? Push him in front of a bus and have done with it."

"It's not that simple. For one thing, he'd just be replaced by someone else we don't have as much information on. There's no shortage of miscreants looking to sell the unthinkable to anyone with enough money. Now that we've isolated him as a potential source, at least we have someplace to start. Up until recently, we didn't even have that."

"The devil you know."

"Exactly. But some of this doesn't sit well with me. I can't explain it, but it just feels off."

She twisted to look at his profile. "What does that mean?"

"I don't know how to describe it. But I've been around these psychos for a long time, and this all seems...I don't know, contrived. It's just an impression."

"Contrived. A group, one of many, that wants to wipe us off the face of the earth."

"It's not that. It's just the speed with which this group's leader went from someone nobody had ever heard of to an international terrorist and media sensation. One day they're nobody, and the next they're issuing communiqués and putting word all over the street that they're trying to get nukes. Oh, and that they're funded by deep, deep pockets. As in state-sponsored pockets. There's no other funding sources that would have the kinds of resources we're talking. While transferring money all over the globe isn't as hard as you'd imagine, it's still hard raising it, and you don't put together billions in a war chest, if they're to be believed, overnight. Certainly not by passing the can at the local mosque or restaurant. That points to a government sponsor."

"But something in your gut is saying this isn't what it appears to be?"

"Like I said. I haven't nailed it down. Or shared my doubts with anyone but you. Then again, you may remember from your days in the field that we're not exactly a chatty bunch."

"I seem to recall something about it." She smiled. "That, and you say you're working directly for the director. So not a big committee to bounce it off of and get a read."

"Normally I would have run it by David. He had the most brilliant strategic mind I knew." Alan paused. "But since that's not an option anymore, I've been left to my own devices, and I've been thinking about it non-stop. I don't know what isn't adding up, but something isn't. That's all I can say right now."

"Let's try that hotel. It looks nice," Jet said, pointing to one across the street from the marina, ending the discussion for the moment.

Alan pulled into the large reception driveway and a valet approached them to take the car. Jet hopped out and went inside and confirmed that rooms were available, and then came back and nodded to him.

"We can decide the fate of the western world better with an ocean view, I think," she said as he got their bags out of the trunk and handed them to the bell captain.

"I've never been more sure of anything in my life. I like the way you think," he agreed as they entered the lobby to book a room for what would probably be their last night in Uruguay until Jet had executed one of the most well-protected and powerful men in Russia.

CHAPTER 18

After getting settled into their room overlooking the marina, they opted for an early dinner at the hotel restaurant, which was empty except for their table. They took their time with their meal, and once they were finished, lingered over coffee, the setting sun creating a dramatic lightshow on the shimmering water. Gulls wheeled over the boats bobbing at the docks in an elaborately choreographed aerial display. Jet stared at them, seemingly in another world.

"She'll be okay. You know that," Alan offered, sipping his drink.

"I hope so. I want this to be finished as soon as possible, so I can come back and start over."

"Seems like you've been doing a lot of that lately. Starting over."

"I know. I just can't seem to catch a break. First Trinidad, then Thailand, and now this. It's a miracle that Hannah's not scarred for life."

"She seems to be made of tougher stuff than that." He paused. "Like her mom."

Jet tore her eyes from the water and forced a smile. "I guess it's time for Mom to prove just how tough she is instead of throwing a pity party, huh?"

"It's completely understandable..."

"Maybe, but I don't have the luxury of wallowing in it. So let's talk logistics. I want to get everything the Mossad has on Grigenko. How long will that take?"

"Probably a few hours on the servers. I just need to get to a connection. So consider that done."

"Let's assume that I'll need to go to Russia to do this. We'll need to plan that, arrange for entry and logistics, weapons, technical support..."

"All of which is a matter of time and money. You indicated that you had plenty of cash, so that's not a problem. What will be is getting through his defenses so that you have a shot at him. He's living in a new villa he just bought, which is a fortress."

"There's no such thing as impenetrable. We both know that. Just degree of difficulty."

"I remember when I looked at this before that it was at the upper end of the scale," Alan cautioned.

"My specialty."

"Perhaps. But we don't want to go into this half-cocked. You're only going to get one chance once we're in, and if you're successful we need a way to get you out in one piece."

"If?"

"Poor choice of words. What I mean is, this will require some careful groundwork. You'll need my help. And my timing is going to largely depend on what's going on with the terrorist cell. I can't be thousands of miles away if they're making a move."

"I understand that. Look, Alan, I appreciate your offer, but beyond getting me the files from the Mossad, you don't have to feel obligated. I'm a big girl, and I can take care of myself."

"I was reminded of that back in Montevideo. Look, like it or not, I'm the only family Hannah has besides you. That brings me into this, and it does obligate me."

She waved it away. "I'm letting you off the hook."

"That's not in your power. I promised my brother as his last wish that I would do everything I could to look out for Hannah...and for you. Maybe you don't need it, but that doesn't free me. I know David. If he had made that promise to me, nothing could have stood between him and making good on it. Nothing. So let's just dispense with this and agree that I'm part of this mix."

"Fair enough. I'm just trying to let you know that you don't have to be."

"I appreciate the sentiment. In the meantime, as part of my digging around, I'll see what kind of assets we have in Moscow. I'm sure we have a decent network there, so finding a source for weapons and specialized equipment shouldn't be a problem. But I will have to be careful and use cut-outs. Remember, like you, the world thinks I'm dead, except for the director."

"So that brings us to where we go next. Uruguay is a small country. No way we can use the airports here. Too easy to have them watched. I'm thinking we'll have to get to Argentina, and then from there, make our way to Europe. The only problem with that is that the system in Argentina is one of the most corrupt in the world, so we can't be sure that Grigenko or the KGB hasn't compromised it, which would flag them when we moved through one of the international airports. I looked into that before settling on Uruguay, and the Argentine clandestine apparatus is as bent as they come."

"Nice to see not much has changed since the Nazis decided to resettle there. But how would they know what names we're traveling under?"

"I honestly don't know. Tell me how they found me in the first place, and I'd be more confident. You know they have photos if they were watching me for days. Let's just say I'm not feeling very confident right now, and don't feel like taking any chances," she said.

"All right. So what do we do?"

"We're going to have some hurdles. I say we ditch the car, take the ferry to Buenos Aires, then take a flight to Mendoza on the other side of the country and take a bus to Santiago, Chile. The border between Argentina and Chile is informal, based on the research I did when I moved here, so we're likely to only encounter a few customs agents trying to move the herd through. Once we're in Santiago we should be able to go anywhere in the world – it's an international hub."

"How long do you think that will take?" Alan asked.

"Couple of days, worst case."

"You want to start tomorrow?"

"First thing. The sooner we're on the move, the sooner this is over."

Now it was Alan's turn to gaze off at the horizon. Eventually his attention returned to her. "We've never really talked about what happened with David. How he died," he said.

"No, we haven't. How much do you want to know?"

"Everything."

She took a deep breath and then sighed.

"That last week, when we reconnected, was like a dream..."

❦

The following morning they rose early, and after a hurried breakfast drove back down the coast to Montevideo, disposing of the pistols in several trash cans along the way. Jet had stripped them and wiped them clean so there would be no chance of finding prints – the last thing either of them needed was to be entered into the Interpol database as suspects in a mass slaying in South America. They stopped at a computer store in town and Alan bought a laptop, and then he dropped her off at the ferry terminal while he returned the rental car and paid for the dents.

Jet approached the ticket counter and looked at the clock – the boat didn't leave for two hours. She purchased two tickets, and then busied herself in the internet café while she waited for Alan to arrive. She was checking on flights from Buenos Aires to Mendoza when she sensed a presence behind her and looked over her shoulder.

"All set?"

"The car company wasn't thrilled with the nicks, but they seemed to settle down when I started peeling off cash. What does it look like on flights?"

"There's a late afternoon flight we should be able to get. We'll overnight in Mendoza and then catch the bus tomorrow morning, presuming the pass is open. The road runs over the Andes, and if there's been a storm it can close for days at a time. But the search engine is showing a bus leaving first thing, so barring a blizzard we should be good to go."

"How long will it take?"

"It says nine hours, but again, sounds like that can change based on the road conditions. Basically we're going to be doing a lot of sitting tomorrow. Buy a book."

"Then once we're in Santiago?"

"We overnight and then hop a flight the following day. Depends on where we plan to go."

"Sounds like we'll have plenty of time to figure that out on the bus."

"That's what I was thinking. Do you want to try to get online?"

"Not here. I don't want any IPs tracking back to Uruguay. I'll wait until we're in Buenos Aires. How long will we be there?" he asked.

"Just under three hours."

"That should be long enough. We'll find an internet café somewhere between the ferry terminal and the airport, and I'll download everything I can find on Grigenko. Then you can make it your bus project *mañana*. Some light reading."

The overhead speaker blared a boarding alert for the boat. Jet paid the clerk and they made their way through the cursory customs area and stood in line waiting for the ship. Once onboard they found their seats, and before long they were barreling at high speed towards Argentina on the huge ferry, the steady thrum of the diesels vibrating as they cut through the waves.

Arrival in Buenos Aires was a non-event, the Argentine immigration clerks having stamped their passports in the ferry terminal before boarding. Once they were on the street, they flagged a taxi from the line and told the driver to take them to an internet café near the domestic airport. Fifteen minutes later they were seated in a coffee shop with dozens of computer stations. Alan powered on his new laptop while Jet ordered coffee and bought an hour of time on one of the PCs, and they settled in, Alan engrossed with logging into the Mossad servers using a proxy mask for additional anonymity.

The coffee arrived and Jet pored over the flight possibilities from Chile, finally settling on a direct flight to Madrid, from which they could easily make it to Moscow. She scribbled down the information and closed the window, contenting herself with browsing the news while Alan went about his search.

It took him the better part of an hour to finish his downloads, and when he was done he leaned back, satisfied.

"It's a tremendous amount of detail. A lot of it may not be of much help in planning a strike, but you've got all the time in the world to absorb it and I figured it would be better to have too much than too little."

"Not a problem. I like to do full immersion before I go after a target."

"We share that trait, then." He glanced at his watch. "Any special requests while we're in Buenos Aires?"

"Not really. I spent some time here with Hannah before we settled in Montevideo. It's a beautiful city, but the financial situation in Argentina is so volatile I didn't want to live here – it's gotten increasingly dangerous as the economy has tanked. As far as I'm concerned, the sooner we're out of here, the better."

"Then we might as well head for the airport."

She nodded as he powered down his computer, saving the data to a USB flash drive and handing it to her.

"Keep that safe. It's everything we have on Grigenko and his organization. I encrypted it – the password is 'Hannah.'"

They paid and emerged onto the large boulevard, cars whizzing by at suicidal speeds, and flagged down a taxi. As Jet watched the driver try to break the land speed record, her mind was racing, the haunting image of Hannah waving to her from the condo indelibly seared into her psyche. She already missed her daughter, and it hadn't even been a full day since she'd left her. The rage seethed as she thought about her predicament, and she vowed again to take down the Russian as quickly as possible so she could return to the normal life she had crafted with Hannah.

Normal life. The thought stopped her, and she wondered whether she was kidding herself to ever expect to be able to have one. Perhaps David had been right when he'd said she would never be safe. She hated his reasoning, but at times like this she couldn't deny the truth of it.

Pushing the thoughts away, she considered the positives. She had a jump on Grigenko and would have the element of surprise. The last thing in the world he would be expecting was a direct attack in his Moscow stronghold. With any luck at all, his combination of youth, recklessness, and overconfidence would prove to be his undoing.

Alan, sensing her agitation, edged closer and patted her arm. Without thinking, she slid her hand over and took his, then realized what she had done. Part of her debated pulling back, but another decided that it felt good. In the end, she decided to leave it. Whatever happened, he was right about one thing. He was the closest thing that either she or Hannah had to family, and right now his presence felt comforting.

They rode in silence to the airport, eyeing the shanty town a mere two minutes from the million-dollar apartments of the Recoleta district, the squalor and desperation like a festering malignancy on the city's skyline, the shabby plywood and brick walls of the precarious structures covered with graffiti, raw sewage running down the center of the unpaved roads. Neither said anything as they bounced past the slum, holding hands, the tentative glow of the unexpected intimacy giving them pause. When they rolled to a stop in front of the terminal, Buenos Aires' high rises looming only blocks away, Jet didn't say a word as she disengaged, the moment over; yet something essential had passed between them – their mutual aloneness had eased with each other's company, if only for a fleeting instant.

It wasn't perfect, and she didn't fully understand it, but for now, it was enough.

Given her last forty-eight hours, she'd take it.

CHAPTER 19

The final approach into Mendoza was turbulent, the wind from the Andes gusting to seventy knots in a freak storm as the jet struggled to stay on course. When the tires smoked against the runway, the entire plane exhaled a collective sigh of relief even as the fuselage continued to rock from the buffeting cross-shear.

Once they made it through the small terminal, Jet and Alan signaled to a cabbie and instructed him to take them to the Sheraton hotel in the town center. Tree branches and dust blew across the road, the grape vines planted on the airport grounds torn by the force of nature's fury. The driver assured them that these kinds of winds hit every now and then but would calm down once the sun set, as if he had a personal stake in the weather's treatment of arriving tourists.

The hotel was clean and modern, with a casino on the second floor, and when they got to their room they were pleasantly surprised to find it looking out over the lower buildings towards the park that was one of the main gathering points in the town. They both took showers, and then went downstairs to get a restaurant recommendation from the concierge.

He gave them two options, both within walking distance, and they set off in the direction of the park, the wind having diminished to a light breeze by the time they made it out onto the crowded sidewalk.

"It's pretty cold. I forgot we're at three thousand meters altitude. I guess I got spoiled by Uruguay," Jet commented as they pushed their way through the throng of pedestrians out for after-work shopping.

"I've never been here. It reminds me of France, strangely enough."

"Or Italy. Only cleaner."

They turned the corner at the end of the block and crossed the street with a group of jaywalkers, cheerfully ignoring the cars racing towards them, and found themselves on a pedestrian thoroughfare clear of vehicles.

A smorgasbord of languages greeted them as they sauntered past the restaurants and shops: English here, Italian there, Spanish everywhere but with the distinctive Argentine accent that was unlike any other in the world, the double *ll* sound, normally pronounced like a *y*, instead pronounced with a lazily-slurred *j*, and the cadence more like Italian than Spanish.

They finally settled on a restaurant located on the main street across the park, and once they were seated next to the glass-enclosed wine room, ordered dinner. Alan seemed distant or preoccupied, and Jet let him have his space until the entrées arrived.

"This looks delicious," she said when the waitress set a succulent filet with a drizzle of truffle reduction in front of her.

"Argentina is known for its beef. Let's hope the trout is as good," he said, nudging his fish with his fork.

Both dishes were heavenly, and as they ate, Jet broached the subject that had been nagging at her.

"How do you think Grigenko's men found me?"

"Had to be the banking. It's the only answer. Believe me, I was pulling out all the stops to get a lead, and I found nothing."

"But how could he have gotten the bank info?"

Alan put his fork down and shook his head. "I know. It's troubling. The most likely possibility is that there's a leak in the Mossad. But whoever it is left no tracks. According to the logs, the only one who has ever accessed that information was David, who created the account, and later, me."

"Can't the system be fiddled?"

"I suppose anything can be, theoretically, but I can't see how. It would be beyond my capabilities."

"What about one of the system engineers?"

"Again, it's sort of a question of what is possible versus probable. If someone got into it, they had insane levels of technical sophistication. The whole point of a log system is that it's foolproof. Otherwise what good would it be? And remember, we're talking one of the most secure systems on the planet."

They finished their meals in silence, Jet considering his point. "I never told you about the mole we found. In the Mossad," she said.

Alan gazed at her without expression. "Come again?"

"David and I. He figured that there had to have been a mole. Grigenko senior got access to the identities of all the team members, and the only possible way he could have done that was with a high-level Mossad contact passing him supposedly inviolate information."

"What? Who is it?"

She shifted uncomfortably in her chair and waited for the busboy to take their plates. "One of the associate directors. I'd never heard of him, but David had. He worked on that side of the fence, so he knew the players. I was always operations, and as you know, we have no reason to know the names."

"But there's the answer. It must be him."

"That's what I was thinking. If Grigenko's people got the information a while ago, it could have taken them this long to track my withdrawals."

"Wait. Why a while ago?" he asked.

She dabbed at the corner of her mouth with the cloth napkin and then set it down on the table. "David and I took him out. The director."

Alan leaned back, shock etched across his face. "You executed a Mossad associate director? Are you completely insane?"

"It was complicated. The safe house had just been hit. All the team members slaughtered. David had been wounded. We didn't have time to screw around."

"Who was it?"

"Eli Cohen."

Alan shook his head. "Doesn't ring any bells."

"Like I said. It wouldn't. He was part of the inner circle – their identities are one of the most closely guarded secrets. Supposedly. Then again, so were the team's. But David, being the conduit and case officer for us, interfaced with him. When the dust had settled, David was convinced."

Alan digested that information as the waitress returned with the check. Alan counted out a few bills and dropped them onto the platter. "I'll have to go with David's instincts, then. He was the best. If he thought there was a mole, then there must have been."

They rose and exited past waiting couples. The wind had completely died down, and the air was crisp, but still.

"I always wondered about Eli, though. David said he had confessed to passing Grigenko information, but I never heard it myself. And we both know that anything extracted from torture is unreliable. That's why witches confessed during the Inquisition and the witch hysterias. You'll confess to anything at a certain point to make the pain stop..."

Alan stopped on the sidewalk. "Wait. David tortured him, too?"

"Before he killed him. Yes."

They retraced their steps back through the park, passing teen lovers on the benches embracing and an occasional hippie vendor selling incense or leather goods. A random gust of freezing air chilled them, and Jet pressed closer to Alan and took his hand.

"It gets cold here, doesn't it?"

"We're right next to the mountains." He didn't pull his hand away. Hers fit comfortably in his, and he swung their arms a few times as children sometimes do, and then the grin on his face faded as they neared the far end of the park.

"We're really in the shit, aren't we?" he asked quietly.

She knew what he was going through. Since the attempt on her in Trinidad she had grown almost used to being in constant jeopardy, every moment bringing with it more danger, able to trust no one. And she knew how destabilizing it was – nothing was ever what it seemed. Jet had been operational for years, on constant missions, but it hadn't prepared her for her life since Grigenko had found her. When you were in the field, at least you knew who the good guys and the bad guys were. Presumably, you were the good guys. But in their current predicament nothing was certain. It was chaos, and the only way she'd been able to deal with it was to simply accept it and focus on the tactical elements she could impact.

None of which she said. It wouldn't help. He needed to figure it out for himself.

"Yes, we are, Alan. Yes, we are."

When they got back to the hotel Alan announced that he wanted a drink, and she accompanied him to the downstairs bar, away from the ruckus of the casino floor. They ordered a half bottle of the local Malbec – just enough for one glass each. Alan didn't say much, and Jet didn't feel any need to make conversation.

Once they were back in the room they prepared for bed, and when Jet crawled under the covers wearing her oversized T-shirt and running shorts, she pressed up against Alan. He seemed to understand her need to be held, and put his arms around her.

For a brief moment everything felt safe.

Her last thought as they drifted off to sleep, his warm breath on the back of her neck, was that the brothers were so very different, and yet each had his strengths. In a weird way, she felt lucky to have Alan, now that David was gone. Perhaps he had known what he was doing, after all – always scheming, trying to control events; maybe his final gift to her, his concession and unspoken apology for his betrayal of her, was to offer up his brother to comfort her in his place.

CHAPTER 20

Jet woke early, restless and jittery. Alan was still asleep, so she pulled on a different shirt and took the elevator to the lobby. After a few minutes of stretching she began her run through downtown, which was largely deserted at dawn.

She pushed herself relentlessly, but noticed that her endurance seemed down a little, until she remembered that she was at a higher altitude, so there was less oxygen.

An hour later, she returned, her sense of the city improved. It really was like a little bit of Europe dropped into South America, much like Uruguay, which made sense given the heredity of the population – mostly European. When all of this was over she would need to take a hard look at Mendoza as a possible resettlement spot for herself and Hannah. It seemed far removed from the big-city insanity of Buenos Aires, with its attendant crime, crowding, fuel and energy shortages, and periodic civil unrest.

When she returned to the room Alan was in the shower, so she turned on the news and searched for any coverage of the Uruguay killings, but didn't find any. Outside of the country it would be considered a local problem specific to Montevideo, and like most news, within a few days, with nothing to keep it alive, it would drop to the second page, and then the back page, and then be quickly forgotten.

Alan came out wearing a towel and motioned to the bathroom door. "It's all yours."

"You need anything else out of there?"

"Nope. I'll pack my gear while you clean up. We need to be out of here in fifteen minutes if we're going to get the bus. Anything on TV?"

"No. Looks like what happens in Uruguay stays in Uruguay."

The water felt good on her skin, its needle-like pulsing stinging her skin, refreshing her. Conscious of the time, she hurriedly pulled a brush through her hair as she exited the bathroom. Alan was just finishing up with his computer.

"I charged it. So you should be good for all the research you can stomach on the ride to Chile."

The bus station was better than most she'd been to, and she made another mental note about Mendoza. So far, all strong positives. They bought tickets and waited twenty minutes, and then the vehicle's door opened with a hydraulic hiss and the waiting passengers tromped sleepily aboard.

As the bus climbed into the Andes the scenery was breathtaking, but Jet was focused on devouring everything that Alan had downloaded on the Russian. She sat by the window poring over the reports, noting that the son looked arrogant in the photos – not surprising given that he'd inherited a vast web of holdings worth many billions of dollars. Twenty-five years old, single, now living in a villa in the most exclusive area of Moscow, protected by a security team of ex-Spetsnaz GRU commandos in his employ. Prior to his father's untimely demise, he had amassed a respectable amount of money after quitting university at nineteen – he'd entered at seventeen, skipped ahead a grade in high school due to academic achievement, but hadn't fit in well once in higher education.

Speculations were that he'd grown bored with academia and had actively developed a crime syndicate dealing drugs to his fellow students, and then rapidly branched out into all the usual ugliness, assisted by his father's network of Russian and Chechnyan mafia cronies. He had disappeared from sight at nineteen, then suddenly re-emerged into the spotlight at twenty-three, the rumored head of a powerful new arm of the mob that specialized in arms dealing, drug trafficking, and violence, including murder.

"This guy's a real piece of work. He's filthy rich now, so he doesn't need to be involved in any of the illegal crap," she commented to Alan as they skewed around one of seemingly countless hairpin turns.

"Some people have a hard time giving up the life. For them it's the kick, the charge of being outside the law. Sounds like your boy is one of those. A sociopath who views himself as the center of the universe and everyone else as objects or things to be toyed with, existing solely for his amusement. I'm familiar with the psych profile workup. Read that next. He's a beauty."

"I'll say. But aside from the fact that he's going to be dead within a week, he's also remarkable in the sense that he's not at all what you would expect from someone willing to do business with terrorists – especially high-risk business like supplying them with weapons of mass destruction. There aren't a lot of things that pretty much everyone agrees is off-limits, but that would be one of them."

"That's why I said to read the profile. Our shrinks' consensus is that he's a thrill junkie willing to risk everything for another adrenaline jolt. It fits. He didn't need to get into the crime game – he could have gone to work for Dad and made his fortune that way, or just waited for his papa to die. Instead he got into the most dangerous possible game, and flourished. It takes a special kind of person to turn his back on billions and willingly wallow with the worst humanity has to offer. That's what he did."

She continued studying the materials, flipping to the layouts of his villa and his office building after reading the exhaustive detail on his personal life.

"This is a bad man. A really bad one, Alan."

"You're singing to the choir. But the one thing we don't have him for, dead to rights, is the arms trafficking. We haven't been able to make any firm connections to the terrorists other than indirect links."

"Fortunately, for me to put him out of his misery, I'm the only judge and jury I need to convince. And I'm already sold. This piece of shit is history. And I thought his father was scum. The son took after the other twin – you know I terminated him, too, right? He was in the arms business as well. Nasty. And also surrounded by impenetrable security. Didn't do him much good, did it?"

"One of our biggest positives is that he's not expecting you to come after him. As far as he knows, you're hiding under a rock somewhere in Uruguay. If you're lucky, you'll already be in and out of Moscow by the time anyone figures out you aren't the hiding type."

"You really think he could have done his research on me and not know I would come after him?"

"I don't think he cares. Remember – this is a sociopath and a narcissist. It's all about him doing things to you, not you doing anything to him. Sounds like he's taken on a blood feud, an oath to kill you as payback for executing his father. Even though nothing ever surfaced officially, you were spotted by enough of his dad's security team on his boat that night that it doesn't take a genius to figure out who took Daddy down. But the notion of you penetrating his defenses and coming for him? Not a chance. That's what we have going for us. He considers himself invulnerable."

"So did his father, as I recall. Smug, snide, sure of his own superiority. Funny, because he died just like anyone else."

"That's always what seems to happen to those that take you on, isn't it? Just remember that his greatest weakness is his arrogance. It makes him overconfident." Alan's unspoken message was clear – *don't make the same mistake.*

She debated firing back at him, but then decided he had a valid point. Very much like David in that regard – always cautioning prudence and humility. They were right, of course. She had seen it time and time again operationally – her targets thought they were insulated from the world, safe from danger. From her. And eventually, that certitude was one of the elements of their undoing.

Two hours later the bus entered the frozen pass near the summit, the Andes towering around them, and it slowed to a crawl as a blizzard hit, snow blowing sideways, blinding everyone on the road to anything more than a few yards ahead. They crawled along in the sleet, the driver being especially cautious – he knew the road well and understood where the worst of the dangers lay.

The lesson slammed home as she took a break from her review of the Mossad's materials. Even though he had traveled the road a thousand times, the driver was wary of the unexpected and was taking nothing for granted. That, in turn, would keep them all alive, and ensure that he lived to drive another day.

Not a bad idea, she reasoned, and filed it away for whenever she felt too cocky.

The afternoon dragged on, and eventually they were over the mountains and descending into Chile, only a few short hours left to go before they arrived at their destination. It had been time well spent for Jet, because now she felt she had a full understanding of the target's habits and motivations.

"We'll hit him at the house. Hit him where he lives, when he least expects it. That's where he's most vulnerable," she announced on the outskirts of Santiago.

"I thought you'd say that," Alan remarked, and then took the laptop from her and packed it away, her research finished for the moment.

They watched the countryside turn into city as they made their way into the coastal nation's capital, ready to depart almost immediately after they arrived, their stay limited to a few hours in a hotel before they flew out on the first flight of the following day.

CHAPTER 21

Moscow, Russian Federation

The streets around Grigenko's ultra-expensive villa were empty at midnight. Located a few blocks from the Christ the Savior church on the Moskva River in the most exclusive neighborhood in Moscow, the quiet area was inhabited by only the wealthiest of the immensely rich, and the sidewalks were jammed with parked Mercedes, Bentley, and Lexus sedans, for those unfortunates who didn't have a private garage area like Grigenko did.

He had bought the villa two weeks after his father's death, upgrading from his prior condominium digs to a residence befitting one of the city's richest new oligarchs. No sooner had he signed on the purchase agreement than he sold his father's nearby home and surrounding residences, rejecting anything that was a reminder of his detested iron rule.

A Porsche rolled down the silent street in front of the villa, stereo blaring, and the security team watched it warily as it sped up and turned the corner at the end of the block.

"Looks clear," Alan said into the ear bud after he had turned down the music, the German sports car purring at his coaxing.

"I'm going to get into position then. I figure it'll take half an hour. I have to contend with the locks, so I need to allow time to disable them and deal with any other unexpected surprises," Jet responded from a doorway four blocks away. She scanned the empty street, then shouldered the black rucksack she was carrying and moved to the manhole cover she'd spied on the sewer plan Alan had gotten from his local contact.

Another glance confirmed that she was still alone, and she wasted no time in prying the cover up with a long steel manhole cover pick she'd retrieved from her bag, sliding the heavy metal disk to one side and then lowering herself down the ladder into the pitch black. Alan would be along in a few moments to heave it back into place, as agreed, while she wasted no time moving though the sewers. The fetid stink of the air caused her to gag involuntarily, and she struggled for control as she breathed through her mouth, focused on slowing her heart rate and limiting the instinctive nausea.

Something scurried across the platform below her and she heard the squeak of one of Moscow's notorious sewer rats – a particularly nasty piece of business that could run to the size of a small dog. She waited a few seconds and then continued her descent, easing down until her feet found the cement tunnel floor. She felt around in the bag until she found the night vision goggles and put them on. As her ears adapted to the eerie echoes, she switched on the goggles – an image in green luminescence jumped into her field of vision.

"Remember the plan. They'll be doing a shift change in thirty minutes. I'll let you know when the new crew arrives – while they're changing out the guard, you'll have three minutes to get in and get out. I'll be by in sixty seconds to close the manhole," Alan's soft voice murmured in her ear. She clicked the ear bud twice to confirm, then fumbled in the sack again until her fingers found the regulator mouthpiece. She put it between her teeth and opened the valve on the attached cylinder, and a blast of blessedly clean air burst from the hose.

They had been in Moscow for three days securing the gear she would need and mounting surveillance, Alan pretending to be a delivery man one day, she a tourist the next. The villa had a round-the-clock security presence, eight men per shift, and they had timed the arrival and departure of the men and were confident that tonight, as with every other night, the graveyard crew would show up at half-past midnight, to be replaced by another shift at eight-thirty.

The giant pipes vibrated underfoot as she crept along the tunnel, following the diagram she'd copied to a split a hundred and fifty yards ahead. When Jet saw the Y junction, she took the right passage until she came to yet another split – this time choosing the left. The texture of the tunnel floor changed, from poured concrete to cobblestones, older, worn by time and slimy from mold. She knew there would be a security grate ahead that she would need to get through, and then another sixty yards and she would be directly under the pump room of the building adjacent to Grigenko's villa – which according to the map was accessible through the tunnel via centuries-old steps.

Another curious rat approached her — she could easily make out the furry shape with her goggles — and then had a change of heart, about-faced, and raced away from her. As she progressed, counting her paces from the last split, she adjusted the rucksack so that it hung more comfortably on the shoulder strap. Inside it she had everything she'd need to terminate the Russian — including a solution for the two locks she was about to encounter.

She reached the gate and paused, squinting at the oversized padlock. Smiling to herself in spite of the toxic stink surrounding her, she extracted a small aerosol can and squirted half its contents into the lock. Wisps of chemical smoke rose from the old steel mechanism, and three minutes later she snapped it open with the manhole pick.

A sharp blow from her shoulder didn't move the grate, so she used the pick to pry at it, eventually shifting it and swinging the grill wide. She hesitated before proceeding, debating pulling it closed, then chose to leave it open for a speedy getaway. Up ahead she could make out two sets of crumbling stairs rising into the darkness at the side of the passage. Two sets. Not one, as she'd been expecting.

Counting her steps, she estimated that the first stairs were the ones she was after and she mounted them carefully, stopping when she arrived at an ancient iron door. She tried the corroded handle, but it didn't budge. Retrieving the solvent again, she emptied the remainder into the lock and waited patiently, then wrenched the handle again. This time it cranked open, and she pulled on it, wincing at the creaking protestation from the oxidized hinges.

Jet stepped into a dank equipment room, oversized pumps positioned in three of the corners — the apartment complex's water and sewage facility. She carefully unpacked the rucksack and removed a backpack and an FN P90 with a silencer, and then prepared to move. When she spat the regulator from her mouth the odor was still terrible, but she could bear it. She stuffed the rucksack behind one of the pumps, closed the door to the sewer, and crept to the room's exit, listening intently.

The building had a doorman and an armed security guard, but they would both be in the front, not in the bowels of the service area. Her strategy was simple: get to the roof, rappel down the side, and get into Grigenko's bedroom on the uppermost of the villa's three floors. She knew from the Mossad reports that the windows were bulletproof glass, but they were also the sort that opened, and any small window lock would take only moments to crack with one more spray can of her secret formula. Then it would be straightforward. Open window. Shoot Grigenko. Exit the way she'd entered, and be back at her hotel in time to get a few hours of beauty rest before leaving Russia forever.

A simple plan. The best ones always were.

She inched the door open and then flipped off the night vision gear – there was enough dim lighting from an overhead incandescent bulb that she could see with no problem. Down the corridor was another steel door that led to the lobby, she knew. The garbage chute dumped into a large metal bin next to it, and just before the garbage were the service stairs that led up, ultimately to the roof.

Her footsteps were silent on the hall's cracked tile floor, and she wasted no time at the stairs, taking them two at a time, checking her watch as she did. The guards would change over in four minutes, giving her just enough time to get into position.

Another squirt from her second canister quickly overcame the lock on the rooftop door, and then she was out in the night air, crunching across the metal and gravel surface to the edge, where five stories below sat Grigenko's villa.

She pulled a length of black rappelling line from her backpack and snapped one end to a steel pipe several yards from the edge, and then pulled up her black sweater and fed the cord through a steel eyelet on the nylon harness she wore underneath it.

At the roof lip, she looked over at Grigenko's home and waited for the go-ahead from Alan to come over the com line. Her heart rate was normal, breathing even. She was ready.

"Abort. Something's not right. They didn't do a normal shift change." Alan's voice sounded strained in her ear.

"Negative. Maybe they're just a few minutes late. Give it a little time."

Alan didn't say anything, and the minutes slowly crawled by with no activity.

And then something caught her eye. On Grigenko's roof. Movement.

She dropped flat and then peered over the edge for a better look, and found herself staring down the barrel of a sniper rifle with a night scope on it.

She rolled away just as the first slug blew part of the roof lip molding off.

"They're shooting. I'm aborting. Stand by. I'll need a pick-up, but I'm not sure where," she said as she catapulted herself to a run, pausing to unsnap the cord from the pipe as she went by and stuffing it into her backpack. She threw the roof door open and switched off the goggles again, and then took the stairs three at a time.

It would be close. They would need to get out onto the street, get into the lobby, and convince the guard to open the steel service door. By her reckoning that would be just about how long it took her to run down five more flights of stairs.

The germ of an idea hit her as she hit the fourth floor, and she quickly retrieved the rappelling cord and snapped one end to the metal stair handrail and threw herself over, dropping four stories in a matter of six seconds, slowing her descent near the bottom before alighting on the ground floor and severing the cord with a flick of her butterfly knife. She was ducking into the pump room when she heard shouting from the lobby, so her estimation was accurate – she'd gained maybe fifteen seconds on them, no more.

She burst into the chamber and locked the deadbolt, then bolted to the door at the far end and retrieved her rucksack from behind the far pump. She slipped on the goggles again and swung the door to the sewer open, then paused on the other side to jam one end of the manhole pick under the door, wedging it in place. Hopefully that would hold for at least a little while. It was going to be close, but between the deadbolt and the jammed door she might have enough of an edge now to make it.

Jet ran down the tunnel, grappling in the rucksack for the oxygen as the methane and sulfur smell threatened to overpower her. That would also slow them once they were in the sewer.

The door behind her shuddered and then slammed twice, flying open on the third blow, and then they were in the tunnel coming after her. She had gained at most a hundred-yard lead, but she had something they didn't: an idea of where she was going. Footfalls sounded from behind her as at least four men raced down the tunnel, but she heard them slow as the air got increasingly foul. She pushed through the old grate, not bothering to close it, and then sprinted, shoes splashing in the noxious puddles that were everywhere. She tried not to think about how much more oxygen she had. However hard it would be on her, it had to be far worse for her pursuers.

Flashlight beams played on the walls behind her, and she ducked into the first intersection, bearing right. Running flat out, she covered the next leg in twenty seconds and took the left tunnel. The sounds from behind her were growing more distant, fading to where she could hardly hear her trackers.

Now the question was, where to exit? There wouldn't be much time. They'd get the police prowling the streets within minutes once they figured out they'd lost her in the sewers.

She arrived at the steel rungs in the wall where she'd descended and cocked her head. Sound was distorted from the echoes, but their footfalls sounded distant and dim – they'd taken different passageways, which would require backtracking once they realized their error, buying her more time. And there was no way for them to know which passages she'd taken, so it would be trial and error. Now the dilemma was whether to wait for them to show themselves, or risk drawing them to her with the noise of the manhole cover.

Her air supply ran dry, making the decision easier. She had to get out of there. Now.

Jet pulled herself to the top of the ladder and regretted having ditched the steel pick. Desperate, she rammed her shoulder against the heavy iron disk and felt it shift, but only barely. She pushed upwards with all her might, and it lifted a few scant inches. She wedged a hand against it, biceps straining, and inched it to the side, and was greeted by a blast of fresh air as she hoisted herself up and out into the night. She rolled the cover back into place, wincing at the loud grating sound it made, and then sprinted down the street as she tapped her ear bud.

"I'm out. Get me at...outside that Cartier store two blocks from my entry point. I should be there within a few–"

She heard the manhole cover crash behind her, and spun, dropping the P90 into firing position as she pivoted, and then sprayed the street with rounds. A man dropped back into the sewer, his skull split open from a bullet, and she heard a shout as his body fell onto others below him on the access ladder. That would keep them busy for a while. Nobody would want to be the next man to poke his head out if there was a slug waiting for him on the other side. She tore off the night vision goggles and dropped them into her rucksack, then tapped the ear bud again as she ran.

"As I was saying. Pick me up by Cartier. I should be there in two minutes."

"Are you okay?" Alan's whispered question tickled her ear.

"No injuries. See you in two."

"Roger that."

Sirens howled in the distance, reminding her that she was still racing the clock. It would be close. Very close.

Her mind raced at the implications of the disastrously aborted hit. Grigenko's men had to have known something was going on. Alan had been right.

Which meant somehow, some way, they'd been tipped off.

She turned a corner and slowed to a walk, then ditched the rucksack into a garbage can half-filled with refuse awaiting collection and adjusted her backpack. Now she was just a nice girl returning from a night of cocktails or a date at her rich boyfriend or sponsor's apartment.

Up ahead at the pedestrian promenade she saw the glow of the red Cartier signs. She was just crossing the street when she heard a revving engine race towards her, and the Porsche pulled alongside her.

"Hop in," Alan said.

She shrugged the backpack off and tossed it into the small rear area behind the passenger seat and then climbed into the low-slung seat. She was just slamming the door closed when a police car with lights and sirens blaring came screeching around the corner a block behind them, heading straight toward them. Alan glanced at her and jammed the stick shift into gear and floored it, and the powerful sports car launched forward into the Moscow night.

CHAPTER 22

"We were blown. They were expecting something." Jet's voice was calm, without inflection, as they weaved through the empty streets, the police cruiser in hot pursuit.

"I got that," Alan said, twisting the wheel and sending the little coupe dizzily around a sharp corner, the back end losing traction for a moment before Alan righted it with a goose of the throttle. The rear wheels gripped and the car jolted forward, accelerating like a runaway elevator, the momentum pinning them both back into their seats.

"Might want to fasten your seatbelt," Alan commented, eyes darting to the rearview mirror, tracking the police car.

"Why, is that a law here?" She smiled and secured it with a click. "I'm just going to have to unbuckle if I need to shoot them to pieces. Waste of energy, the buckling part."

"Probably best if you don't start a firefight in downtown Moscow. Not really low profile."

"Then you better pick up the pace and sharpen your driving chops, because I have a feeling you're going to have more where they came from pretty soon – and you can't outrun a radio."

"Good point. Grab the GPS down by your feet and pull up a map. You can play navigator."

She powered the little device on, then punched the buttons until a map of the area came up. She studied it briefly and then nodded. "Two blocks up, make a right. Go one block, make a left."

"Right, then left. Gotcha. Where are you taking us?"

"To the nearest Metro station. There's no way they have a description of us, just the car. So we ditch it and disappear into the Metro. Split up. Rendezvous later. By the way, next time you're going to steal a car for an operation, pick a different color than red. Just a tip."

"Works for me." He gunned the engine and they flew over cobblestones before he made the right. They were steadily pulling away from the police car, which was now three blocks back. "Besides, I always wanted to put a Porsche through its paces – and this was the only one I could find."

"When we get onto the main street after the left, go up three blocks and then drop me off at the station. Dump the car wherever. Worst case, meet me at the Metropol Hotel in an hour."

"Done. Use that water to rinse off your shoes once you're on the sidewalk – the smell's a giveaway." He motioned to a liter bottle in the back.

"Will do."

Once he had twisted through the streets, following her directions, he pulled to the curb and she leapt out of the car fifty yards from the Metro entrance. He tossed her the backpack and water and tore off again. She sat down on a concrete planter and washed the sewer residue on her shoes away before proceeding to the station, standing calmly on the long escalator carrying her twenty stories below the surface. The air became warmer, tinged with the distinctive smell of subways everywhere in the world, and soon she was standing on a platform waiting for the next train, which she could hear clattering somewhere down the darkened tunnel.

A police officer stepped onto the platform and studied the small crowd of people waiting for the subway, their faces mostly drawn and tired, defeated, ready to go home after a long night's partying. Some teenagers laughed boisterously from the far end of the platform, and one of them yelled at his companion, then stopped abruptly when he saw the cop. The group quieted as he focused his attention on them and everyone suddenly lost interest in creating a disturbance.

The train pulled into the station with a clatter and the doors opened. Everyone on the platform waited for the few travelers to get off, and then they boarded the half-empty cars, grabbing seats where they could. Many smelled like alcohol – she guessed that at least half of her fellow travelers were in some state of substantial inebriation, and some were barely conscious.

The policeman got onto the next car from hers and took a seat. Whatever he was doing, it wasn't looking for her, and she relaxed. She was just one of many millions in the huge metropolis, and didn't stand out in any way.

Except for the ear bud.

Shit. She'd forgotten about it. Fortunately her hair covered her ears, but it was sloppy tradecraft and she mentally kicked herself. She removed it with a tug and dropped it into her pocket – she might need it later to communicate with Alan.

The train rumbled forward and soon they were whistling through the tunnel to the next station. She'd studied the route map before choosing that line, and only had to ride a few stops before she would disembark and loop back around to get to the Metropol, which wasn't far from Grigenko's villa.

The night had been a disaster. Somehow the Russian had been tipped. That meant that she had a huge problem – there was no telling what else Grigenko knew, and worse yet, she'd lost the element of surprise. Without it the odds of success dropped to the single digits.

So her worries had just gotten worse. What should have been a straightforward penetration and termination had turned into a chase across Moscow, and that now involved the police. And one dead guard. Which would mean a murder charge if she was caught.

Spending time as a guest of the Russian penal system wasn't on her bucket list of ways to live out her life, so she would need to be careful – more careful than she'd been up until then. And she needed to figure out how they had tumbled to her plan. That was the priority. Without that information, there was no way to mount another attempt.

Jet disembarked two stops later and switched to the return line, scanning the sparse crowd for any familiar faces from the outbound trip. Thankfully, she didn't see any. She glanced at the time and saw that she still had forty minutes to go before her rendezvous with Alan. She hoped that he would be able to get rid of the car with no complications. Then again, he was a big boy and a seasoned operative, so she wasn't worried.

When she arrived at the hotel she went to the bar, but it had closed an hour earlier. Not wanting to sit in the lobby drawing attention, she asked about internet access and was directed to the business center, open twenty-four hours. Inside she rented time on a computer and scanned the news in Uruguay, then switched to global headlines.

Fifteen minutes later two strong hands landed on her shoulders from behind her and began kneading the bunched muscles.

"I figured I would know where to find you," Alan said with a playful tone.

"You need to see this, Alan. Now." Jet's voice was strangely flat. She turned to face him and he looked into her eyes, and when he saw her expression he moved around her to the screen.

"What is it?"

Jet pointed at the news page and then clicked on a video window.

A figure cloaked in a black headdress addressed the camera in heavily accented English. Below the video was a description describing him as Saif al-Diin, the "Sword of the Faith," leader of the Righteous Light. Alan motioned to Jet for headphones. She wordlessly handed them to him, and he slipped them on and listened to the statement, then watched the footage of a man slowly dying in an anonymous cell.

When the clip finally ended five minutes later, the blood had drained from Alan's face. Jet scrolled down and clicked on a headline, and they read it with dread, each word slamming home with the force of a blow.

Terrorist Group Threatens Deadly Biological Attack, Warns U.S. and Israel of Coming Armageddon.

CHAPTER 23

Jet and Alan played the video two more times and then skimmed the commentary. The early consensus was that the footage was genuine and that the promise of attacks wasn't an empty one. Worried news anchors questioned whatever experts the networks had been able to round up, and one, from the American Center for Disease Control, was especially dour in his outlook:

"We've always known there was the chance that hostile interests would launch a bio-attack. We saw a premonition of the kind of panic it could cause after the World Trade Center disaster, when the anthrax scare hit. People were driving into Mexico to buy ciproflaxin, ordering it from Canada, demanding prescriptions or samples from their doctors. And that was a disease for which there is a treatment. Imagine the effect of a wider-spread attack with a virulent agent like that the video footage purports to show. We are talking every epidemiologist's worst nightmare, and a public health crisis, not to mention an emergency of the most devastating sort. And not just for the U.S.; this will be a world-wide panic, for good reason. Terrorists, once they've let that genie out of the bottle, will see the effect and have a new weapon of choice. All we can do at this point is to be prepared for anything."

The threat level in the United States had been raised to red, signaling the highest possible state of alert. What that meant in practical terms was questionable, but even only a few hours into the crisis the world's most powerful nation was dancing.

CNN featured a different spin, focusing on the domestic disturbances already being seen in many cities. An earnest-looking blonde with sensible hair read from the teleprompter with Shakespearean sincerity:

"Well, Frank, what I can tell you is that many ordinary people aren't taking this lying down. Reports are coming in from all over the country of runs on grocery and gun stores. Apparently the prevailing belief is that it will be best to be armed to the teeth and stocked up on staples. We've seen similar patterns in past crises, but nothing like this in only a few hours. The Righteous Light video is causing a sensation, and the YouTube version already has eighty million views, causing problems with the company's server capacity. And that's not counting all the news outlets with their own feeds."

Jet went to another American news site and viewed a report from two well-fed anchormen with shockingly bad haircuts and sincerity suits, airing man-on-the-street interviews calling for the U.S. to do something, now:

"Damn it. We should nuke the damned Iranians and whatnot. Nuke the whole lot of 'em. Bastards hate us because of our freedom and our way of life. I say blow 'em back to the Stone Age and let Jesus sort 'em out," a beefy red-faced man assured the camera, his baseball cap on backwards as he offered his counsel on international diplomacy.

One of the anchors pointed out that the hazmat suit in the video had been identified as being of Iranian manufacture, causing concerns that Iran was behind the threatened attack, possibly in retaliation for sanctions against their nuclear program.

"Dick, no disrespect, but nobody except the U.S. has ever claimed that Iran was enriching uranium above the twenty-percent level for medical purposes. And multiple agencies have responded to American claims by pointing out that exactly zero of the intelligence that the United States has provided turned out to be true, or even helpful in identifying Iran as pursuing nukes. And Iran itself has claimed multiple times that it is not working on weapons, and all inspections have indicated that nothing in their programs is geared towards nukes."

"That's so typically liberal, Howard. I say we can't afford to take the chance. Of course they're going to claim that they're innocent. But what if they're lying? Then we have nuclear chaos in the region."

"Dick. Please. The U.S. used that logic to invade Iraq. And it turns out the intel was one hundred percent wrong. I guess the question is, what right does the U.S. have to invade sovereign nations and attack them when they're innocent of the claims used to justify the attacks in the first place? Doesn't that set a disturbing precedent?"

"Someone has to man up and keep the peace, Howard. Like it or not, we're the peacekeepers."

"Sounds good, but how is going to war on false pretenses and overthrowing governments we supported for decades 'keeping the peace'? Look, I'm no dove, but even I have to question the government's motives. Our rhetoric doesn't match our actions. For example, in 2006, Bush stated that a pre-emptive nuclear strike was on the table against Iran. That violates international law, where the U.S. and all other nuclear states agreed that a nuclear country cannot threaten a non-nuke country with nuclear war. Does anyone besides me see how messed up that is?"

"I think you're mis-stating what happened, Howard. But anyway, we need to cut to another man-in-the-street segment, this time from New Orleans." The first suited man couldn't terminate the other's reasoning quickly enough.

Alan and Jet continued skimming the news, and then Jet yawned, checking the time.

"We need to get going. Which brings us to the question of what happened, and how we're going to proceed from here," she said.

He rubbed his face, fatigue creeping into his expression, and then sat back. "I think we need to get a few hours of sleep. And I need to contact the director about the bio-weapons threat. This changes everything. I thought this was going to be a drawn-out process, where we'd have more time to figure out what they were up to. Now we don't have to. They've told us. Obviously, that means they're close enough to their implementation date to feel confident that they can't be stopped. So I need to focus on that while you get some shut-eye. Once I've spoken with him, we can discuss Grigenko."

"Before we get ready for sleepy-time, I think we need to talk about how Grigenko knew I was coming for him. I can't think of a lot of ways that could have happened that don't involve the director leaking it to him," Jet spat.

"What? Are you nuts? We're talking about the head of the Mossad. Why the hell would he work with a Russian arms dealer, who might be even now providing our enemies with doomsday weapons?" Alan sounded outraged, and had to struggle to keep his voice even.

"Then what's your theory? David always said there had to be a mole. Maybe he got the wrong man."

Alan sat, thinking, then shook his head. "Impossible. This is a man above reproach, who has devoted his life to the cause. It's preposterous."

"Look, Alan, I'm as patriotic as anyone. But what's the alternative explanation? He would have had the ability to access the bank records. And he's the only one who knows that you're in Russia. If that's the case, then we're screwed, and it's possible he's been feeding him information. Maybe not Grigenko – maybe to the KGB, and someone there is leaking to him."

"I can't believe it. I just can't."

"Then what's your explanation?"

Alan rose and paced to the door of the business center while Jet logged out and paid the listless attendant a king's ransom for her time. "Maybe there's a leak in his office – a confidant who has been compromised? There's no way he's working with Grigenko. But obviously, I haven't thought it completely through."

"Well, take your time. But in the interim, how much detail does he have? Just in the one-in-a-million chance that I'm right?"

Alan considered the question.

"He just knew that I was in Moscow, and...and yesterday I told him that I would probably be done with my project here by tomorrow." Even as he said the words he realized the ramifications. "Which would imply, if he

131

suspected anything about hitting Grigenko...that it would be today or tonight."

She stepped through the business center door and waited for him to follow, stopping in the lobby as he trailed behind her. "You know what I hate? I hate when I have to assume that all the obvious signs are just coincidences. Know what I mean?"

"I'll take that under consideration. But for now, I need to focus on the end of the world as we know it."

"One more question. Does he know what operational ID you're using for Russia?"

He thought about it. "He could find out. Look at who we're talking about here."

"Alan, don't take this the wrong way, but I think I'll be staying somewhere else tonight than at your hotel, then. Call me paranoid. It goes with being chased by gunmen through the sewers of Moscow."

"Then where are you going to sleep?"

"I'll figure something out. It'll be light in a few more hours. Maybe I'll just wander the city seeing if I can entice some muggers to take me on – just to keep in practice."

Even though he was getting tired, the adrenaline surge from the car chase and the terrorism revelation having faded, he managed a smile. "You are so the last chick on the planet I would want to mug."

She gave him a dark look. "What's wrong with me? Although I like being called a chick. That makes me feel like a teen again. God help me."

"Well, I can't see any attempt going well for the mugger. Let's just leave it at that."

"I suppose that depends on who's mugging me. For you, I might not fight that hard..."

He took her hand. "I know this didn't go the way you wanted. And I'm sorry. I'll bear in mind your concerns about the director and won't treat them lightly. One way or another, you can depend on me to see this through. I won't leave you in the lurch. I promise. And not just because I gave my word to my brother." He seemed to run out of words, his voice choking slightly at the end. Jet stood on her tiptoes and pressed her lips softly against his, then pulled away, holding him at arm's length, inspecting him.

"You didn't have to say that. But I'm glad you did," she said, a slight tremor in her tone.

"So am I." He sighed. "We've got a lot to figure out after this is over, don't we?"

She looked off into the distance, out the glass doors at the other end of the lobby. "I've been taking it one day at a time lately, Alan. Don't think too much. Things will take care of themselves."

"One way or another."

"I'll be okay. Go back to the lap of luxury at the Cosmos while I dig through dumpsters for food on the harsh Moscow streets. You have work to do," she teased, turning him around and then marching them both towards the lobby entrance. "Be careful at the hotel. I wouldn't rule out an attack."

"I know. I'm going to change hotels – just go in and grab my stuff and get out. Look for me at the Hilton. Different name." He closed his eyes, trying to remember what passports he had brought with him. "Roberto Guglioni. Italian."

"Roberto Guglioni. Got it. I'll check in tomorrow. Now get out of here and do what you need to do."

They walked out onto the sidewalk and he turned to her one final time.

"Take care of yourself."

She debated kissing him again, and then gave in to the impulse. This time the kiss was more serious. When they disengaged, her heart was racing.

"You too."

And then she whirled and was gone, fading into the gloom in the direction of the Bolshoi Theater. Alan's gaze followed her until the night enveloped her slight form and claimed it for its own.

CHAPTER 24

"Is this a secure line?" Alan asked.

"What do you think?" Samuel Hershod, the director of the Mossad, barked sarcastically, as was his style.

"I'm calling from a payphone, so my end should be good, sir."

"Nice to hear. Now what the hell are you doing about this Righteous Light threat? I thought you were on top of things, and you're in Russia, while the biggest danger to hit from the Middle East in my lifetime goes live. Forgive me if I sound worried that you might be going about this the wrong way."

"I'm getting information as we speak. But I have to confess the timing took me by surprise."

"That's just great. Pumps me full of confidence. Now explain to me why I shouldn't have twenty of our top people working on this right now?"

"Maybe you should. But keep me out of it. I'll deal with the operational side, just like if the team were still together. That seemed to be the most effective approach for years, didn't it?"

"Then that's what I'll do."

"Look, we need every edge we can get on this. The fact that I'm not on anyone's radar is a big win. A lot of deniability if we need to take drastic action, which my sense is, we will. But you'll need to do something official, so by all means convene a task force and put everyone in the Mossad on it. Can't hurt. Just make sure I have access to all the latest reports through the servers."

"Care to tell me what you are doing in Russia? I am the head of the agency, and all."

"You don't want to know. I have a line on the characters who may be supplying the biological agent to the terrorists. So it's related. A wannabe arms dealer. Russian mob."

"If he's selling terrorists germ warfare ordnance I'd say he's more than a wannabe, wouldn't you?"

"But we don't know for sure it's him. I haven't been able to make any firm connection. I know the terrorists were meeting with someone they thought was a Russian, but that's all I got before my asset went dark. I thought I'd follow up on it while nothing was happening in Yemen."

"I think it's safe to say something's happening now. Do you think they're still somewhere in Yemen?"

"That's a tough one. This al-Diin tends to move around more than the average crazy cleric. But my plan is to find out. I'm on the first plane out of here."

Alan heard the director sigh and then groan over the line. "Rain. This is as big as it gets. Don't let us down," he said simply.

"I know."

"If this gets deployed in Israel, it would be devastating. It would embolden all our enemies. Weaken our perceived standing and defenses. It cannot be allowed to happen. Whatever the cost. Am I clear?"

"You are. But I'm not sure Israel is the target. The U.S. is much more vulnerable. Their security is a joke compared to ours, and it's a huge place. If I was looking for maximum impact, I'd hit the Americans."

"That's what I believe as well, but we're still going to be viewed as the root cause. These bastards have set us up. You can already hear the outcry. 'Why is Israel being protected by the Americans? Let them stand or fall alone.' No matter what happens, this will be damaging – I've already gotten a demand to meet with the top brass. It's a diplomatic crisis of epic proportions. But if they release this bio-agent... Expect that to multiply a hundredfold."

"I can only imagine. What's your take on the Iran speculation?"

"Their President just issued a statement indicating that they in no way support any terrorist group, which we know is a lie, and that they have no connection to this one in particular. They sound almost as worried as we do. He went out of his way to say that nothing that's claimed or threatened is in any way related to his country."

"Which he would have to say no matter what. Do you believe him?"

"One thing he said rang true: that he hadn't even heard of this group until a few months ago when they made their first demands. Same here.

And you would think we're about as plugged-in on this as anyone. They appeared out of nowhere."

"Does that remind you of any other groups, sir?" Alan pushed.

"I'm not going to go down that road, young man. We're all aware of the doubts around Al-Qaeda. That's not helpful to this discussion."

The chill was palpable.

"Whatever the origins of this group, you're chartered with stopping them. You've got the latest photographs we have of al-Diin from your surveillance, which puts you far ahead of anyone else. Find him and stop him. Leave the deep thinking to me. That's why I get to wear the cheap suit and sit in the corner office. Figuratively speaking."

"Very well, sir. I'll be leaving Russia tomorrow. I can't accomplish much more here. Just out of curiosity, though, does anyone else know I'm alive, or that I'm here?" Alan framed the question almost nonchalantly.

"What? Why would you ask that? Isn't the whole idea to keep you dead?"

Alan noticed that he hadn't answered the direct question, and considered asking it again, but then decided against it. If Hershod was the leak, he wasn't going to admit it. Perhaps the indirect answering with a question was as definitive an answer as he would ever get.

"That was the plan."

"So there's your answer. Why? What happened?"

"I was mounting a surveillance operation on the suspected arms dealer, and it went sideways on me. I'm trying to figure out why."

The pause lasted one second, then two.

"I presume you're all right since you're calling."

"Yes."

"Any fallout from the surveillance being blown?"

"Not long term. But it couldn't have happened at a worse time, given the stakes." Alan thought he would toss that onto the fire. Perhaps, if the director had leaked information, he hadn't realized Grigenko's role in the larger scheme of things, or he'd been asked by the KGB and it had seemed unrelated or trivial. Alan hadn't ever identified the suspected Russian, so it was a possibility. His mind worked furiously as they wound down the conversation. Was it true? Could it be? He couldn't believe it, but the discussion wasn't going in a reassuring direction.

"Sorry to hear that. But do whatever you need to do to make this go away. You have complete authority to do anything. Anything at all. Whatever resources you need, whatever action you must take, consider me to have already approved it. Don't pull any punches. Is that clear?"

"Crystal, sir, crystal."

When Alan hung up the phone, he was more disturbed than when he had begun the call. He was left with a feeling of distinct unease, and noticed that he was sweating in spite of the cool early morning chill. He hadn't gotten the reassurance that he had wanted, and there was a subtext to the discussion that he didn't like at all; namely that pause and dodging of the million-dollar question, no matter how skillfully the director had done it.

He walked back to his new hotel, having made the call from a bank of phones at a nearby Metro station, and asked himself whether the director's possible involvement with the KGB or Grigenko was even important in the larger matter of the terrorists, and decided that it wasn't – although if there was some sort of clandestine cooperation between the two agencies that he wasn't aware of, it hinted that he wasn't aware of other possibly critical details as well. Details that could ultimately cost him his life.

Once back in his room, he used his laptop to check on flights. First he would get to Europe, and then he'd figure out the cleanest way into Yemen, the source of his current misery. All roads led back to that country, and to the harsh northern desert that this Saif al-Diin called home.

It was at times like these that he most missed his brother's acumen. David had been peerless in his ability to plan, to think ten moves ahead. Alan had never seen anything like it – he could have easily been a world class chess player if he had so desired. Alan was very smart, but not in the same league. That knowledge didn't embitter him. It was fact.

He saw that there was a flight out at one p.m. to Frankfurt. He didn't dare book anything earlier – Jet would need time to get in touch with him and discuss her next move.

Which brought him up short.

Jet.

That he was attracted to her was a given. She was beautiful, exotic, intelligent, and independent – all qualities that were at the top of his list. And she seemed to be warming up to him.

But she was his dead brother's girlfriend.

Sort of, he reminded himself. His *secret* girlfriend...and the mother to his child.

An image of her flashing green eyes and a dazzlingly white smile flittered across his consciousness unbidden, and it was with difficulty that he banished it, recalling her last words. He wasn't to worry. Everything would take care of itself.

He lay on the still-made bed and exhaled noisily, tired to the bone.

Everything would sort itself out.

Easy for her to say.

CHAPTER 25

The following morning Jet and Alan met for breakfast at the Hilton and he took her through the latest developments. She listened attentively, taking it all in as they waited for their food to arrive. The waiter set their plates down in front of them, and after pouring more coffee for Alan, scurried away to attend to other diners.

Jet forked egg into her mouth and nodded as he finished. "I'm coming with you."

This wasn't going as Alan had hoped. "That's not a good idea. Besides which, you need to contend with Grigenko." His eyes darted to the other diners. Nobody cared about his discussion, although three businessmen two tables over were having a hard time keeping their eyes off Jet.

"I can deal with him once we've saved the free world from Islamic fundamentalist terrorists. That shouldn't take too long, will it?" She smiled sweetly, then took a sip of her orange juice. "This tastes terrible. Why can't they get decent orange juice here?" She turned her attention back to him. "In case you haven't noticed, I'm a big girl, Alan. I can take care of myself, and I don't need a big strong shadow to fight my battles for me. And also don't forget that I was the best team had."

"I thought I was."

"They just told you that so you wouldn't get your feelings hurt. Look, can we agree that together, we pose more of a threat than we do separately? Just give me that," she insisted.

Alan took another gulp of coffee. "The coffee isn't a lot better than the OJ."

"I'll take that as a yes. So given that you have the biggest threat to national security of our lifetime, wouldn't it make sense for you, as the man chartered with running this railroad, to enlist the most potent talent you can to bring these A-holes down? Or am I missing some part of this movie?"

He had to concede that she made a compelling argument, but he was unwilling to expose her to any more danger. "That's not the issue. This is simple – you have Grigenko. I have the terrorists. That's how this plays out."

"Sure, but you forget that there's overlap. Grigenko is also involved with the terrorists, up to his neck, if you're right. So he's your problem too. My suggestion is that we work together and deal with both heads of this hydra, but in a reasoned manner. The priority has to be stopping the terrorists, because if I take out Grigenko, they'll just disappear and then pop up again in a few months or years, having gotten a weapon from someone else. Come on. You know I'm right. The sequence has to be, take down the terrorists and then Grigenko, not the other way around." She caught Alan glaring at the businessmen and glanced over, then returned her gaze to him and smiled. "Besides which, even though I'm not with the Mossad anymore, I still believe, Alan, and this affects me as much as it does you. This is a threat to a country I gave everything to, for years. If there's something I can do to stop it, I will."

"What are you proposing?" She was wearing him down.

"I meet up with you in Yemen. We figure out where these scumbags are and then eradicate them. Once that's done, we return to Moscow and you help me put an end to Grigenko. From there...we'll figure it out."

He nodded. "I have to say there's a certain appeal to that."

"What, the kill 'em all part, or the figuring it out bit?"

"Honestly? Both."

She reached across the linen table cloth and took his hand, tracing the laugh and life lines with the fingers of her other hand.

"According to this, you're going to live forever and have a wonderful life."

"Really. Did it say anything about the next few days?"

"Not so much. But I think I've made my position clear." She set his hand down and returned to her breakfast. "So what flights did you book for yourself? I want to ensure I'm on different planes."

Just like that, it was settled, without as much as a whimper from Alan. He'd been outgunned by a hundred and ten pounds of female ingenuity.

It didn't feel all that bad.

The Russian allowed himself to be blindfolded after being picked up at the agreed-upon rendezvous point, and now bounced along in the rear seat of the Chevrolet Suburban, men on either side of him, their pungent body odor sour enough to make him gag. The ride went on seemingly endlessly before they lurched to a stop and he was guided out of the vehicle and into a building. He heard a door close behind him and then hands fumbled with the blindfold. When it was removed he was facing Saif al-Diin, who was, in his fashion, sitting on an ornate carpet on the floor.

"Come. Sit," he beckoned. Hamid, his second-in-command, was standing in a corner of the room, staring holes through the Russian with the burning zeal of the believer, an oversized wad of *qat* leaves stuffed in his cheek in the Yemeni fashion, masticating the plant. *Qat* was a drug with mild stimulant qualities that was in widespread use in Yemen, to the point where it was the largest crop in the country. The custom was to chew the leaves and suck on them, like chewing tobacco, to draw out as much of the drug in the leaves as possible.

"Thank you," the Russian said and then took a seat on the floor across from the terrorist.

"We have run our own trials on the agent, and it is as you said. We would like to place our order, and need to finalize the price and delivery terms," al-Diin began, shifting to get more comfortable.

"I have good news and bad news, then. First, the bad. We cannot make it contagious. It would require far too much time and resources."

Saif al-Diin nodded, having expected the response. "And the good?"

"We can have the agent, as provided in the sample, available for you within a week, possibly sooner, in sufficient quantity to kill ten thousand people, assuming that it is introduced into an indoor area's ventilation system. The effectiveness will vary depending upon the size of the area, of course."

"Of course. I am assuming that we could deploy it with relative ease?"

"Yes. I will provide instructions once we have an agreement and have received half the purchase price in advance."

"That is fair. How much will it cost?"

"Five hundred."

Saif al-Diin's eyes narrowed to slits. "Is this some sort of Russian humor?"

"No, it is not. That is the price."

Saif al-Diin closed his eyes, his face betraying no emotion. When he opened them after several long beats, his anger was obvious. "That is considerably more than we ever discussed. More than double the two hundred you felt would be the number."

"Yes, I know. Apparently when you went onto the web and announced to the world that you were going to use it on a high-profile target, it increased the risk to my master. Risk for which he requires compensation. Frankly, you're lucky he is still doing the deal – we warned you about leaking the bio-agent's existence prior to delivery," the Russian explained reasonably.

"So now that he knows I intend to use it, and require it soon, he has decided to stick it to me, as you say in the West."

"I wouldn't know about that. I simply was instructed to tell you the price if you wish to purchase the product. If you do not, that is also acceptable, and we will wish you every success and hope that you think of us for anything else you need."

Saif al-Diin regarded him with a frown. "Perhaps I should send you back to your master in pieces. Small, bloody pieces. I have a mind to do that, then negotiate with your replacement."

The Russian's gaze was impassive. "I can assure you that would eliminate any willingness to assist you in your endeavor," he said.

The terrorist leader nodded. "I suspect you are right. But then again, I could easily obtain a different agent from one of my other sources. There are still stockpiles of nerve gas that I have located. It would be far less expensive."

"A nerve agent, assuming it wasn't past its expiration point, might serve your purposes; however, I think you are underestimating the level of difficulty involved in handling and effectively deploying it. With our agent, we'll supply a foolproof mechanism for transport and dissemination. It can be remotely triggered with a simple cell phone call or a programmable timer. I think you should consider the value of a guaranteed deployment versus an aborted attempt with an inferior substance."

Saif al-Diin sighed. "This is worth something," he conceded.

"If you would like to think about it, take a day or two. We're in no particular hurry. The price is fixed for forty-eight hours. That is all I have been authorized to guarantee."

Hamid watched the exchange with interest, jittery from the effects of the *qat,* and fidgeted with the AK-47 assault rifle dangling from his shoulder by a leather strap, unsure of whether he would soon be using it or the dagger tucked into his belt.

Al-Diin sighed again. "I am anxious to put my plans into motion, so today is your lucky day. I accept your terms and your price. Now tell me about delivery, as well as about the best form of deployment."

The discussion lasted another half hour, the terrorist chieftain taking mental notes and asking detailed questions, his second-in-command listening, occasionally exchanging thoughts in rapid-fire Arabic. By the time the conversation was concluded, Saif al-Diin felt that he had a working understanding of what would be required, as well as how to select a target where the biological weapon would have maximum effect.

"I wish you could make it contagious," he finished ruefully.

"Yes, well, that is not possible. I'm sorry. But we can probably create a larger quantity if you're willing to wait."

"No. Time is not on my side in this, and I have waited long enough. I will transfer funds tomorrow to the same account. And I expect to see you within five business days, as agreed."

The Russian rose. "Where would you like to take delivery? Remember that it will only be effective for one week from when you receive it. Every day afterwards it will lose fifty percent of its potency – an unfortunate byproduct of its creation."

Saif al-Diin told him, and the Russian's eyes flicked to the side before he nodded.

"Very well, then. We should be able to accommodate you. Will you require any blueprints, identification, or other related items for the target?"

"Can you get those?"

"Of course. Tell me what you need and I shall make it so. On the house." The Russian could afford to be generous at this point.

They talked for another few minutes, and then the Russian strode to the door. "I shall see you within one week."

The terrorist motioned to Hamid, and he approached the Russian with the blindfold again.

An hour later, the Russian was packing his travel bag, ready for the long series of flights that would return him to Moscow. He weighed a satellite phone in his right hand, and walked to the balcony of his hotel room and opened the two glass doors, watching the unit's display until it locked onto a signal.

"They agreed. Money will be sent tomorrow. I'm returning on the first flight out."

Grigenko's voice on the other end sounded gleeful. This was the easiest half a billion he'd ever made.

The Russian terminated the call and returned the phone to his bag, then withdrew a small leather satchel that he placed carefully on the rustic wooden table near the window before taking a seat. He unzipped it and withdrew a syringe and a small vial of white powder. Next to these, he lined up a spoon, a lighter, and a tiny bottle of distilled water. A contact in Sweden got him all the pharmaceutical-grade heroin he wanted by diverting prescriptions – heroin was regularly prescribed in many countries in Europe in order to control disease and crime, and the purity was always constant, eliminating the fear of overdosing due to varying degrees of quality.

The last item he removed was a small votive candle. The veins in his arms had long since collapsed from years of using, so now he injected into the femoral artery in his leg – a practice that carried some risk, but then again, so did facing off violent psychopaths sourcing doomsday weapons. It was all about risk and reward, and he had discovered during his tour of duty in Afghanistan that the magic poppy made danger more manageable without impairing his cognitive function.

He lit the candle and then precisely tapped powder into the spoon, stopping when he had what he knew was two hundred milligrams, more or less. He next poured in a small amount of water and held the mixture over the candle. Once the powder liquefied, he carefully sucked it into the syringe and then injected it with a satisfied groan.

He barely made it from the chair to the bed, and when he collapsed in a state of euphoria his last thought as he listened to the evening call to prayer in the street below was that indeed, *Allahu akbar* – God was most great.

CHAPTER 26

Alan followed the coverage on the terrorist video with near feverish devotion, right up until he had to leave the hotel. Hysteria in the U.S. had built as more of the population had time to consider the ramifications; whereas in Israel, where the population routinely dealt with the reality of being surrounded by hostile forces intent on harming it, the news was greeted more calmly.

The television networks all featured the story as their primary lead, devoting non-stop coverage to an endless stream of talking heads – from highly qualified public health physicians to authors of sensationalistic novels featuring bio-threats. Everyone, it seemed, had something to add to the discussion, and the media feeding frenzy that ensued was stunning to behold. An entire nation held its breath, and communities from the Canadian border all the way to Mexico considered steps to reduce the public's risk, including closing schools, increased airport security, and work stoppages. Bouts of hate crime flared up throughout the nation as Muslims, or those that looked foreign or Middle Eastern, were attacked by the ignorant and the fearful.

Iran came up in virtually all coverage, until the speculation that the country might have been behind the new terrorist scourge became virtual certainty, in spite of voices of reason that pointed out there was no linkage other than a virtual relic of a hazmat suit that could have been purchased from any of countless sources.

Additional study of the symptoms captured on video had led most physicians to agree on the nature of the agent, at least. Alan watched the latest as he packed his bag – a doctor from the infectious disease center at a large New York hospital being interviewed by an anchorwoman who seemed both serious and gleeful that such an epic story had landed in her lap:

"It looks to be a combination of one of the hemorrhagic fevers and bubonic plague. But in some kind of hyper-synthesized form. The speed of disease progression is astounding. It's definitely some sort of lab-generated weapon; but the question is, where did it come from?"

Alan muttered to the computer as he zipped his bag closed.

"Russia, you idiot. One of those labs that the government assured everyone had been neutralized. Who knew that governments routinely lied?" he spat at the television, frustrated.

He checked his watch and realized that he'd dawdled too long. It would be a close call to get to the airport in time to make it through customs and onto the flight. He shut down the laptop, slid it into its padded bag, and bolted for the door, his thoughts on Jet, who was flying out later in the day, also through Germany. They had agreed that they would meet in Yemen in two days, allowing them both time to get their visas and arrange for travel into the civil war-torn country.

In the meantime, he had called the director one final time to let him know he was en route. Both men understood that the clock was ticking, although at this point all the world had was a video and a statement. There was nothing more forthcoming from the Righteous Light, which had been the subject of a media firestorm over the last twelve hours. Hastily thrown together short documentaries had been prepared by several of the news services, and what was most disturbing was the paucity of details anyone had on the organization.

Alan had made some of his own calls and reached several of his Yemeni contacts from his past life – people who didn't know him in the context of the cell he'd infiltrated, but rather were independent from his old assignment. And true to its word, the Mossad had a strike team working on any information it could glean about the possible location of Saif al-Diin.

Everyone was doing what they could, but at the end of the day, there was little to go on. They had to wait for something to break and hope that the terrorists made a mistake – that someone got sloppy or behaved stupidly, creating an opportunity.

The Mossad tech team was working to isolate the location of the video's original upload, and there was cautious optimism that they would track it down – eventually.

He flagged down a taxi and soon was speeding along in a Mitsubishi sedan being driven like a Formula One race car by its surly driver, whose mood had improved significantly when Alan indicated that a substantial bonus was on the table if he made record time to the airport.

As he watched the ugly parade of Soviet-era monolithic buildings whiz by, Alan was glum. Reality was that a motivated terrorist who was willing to give his life could usually achieve a catastrophic result, and that the video threat had been released meant the group was confident in its ability to deliver. Unless they got lucky, he wasn't optimistic, and he had already begun trying to figure out how best to frame his advice for the director – prepare a response based on the presumption of a strike taking place, not on it being stopped.

An ugly but pragmatic strategy, to be sure, but also the most realistic. Assume the terrorists would successfully deploy the agent, a catastrophic event would occur, and the world would keep turning, albeit a different world than the day before.

Nobody wanted to hear that, but it was the most likely outcome.

The taxi almost collided with a motorcycle and both drivers shook their fists at each other before continuing on their way. Alan leaned back in the seat and made sure that his belt was secured, and then closed his eyes, already exhausted before beginning his journey.

Washington D.C., United States of America

Lunchtime at the club was a quiet affair, with the private chef offering a magnificent five-course fixed menu, although he would gladly also prepare something to taste. The group was gathered in the same room, their lunch finished, lingering over coffee.

"I think I can honestly say that's one of the best meals I've ever had," the older man declared, patting his stomach, his hand-tailored suit straining as he adjusted himself in his chair. "Now that we've gotten the nourishment out of the way, let's talk turkey. Where are we with things? Tony?" he asked one of the younger diners.

Tony stood as if accepting an award and consulted his iPad before speaking.

"The video is having even greater impact than we imagined. People are going nuts. Fights are breaking out, there's been some looting in a few communities, and a number of cities have requested federal assistance for possible crowd containment. We're fielding demands for the National Guard in half the states, and that's expected to increase as pressure mounts. This is a replay of 9/11, only no buildings have come down. There's also been a suspicious rush on emergency rooms with people reporting alarming symptoms, so the mass psychology play is in full roar."

"I note that the Iran connection was made early," the older man said, nodding.

"Yes, the hazmat suit did the trick. And nobody is really buying that it's not somehow involved. At least, nobody in the U.S., which is all we really care about. The media is stoking the outrage, and countless experts have declared that Iran is a dangerous supporter of terrorism, as well as presenting the imminent threat of manufacturing uranium enriched enough to be weapons grade."

"The damned International Atomic Energy Agency is still dragging its feet in going along with that assessment, though, aren't they? As are most of our allies. I think many of them feel like they got burned by supporting our contentions about Iraq. It's not going to be so easy this time. People are skeptical. They don't trust their government," the older man groused.

"Fortunately, they'll believe what they see on TV, and right now the TV is hammering on what a threat Iran poses to world peace. I even saw an author, whose claim to fame is a series about a fictional attack by Iranian fundamentalists on Israel, being interviewed by three different networks, as though his opinion had the weight of fact."

"Shades of Tom Clancy after 9/11. Everyone remember that?" one of the other men asked, chuckling. "He was all over the news. I literally couldn't believe my eyes first time I saw him being interviewed – a masterstroke."

Tony ignored the interruption. "Well, so anyway, the video has had far greater impact than we ever imagined. Half the country is clamoring for a pre-emptive strike against Iran, and the other half is too scared to speak up. Only the usual loons have protested any of the spin, and they're easily shouted down," he continued.

"Killjoys," the older man intoned. The whole assembly laughed politely.

"In short, everything is going perfectly. I think it's safe to say that there have been no surprises or loose ends so far." Tony finished and sat down, picking up his coffee cup as he did so and taking a slurp.

The older man scanned the men in the room, some middle-aged, some old like himself, and saw nothing but determination.

"As everyone is aware, the number-one funder of terrorism is, unfortunately, our ally Saudi Arabia. An embarrassment, and one we downplay. As we've seen, if the media ignores it, then the average Joe does too. But we need to be prepared for some malcontents to pop out with annoying information like that. Fortunately, if Iraq and Afghanistan are any examples, that will stay in the background, and anyone questioning the status quo will be branded a traitor or a nut. But we can't get complacent, and we need to have some good responses when the inevitable questions arise. Now, as far as our other preparations, I'd say we have nothing more to do but sit back and wait. The hard work is done, and I have no doubt our team will perform admirably." He took a moment to let that sink in. "Let's not forget that not everyone is going to buy this, and any dissenters need to be spin-doctored into oblivion. The Europeans aren't going to swallow the Iran bio-weapons connection. So we'll need a response, and I want us pro-active. Let's get some stories going about how the French and Germans and Russians all have significant reasons to defend Iran's reputation, none of them honest. If we can stay ahead of this, we can avoid the worst of it."

He took a sip of his coffee and then stood. "This will be our last get-together until D-day, I'm afraid. It won't do to have us in the same room again, no matter how discreetly. I just want to thank everyone for the support and hard work, and especially for the money."

Everyone laughed again, the tension broken.

"Without which, none of this would be possible. I trust we'll see it repaid a thousand-fold in the coming years. It's a smart investment. Nothing more. Now, if you'll excuse me, I need to get back to the White House. Apparently the President can't figure out how to work the teleprompter for the afternoon press conference."

More laughter greeted his jibe, and then everyone rose, the meeting ended.

On his way out of the club, he picked up his cell phone from the tuxedoed maître d' – a long standing rule was that no phones were permitted in the meetings due to their possible use as eavesdropping devices. The technology to activate even a phone that was off had been around for years, and he, better than most, understood that it was better to be paranoid than found guilty.

His driver was waiting for him, and when he emerged into the alley, his suited assistant ran around the car and opened his door. The old man was already making a call, anxious to report the latest to his masters. They would be relieved that everything was going according to plan.

Better than expected, actually.

Now they just needed to be patient.

That was always the hardest part.

CHAPTER 27

Sana'a, Yemen

The video opened with the by-now familiar eyes of Saif al-Diin, leader of the Righteous Light, sitting in the same room shown in the first video, the same banner with inflammatory slogans in Arabic behind him. His measured voice calmly assured the "devils in the West and their minions, Israel" that their time was rapidly approaching, and that the swift, unmerciful arm of vengeance would strike at their heart, forever reminding the arrogant Americans that they were not only vulnerable but targeted by the growing army of the righteous.

"You, who have stolen our right to self-governance, our heritage, and our pride, so that your imperialist aspirations could be satisfied, have smugly believed that there was nothing we could do to fight back. You have behaved as though we, the Arab world, were your whipping boys, your vassals, our countries nothing more than a resource for your corporations to pillage. Well, my supposedly superior friends, I have a message. The message will soon be delivered unless your governments accede to our demands, and it will never be forgotten – the first in a series of prices you will pay for your insolent abuse of our region. Our demands are simple and non-negotiable."

Saif al-Diin reached off-camera for a glass of water, his voice having become hoarse, and after taking a sip, continued.

"The American government must immediately cease its support for the illegal state of Israel. It must stop using its financial power to bully the rest of the world into complying with its agenda."

Saif al-Diin shifted in his seat and cleared his throat.

"Further, the United States must end its policy of harassment of Iran over its nuclear program, which is a peaceful and logical requirement of a responsible nation developing alternative power for the twenty-first century, as is its right, and in fact its duty to its population. What has been construed as a dangerous rogue state is in fact a nation that was supplied nuclear capability by the American government over fifty years ago – the same government that is now arguing that its presence makes it a danger to the region. This has been branded a religious dispute, with Iran being a fringe regime run by religious extremists, but any study of the facts shows a different truth than the one propagated by the Western government-controlled media.

"My message is clear. Force your government through public outcry to end its abuse of the region and support of the true outlaw government, or face the consequences – consequences that will bring the war being fought against our religion and our cultures to *your* shores. Your government lies to you every day, and portrays itself as a benevolent peacemaker. It is not. It foments war, famine, injustice, intolerance, and genocide so that its capitalistic aims are met. It is a tool of Satan, and is itself Satan's embodiment on the earth."

The camera zoomed in theatrically until only the terrorist chieftain's head was visible, his eyes smoldering with barely controlled rage.

"If your government does not do the right thing, there will be no mercy. You will suffer as we, your puppets and slaves, suffer every day under your oppression. And I will unleash upon you a pestilence so horrible that it will never be forgotten. This is your final warning. Ignore it at your peril. Nobody can escape the wrath of Allah when his Righteous Light shines bright."

The footage changed to a view of the same room in which the prior captive had met his fate, his rotted corpse lying on the floor in a pool of noxious fluids. A new man was bound, huddled in the far corner, alternating between crying and begging for mercy – in English. As the screen timer ticked over first one hour, then the next, the progression of the disease took its inevitable course, ending in the same gruesome manner as in the first video, with the decaying remains memorialized for posterity before the segment came to a close.

Jet and Alan exchanged glances in his hotel room in Sana'a. Alan stood, pacing the floor as she read the commentary that had begun seconds after the latest video had surfaced.

"The reaction is what you would expect. The U.S. is saying it doesn't negotiate with terrorists. Israel is denouncing the threats as an escalation of terrorism by its enemies."

"Does any of that surprise you?" Alan asked.

"Not really. Oh, and the American in the video has been identified as a freelance journalist who disappeared in Saudi Arabia over a week ago. Gregory Monk. Working on a story about the regime's current policies."

"A particularly ugly but effective bit of theater. It's one thing to watch a foreigner die in agony, quite another to watch one of your own. Brings the lesson home with brute force."

"What's interesting to me is the blending of lies and truth in the claims. I mean, it's no secret that the U.S. provided the nuclear know-how to the Shah of Iran. But it completely ignores the claims about the current regime abusing the technology to create weapons."

"What, did you expect truth from terrorists? Since when?" Alan chided.

"I think more interesting is that Iran became the focus of this diatribe – it's much more overt here that this group is angry over the Iranian sanctions and stand-off. That weakens Iran's claims that it isn't somehow supporting the group. Although..."

"I know. Go ahead and say it."

"It's just too pat. Too convenient in increasing a connection that Iran couldn't possibly want known, if it was true. If I was Iran, and I was supporting a group that was about to use biological warfare against the U.S. and Israel, would I want to broadcast that fact?"

"One could argue that it's even further proof that they aren't involved. It would be suicide to be associated with this," Alan agreed.

"Yes, and look at the reaction. Already, the U.S. media is running wild with the Iran angle and conducting polls of the population, which now overwhelmingly supports a first strike against Iran. So in the American mind, it's already a good idea to drop bombs first and ask questions later. Remind you of anything?"

"It's pretty scary, isn't it?"

"We have to stop this from happening," she said, clicking on other news sites, surfing the waves of outrage and spin.

"That's what we're here for. It sure as hell isn't out of a desire to have an all-expenses paid vacation in Yemen."

They had arrived separately two days earlier, and were staying in different hotels. Alan had put out feelers to his contacts, developed apart from the ones he'd worked with in the terrorist cell he had infiltrated years ago. But as with all intelligence gathering, it was a slow and confusing process, and even throwing money around with the offer of plenty more, he wasn't hopeful of catching a break soon.

"Something about this doesn't sit right, does it?" Jet asked, as much to herself as to Alan.

"No. But right now, that's not important. Regardless of our feelings about the veracity of this Saif al-Diin's claims or motives, the imperative is to find him and stop him."

"I know. I was just saying."

The commentary from around the U.S. was frightening, where panic had taken hold in some of the larger metropolitan areas, even as the government urged calm. Footage of National Guard troops mobilizing was accompanied by that of frightened housewives demanding that the administration do something, regardless that there wasn't much it could do. Emotions were volatile, and outbursts of violence were on the increase as society's parasites came out of the woodwork and used the threat as an excuse to loot and riot, settling scores with rivals in the confusion.

The net effect was to portray a nation on the brink, although Jet was skeptical of the media's agenda. Sensationalistic reporting spiked ratings far better than the truth, and she had no doubt that the spin was contrived for maximum effect.

Response from the rest of the world was more balanced, although condemnation was immediate, as were expressions of solidarity with the U.S. and Israel. Interesting to Jet was the Israeli response, which was almost a non-response, in keeping with its policy of broadcasting little about its strategy. The fact was that nothing had happened other than a group of crazies making wild threats, which didn't justify commentary. Throughout its history there had always been accusations and threats – this was nothing new. The country was surrounded by countless groups that wanted to wipe it from the planet. Commenting every time one of them issued a press release would be a full time job. Jet wondered why the Americans were so different. Perhaps because they had been insulated from physical danger for generations, other than the difficult-to-internalize threat of the Cold War. Whereas she had grown up with rocket attacks and suicide bombers and hate as daily occurrences, the Americans had enjoyed the distance that only geographical insulation could provide.

She shook her head as she read and watched. So much of the world was out of control with danger and violence. Peace and safety were the exception rather than the rule. It was no surprise that eventually some of the violence would be exported to America. The planet was shrinking seemingly every day, and the barriers to contagion, whether from the flu or the disease of war, were now minimal.

Alan was right about one thing: this was rapidly spinning in an ugly direction, and the terrorists couldn't be allowed to pull off their threat. She just hoped that they would get lucky before it was too late. The stakes had never been higher, and there was no room for failure.

CHAPTER 28

Dust blew down the streets of Sa'dah in northern Yemen, the perennial blanket of arid soil adding to the misery of the inhabitants, which was already considerable given the state of tribal war in which the region had been embroiled for years and the constant battling of various rebel forces vying for supremacy over the mountainous area. A sour smell wafted on the breeze, a combination of sewage, garbage, and unwashed bodies. Sa'dah, the capital of the state, was as war-torn as most of the beleaguered country, and had seen periodic skirmishes between government forces and Houthi rebels, who now effectively controlled the town of fifty thousand. A pawn in a deadly territorial chess match, it existed in an uneasy state of peace – until the next attack came unannounced.

Iran had long been alleged to have been the primary support mechanism for the rebels, a charge lent credibility by the presence of the Iranian navy in the Gulf of Aden, ostensibly to battle Somali pirates but largely believed to be active in arms trafficking to the Houthis. Hezbollah, a terrorist organization also widely understood to be supported by the Iranian regime, was rumored to have supplied personnel to train the rebels in coastal regions, and a week didn't go by when accusations of covert arms drops by Iranian naval forces in the Red Sea along Houthi-controlled coast didn't surface anew.

An uneasy breeze chilled the few residents trudging along the dirt roads outside the city center as an occasional vehicle rolled by, often filled with gunmen staffing the security checkpoints set up by the rebels on the main roads in and out of town. A mangy dog trailed by four thin puppies, starving from neglect, nosed through piles of garbage near the entries of the clay-colored homes in search of sustenance, the canine family's survival dependent upon foraging in one of the most desolate and impoverished wastelands on the continent.

Jet and Alan had now spent almost five days in Yemen, beginning in Sana'a and ultimately leading them into the deadly northern states, following up on information gathered by the Mossad's network of informants. Rumors abounded at all times, and the intelligence was considered to be highly unreliable, but yesterday they had gotten a lead on a house on the outskirts of Sa'dah that was purported to be the Righteous Light's provisional headquarters. Neither of them had much hope that the intel was sound, but they didn't have any other leads to follow, so they had packed into an SUV accompanied by Umar, a local driver and longtime Mossad asset, and worked their way north, their covers as journalists writing a pro-rebel exposé hopefully ensuring that they wouldn't be killed out of hand.

Once they arrived in the dismal mountain city they waited until it was dark, and then they retrieved the stash of weapons they had secured in a compartment under the cargo hold and took up position near the walled compound. Unfortunately there were no nearby structures they could use as surveillance positions, so they were largely blind – and in a small community like Sa'dah, anyone nosing around to find a vacant dwelling would trigger alarms. Northern Yemen was among the least desirable places on earth to live, and there was exactly zero demand for real estate – not surprising given the sporadic outbursts of violence by armed factions that were endemic to the area.

Jet wore the traditional *abaya*, *niqab*, and *hijab* – the black full-body robe, veil, and headdress favored by Yemeni women – and the shapeless folds easily enabled her to hide an MTAR-21 assault rifle with a silencer in its depths. Their plan, such as it was, amounted to watching the home from a distance, with an occasional pass by Jet in her native garb should they see anything suspicious.

When they drove down the dusty road that ran in front of the compound, they spotted two armed men, each sitting on the roofs of the adjacent houses with weapons. In northern Yemen, possession of an assault rifle didn't in and of itself mean anything, but armed sentries deployed around a suspected terrorist hub did. Jet and Alan exchanged glances as they continued on their way in the dark.

"Interesting. Don't see any other nearby homes with guards on the roof, do you?" she asked.

"Nope. Looks like there might be something to this," he confirmed.

"So what do you want to do?"

"I'd say wait and see what happens."

"How do you want to play this? It's not like we can get easy line-of-sight."

"Let's return on foot and find someplace where we can spend the night with the house in view. If nothing happens by first light, we can come up with a new plan," he said.

She looked at him.

"Not really very elegant, is it?"

He nodded, conceding the point. "You got something better?" he asked, afraid of her answer.

"Well..."

⁂

A tapestry of stars glimmered overhead in the clear night, the slim crescent moon's soft glow providing scant illumination as the hour crept towards dawn. An hour before daybreak, a dilapidated brown sedan pulled down the dusty track and rolled to a stop a few yards from the house perimeter wall. Two men got out and approached the front entry, and when the door opened Jet could see with her night-vision goggles that the man inside held an assault rifle.

With a quick glance at the street, the man beckoned the new arrivals inside, and once they had entered, scanned the area again before closing the door.

"I don't think we're going to have much more time unless we want to come back tomorrow night and hope that the bad guy brigade is holding an all-hands meeting. I say we hit it now." Jet was still peering through the goggles from their position in the SUV three blocks away, magnification set on ten.

Alan was torn. If this was in fact the terrorists' base and the leader wasn't there, they would have lost their only chance to catch him. He said as much, and Jet shook her head, the goggles waggling as she did so. Umar sat impassively in the driver's seat, watching the compound.

"That assumes that he's not in there right now, and further assumes that he would be coming back. For all we know he's a thousand miles away right now. Hell, he could be disembarking in Moscow from a private jet, on his way to get the bio-weapon, as we speak. Face it, Alan, this isn't going to get any better, and it's a crappy situation, but it's the one we have, so we need to make the best of it. I think it's now or never."

"I hate to just rush into a situation we know nothing about," he objected.

"Me too. You know me. I'm all about planning. Only sometimes the situation is fluid and you don't get the luxury."

He considered their options and then nodded.

"Fine. Here's what we're going to do."

❧

The two armed sentries watched the woman approach, wearing the traditional head-to-toe black of the devout, carrying a sack bulging with goods of some sort. When she was fifty yards away, she lost her grip on it and the bag hit the dirt with a thump, miscellaneous odds and ends spilling out. She hastily stooped down to gather her things, fumbling with the scattered contents, and when she stood the nearest could see that she hadn't been able to get everything.

The silenced and flash-suppressed MTAR-21 burped three shots and the first guard's head disintegrated. The second was grappling with his weapon when a tiny red dot appeared on his neck and another silenced volley sizzled from the opposite end of the street, cutting him nearly in two.

Jet waited in the road, senses tingling, ears straining for the slightest sound, but the area was quiet again, empty except for her and Alan, whose muffled footsteps thumped towards her as he jogged from his hidden position.

The bag of garbage had distracted the sentries just long enough for Jet and Alan to gain a slim advantage, but from here out they couldn't depend on anything being easy. Alan moved down the side perimeter wall until he was near the entrance, and then Jet removed her veil and robe and placed them carefully to the side of the entry before slipping her MTAR's strap over her shoulder.

"Ready?" she whispered, the ear bud picking up her question.

"Go," Alan responded.

She sprinted for the twelve-foot high wall and ran sideways up its face for a few yards, her right foot finding a joint where a structural beam ended, and used the cranny to propel herself to the top, her hands reaching overhead for a hold. She grappled till her fingers found a grip and pulled herself over, landing on the inside in a crouch. She whipped the MTAR back around into firing position and swept the area, ready to shoot. A two-story dwelling occupied the far end of the courtyard and she could see lights on in two of the windows.

Jet moved to the door next to the gate and hissed into her ear bud. "Opening the door."

She leaned against the bolt and slid it free, and Alan slipped in, his MTAR also ready for action, its futuristic form hinting at its deadliness.

Jet pointed at the house and motioned to the front door, then pointed at him and gestured to the rear of the two-story structure. Squinting in the gloom, she hesitated and then edged next to him.

"I'm going to try the second story first. If I can get in, they'll never expect it. Stand by for my signal by the front."

Before Alan had a chance to respond she was off, tearing for the house at flat-out speed. She threw herself at the wall near the side, repeating her sideways run, and pushed off, twisting in mid-air, and clutched at the second-story stone window sill. Alan watched as she seemed to defy gravity, swinging her torso ever up, and then pushed open a window and slid through in as much time as it took for him to make it to the front door.

Jet took in her surroundings in a heartbeat: an empty bedroom with a cool tile floor, door closed, a travel bag with an assortment of robes on a chair near the bed. From downstairs, the murmur of male voices drifted upwards, audible even through the heavy wooden slab.

"I'm in. Room's empty. You want to try to get in this way, or go around the back and look for a way in?" she breathed into her ear bud.

"Round back," Alan replied curtly.

She stepped to the door and brought the MTAR around into firing position, one hand on the grip and trigger, the other reaching for the door latch. Carefully, she twisted the lever, and then hesitated – the hinges were ancient, and there was a fifty-fifty chance that they'd creak when she opened it.

Jet took two deep breaths, the oxygen thin at their altitude of over six thousand feet, and then pulled it open a crack; then after a few seconds, another few inches. The hinges protested, but not loudly, and she hoped that the men downstairs were so engrossed in their discussion they wouldn't notice. They were directly below her, the second story consisting of three bedrooms and a landing with a concrete and mortar half-wall running its length, the area over the living room and dining room open, creating an atrium effect.

The bedroom door at the far end of the hall opened and a man exited, yawning and scratching himself. His eyes were widening in disbelief and he was preparing to yell when a razor-sharp steel blade flashed through the air and lodged in his throat, his mouth still open and working spasmodically like a landed carp; a gush of blood poured from his lips as his knees buckled. She darted to him, catching him as he fell forward, and his eyes glazed over as she laid him gently down for his final rest.

She waited for a few seconds as he lost consciousness and then a leg jerked, scraping the tiles beneath his feet. A voice called from below.

"Amir? Hurry up. We need to get going soon."

She heard a muffled comment and then some laughter.

She stood and considered her options, and then another call for the dead man decided for her.

"Amir? What's going on up there?"

❧⸲

Three men sat at a crudely built round wooden table, sipping tea and chewing *qat*, their guns by their sides leaning against the walls or the fourth empty chair. One of the men, Hamid, the second-in-command, glanced at the stairs again, annoyed with his companion for running late.

"Ami–"

His cry was interrupted by a body falling from the upper floor, the table exploding with a crash as Amir's inert form slammed into it. The men toppled backwards in their chairs in surprised fright as they scrambled for their weapons.

The man closest to the rustic kitchen reached his AK-47 first and was bringing the barrel up when the red dot found his forehead and the deadly MTAR spat forth its lethal load. Brain and part of his skull splattered the wall behind him and his partner screamed in horror as he clutched for his rifle. Another burst of slugs tore through the second man's torso, shredding his robe as he jerked like a macabre puppet before falling to the floor. Hamid had his hands on his weapon when another figure plunged from above, the dead man's sprawled body cushioning the drop, and then a

161

woman dressed all in black was facing him, the wicked snout of her weapon pointing squarely at his chest.

"Don't. It's over. Let go of the rifle. NOW!" she screamed in Arabic, raising her gun for emphasis. "Drop it or you're dead."

She saw it in his eyes, the split-second calculation, the sidelong jitter, and then the image seemed to slow to a crawl as he scowled, dropping to one knee as he wrenched the Kalashnikov from its resting position against the wall and tried to cock it in preparation to fire. Jet stepped forward and slammed him in the side of the head with her weapon and his neck snapped back, the rifle clattering uselessly at his feet as he went down hard, his head hitting the stone floor with a sickening smack. A pool of blood began spreading behind his skull as if in slow motion, and then time resumed its normal pace – the sudden violence finished, everyone lying still, Jet the only remaining body in motion.

Her ear bud crackled.

"What's going on in there?" Alan demanded in a hoarse whisper.

"It's over. One's still alive, but I don't know for how long. I'll get the door for you," she said in her normal speaking voice, and she thought she saw a flicker in the surviving terrorist's eyes as he heard her speaking Hebrew.

"That's right, you spineless dog. Looks like you aren't so tough when your targets have a gun in their hands, huh?" she spat at him, then took four long strides to the front door and threw it open.

Alan stepped in, gun at the ready, and when she shook her head, lowered it as they approached Hamid's collapsed form.

The blood beneath Hamid's head had expanded to a puddle four feet in circumference. Alan looked down at him without pity, and their eyes locked, hatred radiating from the terrorist's with startling intensity.

"Where is Saif al-Diin? The game's over," Alan snarled.

Hamid glared at him, unable to move.

Jet shouldered her weapon and moved towards him, then reached below his head to raise it so she could staunch the blood flow, but then withdrew her bloody hands when she felt the soft back of his skull. She glanced at Alan and shook her head almost imperceptibly.

"You have failed. Where is he? Where is the bio-agent?" Alan demanded, then pulled his commando knife out of his pocket and flipped it open.

"I...have failed? It is you who have failed. Soon your filthy country will be begging for mercy along with the Americans," Hamid hissed.

"Lies. You've lost. It's just a matter of time before we eliminate your great leader like the fecal speck he is," Jet spat, rising to her feet, walking to one of the dead men, and wiping her hands clean on his robe.

"Ha. In just a few days you will feel the wrath of the righteous. And then it is you who will learn what hell really is. Your people will cry as their flesh falls from their bones. I have nothing to fear, and am going to my reward. But you will watch as your world collapses around you..." Hamid warned, his energy waning at the end.

"One final time. Where is he? If you don't tell me, I'll ensure your last minutes on the planet are your worst. You will die like a dog, but not before begging for mercy," Alan said, and then waved the knife close to the terrorist's right eye. "Do you want to go to your virgins in the afterlife blind and disfigured? I can arrange it."

"You have no power over me," Hamid snarled.

Jet shook her head and walked to the door. "Cut him up into small chunks. I saw some dogs outside that could use a meal. At least this miserable piece of shit will serve some useful purpose, if the stink of his fear doesn't sour the meat. Have a nice eternity in hell, you bastard," she growled, then moved through the door and out into the pre-dawn.

Alan emerged five minutes later.

"Did he tell you anything?" she asked, without much hope.

"No. I don't think he knew much. But I got the impression that he wasn't worried about us catching his glorious leader, so that tells me he's not going to be back here."

"Which leaves us no better off than when we started."

"Not exactly. I took photos of them and will e-mail them to the Mossad as soon as I have a cell signal. Maybe they'll come up with something. If they're known terrorists or have been sloppy, they'll be in a database somewhere. It's a long shot, but it's more than nothing," Alan said, his voice conveying defeat even though his words were defiant.

"Then our best bet is to get back to Sana'a as soon as possible so you can send the photos off."

"Yes. And I scanned their fingers, too, so they can run their prints. Maybe one of them has a record."

"For all our sakes, let's hope so. Although I've given up on hope as a viable strategy."

"Me too. But sometimes hope is all we have."

"I know," she murmured as they moved towards the compound entry. "And God help us all."

CHAPTER 29

The return trip was anti-climactic. On the way north to Sa'dah they'd had the chance that they were headed for a showdown with their enemy; whereas now, tearing along as fast as the roads would allow back to Sana'a, they were headed into the unknown. The terrorist had been too confident, even as he died, that they were doomed – his unshakable conviction was obvious, fueled by hatred. He had gone to his grave sure that their world was about to come apart and so his death hadn't been in vain. You couldn't fake that type of faith. He'd believed they were only days from Armageddon.

Half an hour north of the capital, Alan's iPhone finally displayed a signal, and he sent all of the data he'd collected to headquarters, where the images would be compared to thousands of known terrorists and the prints run through every database in the world. The Mossad had a powerful network it could leverage, and if there was any chance of any of the dead men being identified, they would do so. Alan knew their capabilities and was optimistic.

Jet was glum. She had the sense they'd wasted their time, but she tried to remain upbeat even as she sank despondently into the passenger seat, her robes back on, her veil and headdress in place.

They arrived at Sana'a after rush hour and the driver dropped Jet off in the center of town – she didn't want anyone knowing where she was staying, no matter how trusted by Alan they were – and she made her way gratefully to her room, exhausted after a sleepless night of hyper-vigilance. Even though it was only late morning, she decided to get a few hours of sleep so she'd be rested if Alan needed her later.

The traffic outside her window roared and revved as she pulled the curtains closed and prepared for bed. Sputtering cars battled for supremacy with delivery trucks and swarms of motor scooters with a death wish. Dropping onto the mattress, she resolved to be out in seconds, but even as she drifted off she was struck by a sensation that something wasn't right.

They were all missing an important part of the puzzle.

What it was, she couldn't say, but she was sure of it.

And she was rarely wrong.

෮෧

It was late afternoon, and Alan looked like he hadn't slept in a week, fatigue wearing at him as the pressure of the mission mounted. Jet had checked online and the furor over the terrorist threat had grown to colossal proportions, with civil unrest in New Orleans and Philadelphia threatening to bring the cities to a halt.

"You look like crap," she offered when he opened the door to his room.

"Nice to see you, too," he replied with a hoarse voice, stepping aside so she could enter. "You really like that outfit, huh?"

She twirled in her *abaya*, *niqab* and *hijab* as if modeling for him. "This is the racy version – they call it sexy nurse. You can almost catch a glimpse of my toes."

"They're very nice," he observed.

"Anything new? You break this wide open yet?" she asked.

"Not exactly. I have a call set up a few minutes from now. Sat phone. I'm hoping that we got a match on the IDs that will take us in a different direction."

"Other than stalled."

"Dead by the side of the road."

"*Finito.*"

"End of the line."

They both giggled, sleep deprivation and tension starting to show.

"You check the news?" she asked.

"Not much else to do, is there? Looks like all hell is breaking loose. Iran has issued another statement offering to allow in an international team to inspect their nuclear facilities. They're worried. Which they should be. Whether or not they're involved in this threat, they're being treated as though they are by the U.S.."

"If the terrorists are successful, Iran will wind up getting hurt far worse than the U.S., and they know it."

"It's definitely an ugly position to be in. I mean, they're probably guilty of a lot, but I'm unconvinced that they're guilty of this," Alan said. "Let's hope we can cut this off before it goes ballistic. Which I'm working on. Can you wait for me in the lobby? I need to prep for this call."

"Sure. I love sitting in Yemeni lobbies waiting for mystery men."

"That's how I was hoping you'd feel."

Jet obligingly went downstairs and took a seat on one of the leather sofas, and after reading several of the tour brochures offering trips around the country, fished a cell phone from the depths of her robe. She pressed a speed dial number and then listened as the tremulous ring sounded in her ear.

"*Hola!*" Magadalena's voice sounded distant, but excited.

"Hello, Magdalena. How are you?"

"Oh, *Señora*, very good. I want to thank you again for everything. This is like a dream come true."

"I'm glad you were able to help me, Magdalena. How's Hannah?"

"She's already made new friends in the building and across the street in the playground. But I can tell she misses you..."

"That's great about the friends. Is she there? I'd like to talk to her."

"Of course. Just a moment." Jet heard Magdalena call Hannah, and then rustling as the phone was handed to her.

"Hello?" Hannah's voice sounded tiny and tentative.

""Hello, sweetie. How are you?"

"Mama! Hannah is good. I play lots!"

"Magdalena told me you met some other kids?"

"Two. Two kids!" Hannah enthused.

"Well, that's wonderful. And are you being good?"

"Yes, Mama." She sounded indignant that her behavior could be questioned.

They talked for another two minutes, and then Alan emerged from one of the elevators, his face animated.

"I have to go now, sweetie. Mama will be coming home soon. I love you, Hannah."

"Hannah love Mama!"

Her heart felt like she'd been dropped off a building as she terminated the call. She turned to Alan, who had taken the seat across from her.

"How is she?" he asked.

"Good. Enjoying her vacation. Sounds like Magdalena is spoiling her rotten. Now tell me how the call went."

"I think we may have just gotten the break we'd been hoping for. I don't want to get too excited, but one of the terrorists was in our databases. He's Yemeni, which is no surprise, but he's also a known associate of one of the lowlifes in the cell I had infiltrated. A character by the name of Abdul Nasr."

"That's great news. But how does that help us?"

"Before I blew up, Nasr was dissatisfied because he felt that the cell wasn't taking large enough steps, and was hinting that he was thinking of taking his brand of murderous extremism elsewhere. To a new group. The guy's a frigging nutcase, but he's considered dependable, if extremely violent in both behavior and ideology."

"And you know where he lives?"

"I do indeed. Or rather, I know where he lived five months ago. But I doubt he's moved. People don't change their ways here for no reason. My guess is we can find him, and then watch him. It's not a guarantee, but it's better than anything else we've come across."

"Small world in terrorist circles, huh?"

"Which isn't unexpected. Especially in a region like Yemen. The truly extreme are a relatively small bunch – most everyone with a desire to maim and kill joins the rebels. So there's an outlet for the homicidal. But I'd bet that most of the really devoted know each other. Like minds think alike, and all."

"Too bad you can't get a whole surveillance team in."

"That's a problem. Remember Yemen isn't exactly sympathetic to our cause. And with the civil war, they'd probably spot a bunch of Mossad personnel flying in. Besides which, we're running out of time. We need to start now."

"Fine. Do you have a dossier on the target? Photos? I can take first shift if you want. Between you, me, and the driver, that would be four hours on, eight off, which is manageable."

Alan stood. "Upstairs. I have everything."

"Why, Alan. Are you just trying to get me into your room?" Jet teased, batting her lashes, the veil hiding everything but a small strip of eyes and the bridge of her nose.

"I wish it was a social visit. Believe me."

They waited for the elevator in silence, and when they got in, Jet took his hand. "You really look beat, Alan. Just give me the information and get a few hours of shut-eye. You're not going to do either of us any good if you're too tired and start making mistakes."

He squeezed her hand. "I never make mistakes."

"So I've noticed. But you have to be exhausted. Just point me at him, and I'll take the first watch. The likelihood that anything will happen is pretty slim in any four-hour period anyway. You get some sleep, have Umar take the second shift, and if there's anything worth reporting he can call you, and then you can call me. We still have our arsenal, so I'd think we can take on a few lousy amateur-night Yemeni terrorists, don't you? I mean, I single-handedly cleared the last house and didn't break a sweat."

"You make a compelling case."

The elevator door opened and they walked to his room. Once inside, he moved to his little desk and pulled up a series of images on his laptop.

"This is the guy. He shouldn't be that hard to spot. He's got a slight limp – birth defect. Left leg's shorter than the right. Probably why he went the terrorist route."

"Not enough breast feeding when a baby."

"Nobody understood him."

"None of the other terrorists wanted to play suicide vest with him."

They laughed while she studied the shots.

"How old are these?"

"Less than a year. I took them. I've known the creep for over three years, and he's always looked the same, so you should be able to pick him out pretty easily. He has a room in a dump over by the Al-Thawra Stadium. Here's the address and a photo of the exterior." Alan switched to another shot.

"Does he have a car?"

"No. Motorbike. He's pretty low on the financial totem pole."

She nodded. "Fine. Send all these images to this email address. I can access it from my cell phone." She scribbled on a piece of hotel stationery. "I'll get over there right now. I'm guessing you have a car?"

He handed her a valet stub. "Green Toyota Highlander in the lot. I can get another car, and Umar has his Land Cruiser."

She studied his face, several days' stubble darkening it, and reached up and laid a cool hand on it. "Get some rest. Really. Even if it's a couple of hours."

He nodded, hesitating, then thought better of whatever he had been going to say and grinned instead.

"You'll probably want your weapons, right?" He went to the duffle in the corner and unzipped it, extracting an MTAR with four extra magazines, a silenced pistol, her night-vision goggles, a complement of knives, and an empty black nylon backpack.

"All that for me? You definitely know how to win your way to a girl's heart. Did you reload the magazines?" she asked, moving towards the bed, where he'd placed the weapons.

"Yup. All full. But don't do anything until you call me and everyone is in place. Please. Promise me that."

She slipped everything into the backpack and then hoisted it over one shoulder, the MTAR barely fitting inside the oversized backpack.

"I'm good to go. With all this firepower, I can take on the whole city."

"Remember, anything suspicious, you call me."

She moved to the door. "Anything else?" she asked.

"Be careful."

CHAPTER 30

The neighborhood was seedy, the homes crumbling and the roads decrepit. This was an area where only some of the larger arteries were paved, with the majority dirt. Trash lay strewn across the rutted streets, and the area had a lingering stench of rot, made worse by puddles of murky fluids of suspect origin. Jet looked around as she drove, and the further she moved from the main intersection the more buildings were either abandoned hulks or bare cinderblock dwellings with bars on the windows and laundry hanging on clotheslines.

She checked the time. It would be three hours before dusk came. Once it was dark she could park closer and watch the address from behind the wheel, but right now it would be conspicuous, and she opted to leave the car a block away and reconnoiter on foot, her robes rendering her unrecognizable from the dozens of other Yemeni women moving like black ghosts along the squalid streets.

Jet left the MTAR in the vehicle, covered with a local blanket, and shuffled towards the barren house, a simple two-story cinderblock rectangle with windows, where Nasr rented a room. Flies buzzed around her as she meandered along the dirt road, carrying the backpack like it contained shopping. She had pocketed two of the throwing knives and slipped the silenced pistol into the side pocket of the lightweight cargo pants she wore under the robe, so the backpack only had the goggles and the magazines in it.

Two other women in full garb were walking carefully along the side of the rustic street, approaching her, and with a flash of inspiration she realized that Alan's concerns about being recognized on his watch were unwarranted. She dug her cell from the depths of her robe and placed a call.

"Are you asleep yet?" she asked when he answered his phone.

"I swear I'm just lying down," he lied.

"Well, add an *abaya*, *niqab*, and *hijab* to your shopping."

"Why, did something happen to yours?"

"No. For you. If you slouch you can pass for a tall woman. Nobody can see anything but your eyes. As a woman, nobody will give you a second glance, so when you're in the car, you'll be as close to invisible as you can get. No chance of someone placing you. It's perfect."

"A woman..."

"Correct. Nobody suspects women. I've been using that to my advantage for years. If it will help you get into character, shave your legs and wear something pretty under the robe."

There was silence as he considered her odd advice. "You know what? That actually makes a lot of sense."

"Even a broken clock's right twice a day," she reasoned.

"I'm going to lie down now."

"Nice neighborhood, by the way."

"I imagine it's improved since I was last there."

"The dirt has dirt on it."

"Maybe it hasn't improved that much."

"Is Umar taking the next shift, or are you?" she asked.

"Umar. I'll be working graveyard."

"I'll watch for him, then. Nighty night."

Jet punched the phone off and drifted towards the building. A few ancient SUVs that looked like they had gone through a war sat rusting near it, but as she passed the graffiti-covered cinderblock perimeter wall and open gate that led to the parking area, it was empty. Glancing up, she saw that the window of the room Alan had identified as belonging to Nasr was open. No guarantee, but that probably meant that he was there.

She continued along the grim road until she came to a small market on the corner with an extremely fat, sweating man sitting behind the counter chewing *qat*, watching a small black-and-white television, a fan blowing stagnant air from the front of the tiny store to the back. She purchased a bottle of water, and he didn't even look up from his show as he felt for the coins she had left for him and nodded.

Her return trip to the Highlander was equally uneventful. There were few signs of life other than the screeching blare of tinny music from the second story of what appeared to be an abandoned building, and a woman's voice screaming at her children from the house next to Nasr's.

It was going to be a long four hours.

Jet reached the vehicle and got behind the wheel, far enough away to not be spotted but still close enough to see anyone coming or going from the building. A niggle of unease worried at her stomach as she thought about her abbreviated discussion with her daughter and she pushed it aside, preferring not to dwell on the unpleasant. They would be reunited soon enough and would make their way to a new area to live, and hopefully never be endangered again. It was a shame, because she genuinely liked Montevideo, but Uruguay had become too hot for them to stay. Maybe she'd try Mendoza next. It was worth a shot.

Two hours later, men began appearing on the road, on their way home from work, clothes dusty, with the defeated gait of the downtrodden and perpetually hopeless. A few glanced at her in the car, but most ignored her, their battles with life so consuming that they didn't notice their surroundings. Four adolescent boys appeared near Nasr's dwelling and began kicking a soccer ball around in the dirt, laughing and screaming at each other as the orb sailed through the air, brown legs and arms flailing as they battled one another for possession. Another pang of longing struck her as she watched. Even in this hellhole, kids managed to have fun – as Hannah did even when her mom had to go fight for their lives.

She was jarred out of her melancholy when a limping man exited the house pushing a motor scooter, then kick-started it and bounced past her, the motorbike's engine snarling as he went by. She cranked the ignition, put the Highlander in gear, and reached for her cell phone. Poor Alan wasn't going to get much sleep today. The man on the scooter was Nasr.

❧❦

Jet wove her way through traffic, which fortunately wasn't that heavy on the outskirts of town, most of the flow going in the opposite direction as the evening commute started. The motorbike wasn't particularly fast, which was good, because Nasr piloted it in the daredevil fashion that was the local custom, and it was all she could do to keep pace.

After fifteen minutes the scooter slowed and then pulled to the side of the street next to a large home near the perimeter wall that encircled the old town, and Nasr made a call on a cell phone. The iron gate of the complex's main entry slid open and he eased the motorbike in, then the gate rolled shut again, sealing off the street behind a ten-foot-high wall topped with

173

broken glass. She continued past it, noting the security cameras mounted on both corner posts, and then parked on the opposite side of the road eighty yards away, out of the cameras' fields of view.

Alan would be there within twenty minutes, at which point they could do a more covert surveillance using at least two vehicles, so that anyone watching in the house wouldn't see the same car parked nearby. This was a traveled-enough area that there were a fair number of cars parked, but she wanted to take no chances.

Minutes ticked by excruciatingly slowly as the light began to fade, and then the gate rolled open again and Nasr pushed his bike out onto the street and started it. Now she was torn. Did she stay there, or continue to follow him? He revved the throttle and rolled off with a puff of blue smoke. Jet cranked the ignition. Alan knew the address. He could pick up where she'd left off. She dialed him and told him what was transpiring, then took up position tailing her quarry, secure in the knowledge that Alan would be there in a couple of minutes, tops.

Three minutes later her phone rang. Alan was outside the compound.

The motor scooter traced the surface streets, going slower this time, and soon the area began to look suspiciously familiar – he was going home. Just as she was convinced that was the case, he turned a corner and parked at a mosque a few blocks from his house, where the devout were entering for the evening prayer. She called Alan again and relayed the information, and he told her that he would send Umar to the mosque to keep an eye on Nasr while he was inside, in case he met with someone. She couldn't do so, because the women's area was segregated from the men's. Alan said Umar would be there within ten minutes, and to wait, and then he would take over the surveillance.

The mosque was just closing its doors when Umar's SUV rolled to a stop and he leapt out. A man at the entry motioned to him to hurry – the devotion was getting ready to start.

She waited until he was inside and then pulled away, urging the Toyota through the tangle of cars, back towards where Alan was waiting.

When she was a quarter mile away, her phone vibrated.

"Yes?"

"We have game on. A blue van just pulled up, and Saif al-Diin got out and went into the house, accompanied by a nervous-looking entourage. Looks like they must have gotten word about the house in Sa'dah."

"I'm a few minutes away. What do you want to do?"

"I want to hit it as soon as we can. Now that we know he's inside, there's no reason to wait. He may not even have the agent yet, but that's immaterial. He can't murder thousands if he's already dead. Make sense?"

"Part of me thinks we should wait and see what he does, but the other part agrees with you. What kind of backup do we have?"

"Just you and me. Umar isn't a fighter. I really wish we could get a team of wet operatives here, but that's off the table." The frustration in his voice was palpable. "I hate these last-minute ops."

"Me too. But at least we know where he is. That's better than we had when we started the day."

"All right. It's almost dark. I say we wait until traffic slows to a halt and dinner time arrives and hit them while they're eating."

"You got it. See you in about five."

CHAPTER 31

The night was still, the pall of dust and smog that hung over the city blanketing everything with a toxic tinge of exhaust and chemicals. Jet had done as much nosing around as she could without being obvious, and felt like she had a reasonable sense of the immediate area around the house. It backed onto a small alley, on the other side of which was another compound wall, shielding it from intruders. The house Saif al-Diin was in was relatively large, but that could work in their favor – more entry points.

One thing she didn't like was a rear gate in the wall as well, which would make securing the compound more difficult with only Alan and herself. Not that it would matter if they hit the house quickly enough – by the time the inhabitants could mobilize, everyone would be dead.

She walked down the street carrying the backpack, her MTAR concealed in the folds of her robe, where she'd made a slit for that express purpose. Alan was also dressed as a woman now, and they walked together as if a pair huddled for security, alone on the street – a common sight.

As agreed, when they reached the first camera Alan continued on, and Jet sprinted to the neighboring house's wall, sprang against it, then twisted and grabbed the top, which thankfully had no glass on it. She pulled herself up and inched across to the post with the camera mounted on top, out of the field of view, and then flipped open her combat knife and snipped the wire in the back. Wasting no time, she somersaulted into the target house's front courtyard and flitted like a ghost to the gate. It groaned as she pulled it open, and Alan was barely through it when the night exploded with gunfire, and slugs pounded into the wall behind them.

Alan uttered an expletive and then she was rolling, firing at the house as she moved towards a nearby Nissan pickup truck. She heard Alan's MTAR join hers in harmony as they fired burst after burst at the muzzle flashes in the windows.

This was a bad situation – taking fire before they'd even made it to the house. The plan had been to sneak up on it, as they had in Sa'dah, but obviously something had gone wrong. Either there was another camera located somewhere they hadn't seen, or there was a motion detector concealed on the interior of the gate she'd tripped; or, most likely, there was a sensor that alerted the house when the gate was opened – one of the problems with a hurried approach was that they hadn't had the chance to do their homework, and were going in essentially blind.

Her MTAR burped death at the house as incoming rounds slammed into the truck's chassis and engine. She heard men yelling, and peeked her head around the fender in time to see four gunmen dart from the home's front door and take up positions behind a short wall near the entry. That would make getting inside even harder. Never mind that any surprise they'd had was now gone.

A barrage directed at Alan's position greeted his fire, and she tried to alternate her volleys with his, trying to buy them some breathing room. The best thing they could hope for now was that the shooters would do something stupid, like try to rush them – or that the Yemeni military would show up, drawn by the shooting, which would pose its own set of problems.

An errant round hit the Nissan and she smelled gasoline. She glanced next to the rear wheels and saw a small pool of fluid accumulating below the truck. Maybe there was some way to use the vehicle as a diversion – a bomb? More rounds shattered the truck windows and she instinctively ducked, the spray of glass falling harmlessly on her robe and the ground next to it.

She peered around the fender and saw a gunman's head sighting down a rifle barrel and firing at Alan, and her red laser dot was bouncing across his face when she gently squeezed the trigger. The little gun bucked as it coughed its staccato chatter and she saw the shooter drop back behind the wall, his weapon tumbling on her side of it.

One down.

A grunt greeted her over the ear bud. Alan.

Gunfire continued to rain a hail of slugs around her, and she tapped her ear bud.

"You okay?" she whispered.

"Fine. I've got decent cover from these concrete blocks. One of them got lucky and a ricochet grazed my shoulder, but I'll live. That's not our biggest problem. They have us pinned down here. Barring a miracle, we're screwed."

"I know. I'm fresh out of miracles tonight. Any ideas?"

He hesitated. "I have two hand grenades."

"That's right. How's your arm?"

"Not good enough to go all-pro, but I think I can reach them."

"No time like the present. Let me know when you want cover fire and I'll burn a magazine for you," she offered.

"On the count of three."

She ejected her half-spent magazine and slammed home a full one, then switched the weapon to full auto.

"One. Two. THREE." Jet fired at the wall shielding the gunmen, the magazine emptying in only a few seconds, and then a *whump* rent the night as the first grenade detonated behind it – Alan's pitching had been more than adequate. Her weapon exhausted, she dropped the spent magazine on the ground and then slapped another home, switching to burst mode so each pull of the trigger fired three rounds. She rarely used full auto mode, because a typical assault rifle would be empty in no time with thirty round STANAG magazines and a rate of fire of seven to nine hundred rounds per minute.

The shooting from behind the wall stopped, and Alan's voice murmured in her ear, still ringing from the blast. "Let's move."

She was just rising to her feet when a massive explosion inside the house blew through the windows in a molten shower of glass, and fireballs belched from the apertures in a blinding flare. Both she and Alan were stopped in their tracks by the detonation, and then two smaller explosions from inside followed before the propane tank blew.

Flames licked from the windows as black smoke poured into the air. Jet shook off her surprise and ran in a crouch to the wall. The three remaining fighters had been torn apart by the combination of the grenade and the blast.

"I'm going around to the back. What the hell was that?" she asked.

"They must have had the house wired with explosives. Either that or they had a bunch of Semtex lying around and someone got careless with a detonator, trying to improvise a bomb intended to take us out."

She took a deep breath and moved, first to the house and then along the wall to the rear of the structure, which was also an inferno. She tried to approach the back door, but it had been blown half apart and flames were pouring through it from the interior.

"No way anything is still alive in there," she said.

"That's my take."

Sirens ululated in the distance, the music of their wail sounding a familiar tune for the beleaguered city.

Alan joined her as she moved to the rear wall exit.

"Let's get out of here. I don't want to have to explain what a couple of Mossad operatives are doing dressed like women in terrorist country."

"Sounds good. Out the front or the back?"

"We'll probably have an audience out front. Let's go," he said, and trotted to the iron rear door.

Two minutes later they were back at his car, trying to make sense out of what had just happened.

"Unbelievable," he said, shaking his head, pulling his veil off.

She studied his unshaved face and smiled. "Well, that was subtle. I think it went well. And quite the fireworks display, huh?"

"I wish we could take credit for killing the bastard, but he did it to himself. Where do these freaks get their death wish? Can you imagine?"

"I would go down shooting before I blew myself up. Then again, we don't know whether it was an accident or not. It's fifty-fifty that they had the house wired. Wouldn't surprise me, though. Not a bit." Jet smiled behind her veil. "You don't make a bad-looking woman, you know. Big hands, but other than that…"

"Nice to hear I've got options."

She looked him over. "How's the shoulder?"

"It's already clotting. Like I said, just a scratch. I'll seal it up with some Dermabond and be good as new. Not like I haven't had to do it before," he assured her.

The sirens were close now. Jet swung the door open, leaving her MTAR on the car floor.

"See you later. You going to be busy tonight?" she asked, her tone neutral.

"I'd invite you over, but I have a feeling this is going to be a long one. I have to call the director immediately and file a situation report, and then assess where we go from here. Can I take a rain check?"

She paused at the question. "You always have a rain check with me, Alan."

And then she was gone, the door closing behind her, a black wraith disappearing into the gloom, as silent as death.

CHAPTER 32

"How soon can we get out of here?" Jet asked at lunch the next day. "I still have a date in Moscow I need to make."

"I don't see any reason to hang around. Unless you've been waiting for a guided tour of Sana'a's hotspots."

"Did you see the news?"

"Yeah. They're calling it a rebel stronghold that blew itself up by mistake. Playing without adult supervision around explosives. A sad cautionary tale."

"I saw that on TV. Kind of ignores the reports of an all-out gunfight before the explosion, doesn't it?" she observed.

"This is Yemen. Come on. You going to let a few annoying facts cloud an otherwise seamless theory?"

"What did the director say?"

"'Congratulations.' As far as he's concerned, this ugly chapter is now behind us. He actually couldn't have been happier. I suppose when your nemesis blows himself up it's time to break out the cooking sherry a little early, no?"

"Still, it's not what I was expecting."

"I know. It's surreal. But that's what keeps the job interesting, right? Anyway, it's over now. And as you pointed out, you have a Russian to attend to."

"You're coming, right?"

"Are you kidding? I wouldn't miss it for the world. Besides, being a dead guy, I don't have a lot else to do..."

"I know the feeling. How's the arm?"

"Tip top. I'll be playing tennis by the weekend."

They ate in silence, each processing the night's events, and when the server came for their plates, she waited until he had left before continuing.

"So, separate flights. Rendezvous in Frankfurt, or in Moscow?"

"Moscow. Safer if we don't travel together. Besides, unlike this little disaster, we'll want to plan that carefully. We already blew one shot at him," Alan reminded her.

"Which brings me to the part where I swear you to secrecy. You can't tell anyone we're in Russia. Not the director. Nobody."

"I got it. I still think you're wrong about him, but it's not worth taking the chance, I agree. As far as he's concerned, I'm taking a few days from the terrorist beat before I decide what to do next."

She took his hand. "Thank you for helping with this, Alan. I really appreciate it." She stared deep into his eyes. At times, like this morning, he really reminded her of David – some of the mannerisms. Must be in his genes, she supposed.

"Sort of reciprocation, wouldn't you say? Quid pro quo? You were here for me when I needed you. You can expect the same from me..."

"All right, so we meet up in Moscow. Tomorrow? The day after?"

"Probably the day after. I'll stay at the Hilton again. I liked it there. I'll try to get out tomorrow, but don't count on it. You'll be lucky if you can get a flight."

"I know. I checked, and there was nothing open for today going anywhere I could easily connect. What name will you be using?"

He thought for a few seconds. "Richard. Richard Davis. A Brit."

"All right, Richard Davis. I'll be on the first plane out. Paris, Frankfurt, Madrid, doesn't matter. I can connect wherever. Are you going to be busy the rest of today?"

"Yeah. The director wants me here in case they find anything in the rubble that we can use to identify who sold them the agent, assuming it was in there. We won't know for sure until tomorrow, but I've got to start spreading money around and see if we can get any information. The local cops always have their hands out."

"Then I won't make any plans with you for tonight..."

"I'm afraid not. I have no idea where I'll be or for how long. I'm sorry," he said, rubbing his face.

He was unable to read her expression. She reached over and patted his hand.

"So am I, Alan. So am I."

❦

The plane banked on final approach, bumping through the heavy cloud cover blanketing Moscow, turbulence jostling the passengers as the jet bucked and fell with the vicious downdrafts. The man next to her looked gray and was gripping the armrest like it owed him money; the odor of too many scotches on the rocks drifted from him, mingled with the stench of fear.

She watched out the window as they broke through the final layer and drifted down towards the runway, the wings slicing through sheets of rain hurled at them with all of nature's possible force. When the wheels struck the tarmac and the thrust reversed to slow it, the plane shuddered as though the engines were going to tear off, and for a few jarring seconds the fuselage began to twist, threatening to skew sideways, before it righted and slowed three quarters of the way down the tarmac.

Customs was the usual circus she had come to hate about the country, taking three times longer than anywhere else in the world, a throwback to the lightning efficiency that had made the Soviet Union a triumph of modern ingenuity. When she finally made it through to the arrivals area she was ready to turn around and fly back out – the only thing that kept her walking towards the exits was the errand she needed to take care of to keep her daughter safe.

She decided to stay at the Metropol, liking the central location as well as the grandeur of the hotel, and the fact that it wasn't that far from Grigenko's home and offices. She'd made mental notes the last time she was in Moscow and had decided that an attempt on the villa again wouldn't work. Armies were always ready for the last war, not the next one, and she knew that if there had ever been a chance getting to him by rappelling down the side of the adjacent building and entering through a window, that train had left the station. Which left her with only a few choices: try to hit him while in transit, or somehow penetrate his office building.

Her room was ornate but worn, which suited her mood as she looked out the window at the cold gray sky. She traced a design in the fog on the inside panes, absently pondering the origin of the melancholy that had enveloped her since she'd set out on this trip. Perhaps it was being away from Hannah, or the feeling that she'd never be able to settle down in one place without enemies from her past coming for her, or...it could have been that for all her tough exterior, there was a part of her that was lonely. She had never minded being alone, but what she was feeling was something else – a vacuum that she'd somehow suppressed awareness of before she'd gotten her daughter back, when she thought it would always just be her, by herself. But now she had Hannah, and something inside of her wanted more.

Her thoughts wandered to Alan as she unpacked her few belongings and hung her clothes up. What did she feel about him? She had gotten past the hurdle that he was David's brother – that past seemed a lifetime away now, after Thailand and Uruguay and the healing distance of time. He was definitely attractive, and was interested, and there had been a spark when they'd kissed – but mostly, she liked holding his hand and bantering with him, and the way he smelled when he was close. She felt secure when she was with him, even if security was an illusion. Mirage or not, it felt good, and made her feel somehow...complete.

Jet rarely felt regret over the life she'd chosen. She'd done well by her country, honoring it with selfless service, doing what needed to be done even as she sacrificed everything. But now, she was conflicted between not daring to hope for a better future, and imagining one, perhaps even as part of a fragile family, remote as that had seemed only a few short months ago. Was it possible to wash away the sins of the past and start anew, or was that some sort of romance novel tripe that never happened in the real world?

She threw herself down on the bed and stared at the molded ceiling.

Could everything be different after this final operation? Was there a way to find that elusive dream she thought of as a normal life, where the only concerns were doctor visits and grocery shopping and playground cuts and scrapes...and yes, the feel of a strong man by her side?

When her Russian disposable cell phone rang it jarred her from her thoughts, and she stabbed the call on button as she raised it to her ear.

"Yes?"

"Sorry. I'm not going to make it out. Too many loose ends to tie up. I'll be traveling tomorrow, so I'll either see you tomorrow night, or the following morning. You make it okay?" Alan asked, sounding contrite.

"I'm here in one piece. It's pouring down rain, but maybe you'll bring some sun with you when you fly in."

"I hope so. Let me know if you need anything in the meantime."

She thought about that. What did she need? Besides this nightmare ordeal to be over, and her daughter in her arms?

"I'm good. I'll be waiting for you to get here. Everything okay on that end?"

"Yes. Nothing to worry about. But apparently it's not like the old days, where I could walk in, blow the town up, and walk out. Management sucks," he groused.

She laughed. "Yes. But you get free pencils."

"Some incentive."

"Nobody said life is fair."

"I have to read my warranty. I want a refund."

They signed off after agreeing to meet for dinner the following night at the Hilton, and Jet realized that she felt better after the exchange.

Maybe that was a sign. Even if there were no fireworks going off like with Matt, maybe the fact that talking to Alan made her feel good was enough.

Maybe that was the secret to happiness that had been eluding her.

She definitely had a lot to mull over, she thought, as the rain drummed against the glass, a reminder that things could always be worse. A few hours ago she had been out in the downpour, and now she was warm and dry in her suite.

Waiting for the storm to pass.

And for Alan.

CHAPTER 33

Sonora Desert, Mexico

The desert heat was broiling, even inside the van, the meager air-conditioning inadequate to keep the interior cool in the best of circumstances, much less with ten passengers seated on the floor, their bundles of belongings and bags clutched tightly to their chests. The van's springs strained as they rocked down the dirt road into the wilds of the Sonoran desert, nightfall approaching rapidly as they moved north from Mexico towards the U.S. border.

Everyone in the van had paid top dollar for this trip, which meant at least two thousand dollars, and in some cases considerably more. The 'coyotes' that trafficked in humans, leading them from Mexico across the border, were a ruthless but pragmatic bunch. This gang was one of the most expensive, and reliable; meaning that if they thought they could put a bullet in your back and steal your valuables, they still might, but not if there was a chance of any retaliation – like if you were connected to the cartels or some other criminal syndicate. Others were more murderous – they charged more in the range of five hundred to a thousand dollars, but would occasionally abandon truckloads of unfortunates to cook in the desert when they had a mechanical problem and couldn't fulfill their contract.

The passengers had climbed aboard in Caborca, Mexico, sixty-six miles south of the Arizona border, at ten-thirty at night, and under cover of darkness had traversed the dirt roads through the mountain desert, averaging barely twenty miles per hour. Nobody spoke during the trip – there wasn't anything to say. They were a hardscrabble lot; for most, this dangerous trek was their last resort to escape to a better future, usually after paying their life savings, or the savings of their family, to get them into the States. Although since the financial crisis, for the first time in decades, outflows of illegal aliens returning to Mexico outpaced inflows to the U.S., there was still an allure to making the trip north, and for many, this was their final chance.

The coyotes had explained everything before they got under way. The area of the border they were going to was desolate, nothing within thirty miles except scrub and cactus, sometimes manned by the border patrol, though more often not. Arizona didn't have the resources to police every foot of border, and even with a fence in place, large tracts were porous, with traffic in both directions uninhibited despite the best efforts of the border patrol.

A well-known reality in Mexico was that if you had the money, getting across the border was relatively easy, although it had gotten more difficult over the last week due to the terrorism hysteria. But that seemed distant in the sweltering night, the temperature still over a hundred degrees hours after the sun had set.

The man in the passenger seat, swarthy, with a poorly trimmed moustache and several prominent steel teeth in his reptilian smile, turned to face his human cargo.

"There are rattlesnakes in the bushes and anywhere off the road, so once you're across, stay out of the brush unless you see cars coming. Every now and then the Americans might have a helicopter in the area, but that's not often, so your chances are very good of making it. Some of you have paid for a guide on the other side, who will take you to Nogales. It's a rough journey, and you'll have to be brave – it can take many hours. At least most of it will be in darkness. When the sun comes up, it gets hotter than hell." He lowered the window and spat, the blast of hot air like a furnace, then hurriedly rolled it back up. "Those with a guide, go right along the fence once you're through. Those without, don't try to follow them. You're on your own, and you can't tag along. Make your own way."

The passengers rocked back and forth, staring at him wordlessly. Everyone knew the arrangement. Some had paid the extra to be taken into Nogales, some were going to chance it on their own. One had made different arrangements, and so was unconcerned by the dire warnings.

They continued bouncing along, and then twenty minutes later the old van ground to a halt, its headlights off, guided by the slim light of the gibbous moon. Both of the coyotes got out of the car, and the driver moved to the rear cargo door and swung it open.

"All right. This is it. Hopefully you all brought water as I recommended. If not, I can sell you some for twenty dollars a bottle. You'll be walking thirty to fifty miles across some of the most difficult desert and mountain terrain you can imagine, in extreme heat, and that can be the difference between life, and death. Don't be cheap and stupid."

One woman looked panicked, and dug in her pockets for the last of her money – only a ten-dollar bill. The coyote grinned murderously and shook his head. Not good enough. She fumbled in her pockets, searching for more, but had nothing. The rest of the group pushed past her and climbed out of the van, anxious to be on their way.

"Over there. Two hundred yards. You can see the fence. There are at least three spots you can get through. Just push along the base until an area gives, then push it back in place once you're through. And don't make any noise. Be quiet," the driver whispered.

The woman had found three more one dollar bills, and looked at the driver imploringly. He shrugged and his partner walked back to the cab and got a one-and-a-half-liter bottle of water and handed it to her.

"It's your lucky day. If you were better looking, I'd make you work off that seven dollars, but it's not dark enough out here to make that appealing. Now get out of here. Go."

The passengers moved towards the fence, and the driver grabbed the arm of an older man who hadn't moved.

"Your guide will be on the other side, five hundred yards up the road. He'll have an ATV. Tip him well once you're in Nogales," the driver murmured, eyes scanning the gloom for any signs of the border patrol. "Let them get through, and they'll go to the right. Just start walking up the road and my man will find you."

The man nodded, then moved off after the rest of the group.

Once across, two of the travelers moved to the right of the fence, looking for their guide, and the rest followed them, more out of instinct than anything. The man waited until they were out of sight and then began walking up the road, his dark blue jeans and shirt acting as natural camouflage in the night. After five minutes of walking, a voice whispered from fifty yards off the road.

"*Yo. Jefe*. Taxi?"

The man turned to face the guide, his backpack bulging, and said nothing.

"I'm José. Your ride to freedom. Here's how this will work. We can make it to Nogales before dawn, and then you're on your own, unless you have some extra cash – in which case I can get you to Tucson. I'll drive, you hang on. Ready?"

The man nodded.

"Not very talkative, are you?" José shrugged at the lack of response, climbed onto the waiting ATV's seat, and motioned to the man to climb on behind him. The engine started with a purr, and then they were racing down a trail towards civilization, navigating by the light of the moon and stars.

The man exhaled a sigh of relief as the hot air blew across his brow. He'd thought this might be worse. This was nothing. The Mexicans thought this was hot? Any respect he'd had for them as hardy quickly faded. They were whiney children, like their neighbors to the north.

Once they were within sight of Nogales, he'd stop the driver on a pretense and then break his neck before he was off the seat. He'd find his own way from there. He'd already arranged for a car to transport him to his ultimate destination – Los Angeles.

He'd never been to the U.S. before, but he wasn't worried. His English was more than passable, and there would be plenty of support once he was in LA to ensure he assimilated for his brief stay without any issues.

The ATV cut across a ravine and skittered along the edge until they came to another trail leading east.

Border security was a joke. A baby could have gotten through.

He watched the scrub rush by and grinned to himself.

So far, so good.

CHAPTER 34

Jet sat at a small table on the sidewalk a block from Grigenko's building, squinting up at the towering thirty-story edifice in the new light of a clear morning. She liked what she saw – some buildings were harder than others, but this looked like it had been built fifteen or so years ago, in a style that was well-suited for her purposes.

She was drinking coffee, watching the garage area next to the front entrance where underground parking sheltered the building occupants' vehicles, and sat up when a stretch Mercedes limousine pulled to the curb in front and several muscular goons in suits trotted from the building entrance to be joined by eight more from the two SUVs that trailed the limo.

She pulled a pair of small binoculars from her purse and peered through them, leaning back into the shadows as she did so. She recognized Grigenko from the photos. He strode into the building like a peacock, his men forming a protective entourage. She checked the time. Precisely nine a.m.. The intelligence Alan's contacts had provided was golden – she knew from the reports that he went to work at nine in the morning and stayed until nine every night. She also knew that he had a gym, steam room, and hospitality suite as part of the three floors that housed his empire.

The reports had been clear: The building's security was impenetrable. Access to Grigenko's two private top floors was only available via his private elevator. The floor below it that housed his public offices was no good for her purposes – there was no way to get from those offices to his private floors above them.

Shooting her way through the lobby security wouldn't achieve anything. The private elevator had security cameras inside that could be controlled from the top floor and stopped by Grigenko, and also required a security code for access that changed daily. When he purchased the building after his father's death, he'd immediately had the top security firm in Sweden fly in and work with local contractors to turn his realm into a fortress, and they'd spared no expense. A brute force entry from the street level was out of the question.

Cursory research from her last Moscow adventure had yielded no encouragement from the air. Airspace was tightly monitored, so a helicopter wasn't an option, and neither was a high-altitude parachute drop – the roof was equipped with motion sensors designed to alert both security and Grigenko if anything larger than a bird got within a hundred feet, creating a sonar envelope in the airspace over the building from ten to a hundred feet above the roof.

Security precautions in Moscow among oligarchs was akin to Patek Philippe or Rolex watches among Hollywood producers – the stuff of bragging rights. When you had billions, a Ferrari or new Bentley didn't move the needle, and the number of sixty-million-dollar Gulfstreams at the airport was silly. But spend a hundred million on equipping your lair with the very latest and best to keep your enemies from killing you...now that was something worth tossing out at the club.

A rocket strike was an option, but not a terribly good one, as Grigenko had reinforced the exterior walls with two feet of high-density concrete and rebar, with the windows double-pane bulletproof glass, and his private office walls were constructed of half-foot-thick steel – making him safe from everything but a large guided missile. Never mind the difficulty of obtaining one, unless she wanted to try to buy one from him. The irony appealed to her, but she wasn't feeling particularly patient, and wanted this over with within a few days, not weeks or months of subterfuge to set up a dummy corporation and get operatives to pose as buyers. Even then, with that amount of reinforcement, it would be hit or miss. The man had created a bunker – a contingency born of paranoia, which in this case was entirely justified.

She'd debated a rocket attack on the limo, but that was even more problematic – according to the surveillance, he took different routes each day, and the heavy car was armored to the point where it resembled more a tank than a luxury cruiser. While it was possible she could hit him once he pulled up to the building, she had the same problem as using a rifle and taking him out with a sniper round – no convenient place to fire from with decent line of sight, no buildings in the immediate vicinity that were high enough to make a guaranteed shot.

The sewers were out. Even if they were stupid enough to leave an opening there, which she doubted, the area was a newer system without the sorts of access that the area around his residence had.

Shutting off the power would do nothing – the facility was equipped with fail-safe backup generators.

Which left only a few options. An explosive on the car, which was inspected for precisely that before it picked him up every morning and evening. A fire somewhere else in the building to drive him out – but he would likely just call a helicopter if he was trapped in his suite. Gas was out of the question – she'd need to be able to access the maintenance areas to use it, and they benefitted from the same Swedish company's thoroughness as the rest of the building.

She doodled some notes to herself on a little pad she'd bought from a street vendor and then flipped it shut when the waiter approached to ask whether she wanted anything else. She shook her head and asked for the bill. When he departed, she studied the building and its neighbors one last time, then slipped the opera glasses back into her purse. Jet had a couple of ideas that could work. As she well knew, there was no such thing as a completely secure location, regardless of how much was spent to render it so. She'd spent her career slipping past supposedly impenetrable security, so the building actually only posed an intellectual challenge for her, nothing more. That she would get in was a given. The only question was how.

Back at her hotel she pulled up all of the information Alan had given her and studied the building blueprints, taking her time, skipping lunch in favor of memorizing the layout. Mid-afternoon she spotted the weakness.

It was so simple.

And all it would require was tremendous skill, nerves of steel, the physique of a triathlete, and a modicum of luck. Plus the cooperation of the weather. Rain or high winds would be disastrous, so she would need a clear, calm night.

She got online, checked the forecast, and confirmed that the next two days would be relatively warm and dry, with no more than a light breeze. As she thought through the kernel of a plan that was beginning to form, she grew more excited.

It could work.

No, with a little preparation and refinement, it *would* work. She'd see to that.

 ❧❧

When Jet walked through the glass entry doors into the lobby of the Moscow Hilton, Alan was waiting for her on one of the sofas. He stood as she approached him, looking dashing in olive slacks and a pale blue dress shirt, and she spontaneously threw her arms around him and kissed him in welcome. He kissed back, and after a brief eternity she pulled away, leading him to the restaurant by the hand.

"I'd say get a room, but we already have one..." she said with a smile. She hadn't realized how much she'd missed him until he'd stood to greet her.

"Good point, as usual. You hungry?"

"Very. What's the latest?" she asked as the hostess showed them to a dimly lit corner table.

"Nothing earth-shattering. Just beat after traveling all day. What a pain, as you know."

"I hope when I fly out of here that it'll be the last time I ever see Sheremetyevo Airport. I mean it," Jet said.

"Still not a big fan of the Russian people, I see."

"I'd say I'm definitely biased. Something about how whenever someone shows up to kill me they're Russian has made it hard to love them, you know?"

"Hmm. I kind of see what you mean. Now tell me about your day. Any breakthroughs?" Alan asked.

She was just getting ready to tell him about her idea for penetrating Grigenko's building when his cell phone jangled.

"Hang on. I need to take this," he said, looking at the display.

He answered, and then after a few seconds held up a finger and stood, moving back through the restaurant towards the lobby. The waiter brought them menus, and she skimmed hers as she waited for Alan's return.

When he sat down, he looked like he had been sucker-punched. "I'm sorry. I have to go. Right now. Grab my bag and head to the airport. If I can get to Germany I can get a plane across the Atlantic late tonight."

"What? The Atlantic? What's going on?"

He looked around. "That was the director. The Mossad got a tip that Saif al-Diin is going to be in Los Angeles tomorrow evening to release the bio-agent," he whispered.

She digested the news, then frowned. "That's impossible. We saw the explosion. Nobody could have survived that."

"Agreed. He must have slipped out the back while we were shooting up the front. Either that, or he had a tunnel."

"They didn't find a tunnel, did they?"

"No, so the likeliest is that he was running out one side while we were fighting his gunmen on the other," he explained.

She shook her head. "Why would someone tip the Mossad and not the U.S.? That makes no sense."

"Apparently because the tipper is afraid that the Americans will either leak the information or will screw it up, and then he'll just move to a different target."

"What the hell are you supposed to do? Los Angeles is huge. Were there any specifics?"

"Not that I know of. But he wants me in the air. Now. The tipper said he'd call tomorrow with detailed information on where he plans to strike." Alan stood, and Jet rose with him.

"So you're serious."

"Absolutely. I have no choice. But I already touched base with my contact here, and he's sourcing the list of weapons you sent me. Will that be enough?"

"It should be." Jet clearly wasn't happy.

He looked at his watch and shrugged. "I have to go. I'll call you on the way to the airport. I'm sorry..."

"No need to apologize. I know the game. Besides, you probably would have just slowed me down, anyway," she said, and then tiptoed to kiss him again. "You don't know what you're missing."

"I have a sneaking suspicion that I do, and I hate to go, but I should have been walking out the door sixty seconds ago. I...I know this sounds dumb, but can I take another rain check?"

"Get out of here. Go. And be careful. I don't like the sound of any of this. Anonymous tips scare me. How do you even know if there's any validity to it, and it's not a trap of some kind? Doesn't this strike you as extremely odd?"

JET III ~ VENGEANCE

"Everything does these days. But it's not like I can argue. The director ordered me to go to Los Angeles, so that's where I'm headed." He froze. "Shit. How are you going to get Grigenko? I got so caught up in this..."

"Don't worry about me. I can take care of him without you here. I actually think I've got the perfect plan."

He gave her a skeptical look. "You do?"

"Sure. But before you go, tell me. Any ideas on where I can get a blow torch around here?"

CHAPTER 35

Alan passed through customs at Los Angeles International Airport without any problems, thanks to his Israeli diplomatic passport, and was met by Jeffrey, one of the attachés at the consulate – a popular cover for members of intelligence services all over the world. They exchanged a few pleasantries and then walked silently to his vehicle, a non-descript gray American sedan.

Once they were out of the parking structure, Alan used his satellite phone and called the director to find out the latest developments while he had been in the air.

"We got the second call. Traced it to California, but it was too fast – we couldn't get it any more precise. It's going to be tonight, in just a few hours. At a large indoor sports arena in downtown Los Angeles. The caller said that al-Diin will be dressed as a maintenance man. There's an ice skating competition that's being televised on national TV – lots of children and old people in the crowd. This guy is one sick bastard. The outrage will be...I don't have to tell you." The director proceeded to fill him in on the details. Alan looked at his watch. He had three hours.

When he hung up he stretched his arms over his head, trying to work out the kinks in his neck from sitting on airplanes for almost twenty hours, and stared out the window at the smog layer hanging over LA. They stopped at an intersection leading to the freeway, which was gridlocked from early rush hour, and Alan turned to Jeffrey.

"I'll need a gun, and a few other items on short notice. An LAPD badge and ID. Would the consulate have something like that lying around?"

Jeffrey grinned humorlessly. "We're in the land of guns, so that isn't a problem. As to the badge...I think we can help you. Let me make a call. Anything else?"

Alan told him, and he nodded and raised a cell phone to his ear, in violation of the law prohibiting using one while driving, and began speaking in a soft voice.

☙❧

The sidewalk outside the sports arena was thronged with mothers and their little girls, aspiring skaters in their Sunday best there to see some of the marquée names take to the ice. Television crews in vans sat munching sandwiches in preparation for the show to begin – the event was being televised across the country on sports channels and a few specialty channels, but the work for the grips that moved the cameras and hardware into the huge venue was done until the show was over. Most of the fourteen thousand attendees were already inside, anxiously awaiting the start of the traveling pseudo-competition that showcased the talents of the Winter Olympic medalists past and present. Capacity of the arena was almost twenty thousand, but a significant number of ticket holders had canceled their plans after the terror scare, despite the oft-repeated counsel from the government to keep behaving as though the situation was normal, or the terrorists had already won.

A maintenance technician shouldered past the line of little girls holding hands with their moms and approached the trade entrance, where a couple of bored LAPD officers in uniform were standing talking to four security guards, all off-duty policemen hired for crowd control – about the cushiest job you could get, given that ice skating shows weren't the kind of sporting event where the crowd rioted after their favorite lost.

The maintenance man flashed a laminated card suspended around his neck on a lanyard at the men, who waved him through with hardly a glance, his age and uniform placing him in the lowest of possible threat profiles. He shambled past the guards and then was inside, toting his large toolkit as he headed for the bowels of the mammoth enclosed stadium.

He had hoped to be able to get into a more visible venue, like JFK Airport in New York, or perhaps Grand Central Station, but the risks were too great – those were natural target assumptions for the authorities, and they were crawling with security forces after his two videos. Still, the horrific death of almost fifteen thousand, on national television, would get more than enough attention, especially as the crowd moved as one for the exits when the symptoms began hitting three quarters of the way through the show.

By that time, he would be on the road, halfway to Palm Springs, well away from the nightmare that would follow his actions. The fallout would be extraordinary, unlike anything ever seen, and he allowed himself a small smile on his newly shaved and bleach cream-lightened face. Even if they had distributed photos of him, those would have shown a dour man with a heavy beard, as unlike the maintenance man as anything could be.

Two janitors approached him from the opposite direction and one of them nodded at him, offering a *whassup* in passing – some sort of traditional American greeting, apparently. Saif al-Diin, the Sword of the Faith, grinned back at the man like an addled moron and continued on his way, his heavy work boots clumping down the ramp to the lower level and the equipment rooms.

A red steel door marked *For service personnel only* yielded a concrete stairwell that went down one additional level, and al-Diin paused before he opened it, glancing around to ensure that he wasn't being watched. Satisfied that nobody was paying any attention, he eased it open and slipped onto the landing before descending to the rooms that were his ultimate destination.

Music from the ice rink above echoed through the long winding corridor of the basement level, barely audible over the muted roar of the massive generators that powered the refrigeration equipment that kept the stadium floor frozen. He took another quick look at his phone screen and counted doors until he arrived at the one that was his target. Yellow paint on the red door proclaimed *ventilation – restricted access* in six-inch high yellow block letters. He tried the handle but it was locked, which he was prepared for. He felt in the pocket of his overalls and pulled out a key that had been provided by one of his American compatriots, a true believer who had been working at the center for months in preparation for this glorious day – the day that everything changed for America and, ultimately, for the Middle East.

The key slid into the lock and he turned the lever, the door squeaking as he stepped inside the large room, machinery and large pumps mounted on concrete bases vibrating as they thrummed. At the far end giant fans powered the air up into the arena, massive filters cleaning it as it was re-circulated and mixed with fresh air sucked in from outside through ducts.

When he'd questioned the Russian worm about the best delivery system, al-Diin had been particularly interested in a scenario like the one he now faced, where he had a single canister that he could position to flood the stadium with the lethal agent. The disbursal through the ventilation system would ensure that everyone in the hall was exposed within ten to fifteen minutes maximum, although the Russian had felt that the job would be done within five.

He studied the endless rows of ten-foot-high pump assemblies and saw the area he was looking for – a row of huge fans that were driving the air up into the coliseum. He moved to the center one and kneeled, then opened the tool box and extracted the blue canister, disguised as an aerosol can of solvent. Deft fingers removed the top and then screwed it into the female end of a valve assembly. After checking to make sure it was tight, he reached into the toolbox, lifted out the false bottom, and extracted a compact silenced pistol and a device the Russian had provided – a small regulator that operated on a digital timer, which would release the canister contents when the timer reached zero. He stuck the gun into his belt and then carefully threaded the regulator onto the valve assembly, twisting it to ensure it was secure.

After studying the fan lineup for a moment, he stepped up onto the concrete curb and placed the device behind the metal cowling that protected the center fan's whirring blades, and as he'd practiced numerous times when testing the timer, punched in a series of numbers. Peering at the little LED readout, he nodded and then flipped the red switch that would activate it. The timer began counting down, and he stood and turned, moving hurriedly to the tool box and closing it before picking it up and trotting for the door.

He was fifteen feet away from it when the handle rattled as someone tried the lock, and then the metal by the door jamb exploded inward as three bullets destroyed the latch. He ducked behind some machinery just as the door slammed inward from a kick, and a tall blond man in a charcoal blazer and black slacks stepped into the room, holding a pistol.

Alan's grip on the weapon was unwavering. He swung around, searching for a target, then walked slowly to the fans. Halfway there a voice called from behind one of the large pumps.

"Stop where you are, and slowly, carefully, put the gun on the floor."

Alan froze and debated his next move, but then the voice spoke again.

"I have a gun on you. Either do as I say, or I shoot you in the back."

Alan slowly kneeled and placed his weapon on the floor, then held his hands above his head.

Al-Diin stepped out from behind the pump, his small pistol trained on Alan. "Turn around."

Alan did as instructed.

"Who are you?" the terrorist demanded in accented English.

"What do you care?" Alan asked in fluent Arabic.

"I asked you a question. Who do you work for?" He raised the pistol, waving it at him for emphasis. "Who are you? You aren't Homeland Security. No. Not American." His eyes widened. "Could it be...Mossad?"

Alan didn't respond to the question.

"You have no concept what you're dealing with, do you?" the terrorist asked, more statement than question. "You think you're saving Israel, and the world, from terrorism, right? Fool. You know nothing."

"I know enough to have this building filled with agents. You'll never get away with this."

"Perhaps. But my guess is that you haven't told the Americans anything, am I right?"

Alan's eyes narrowed, but he stayed silent.

"Ah. As I thought. If you had, I would have heard about it." Al-Diin regarded Alan's look of surprise. "That's right, you cretin. You have no idea what you're involved in. No idea." He shook his head in disgust. "I would have heard because I'm working for the Americans."

"What?"

"Yes, I thought that would get your attention. I suppose it doesn't matter, because I will have to shoot you anyway. But this isn't about anything you think it is. You think I'm some rogue terrorist, eh? You're an idiot, and your masters are fools. You are pawns in a much larger game than anything you realize," al-Diin hissed.

Alan calculated how many steps it would take to reach the terrorist.

"Don't even think it. Everyone in this building is already dead. You. Everyone here. The agent will disburse in a few minutes, and the awaited terrorist strike will have taken place. But you don't know why, do you? Of course not. You're too busy believing that it's all about you. So what do you have to say to that – that I work for the Americans?"

"I don't believe you work for the government."

"Oh, maybe not the government, but the power behind it, certainly. You really don't have a clue. I'll give you a hint. It's all about Iran."

"What is this, some fantasy about oil? I can read that all over the internet. You're lying," Alan ventured.

"Not oil. Money. The dollar."

"What about it?"

"Iran is dangerous, but not the way you think. It means to stop trading in dollars for oil. It's pushing for a gold-backed dinar. If that happens, the dollar is doomed, and the American bankers will lose all the power they accumulated after World War II, when the dollar became the world's reserve currency – and oil began trading in dollars."

"Wait. So all this is to justify overthrowing the Iranian government?"

"It's bigger than that, but you have the right idea. There were two other countries in the Middle East that had national central banks that weren't owned by the private bankers behind the Federal Reserve. They too wanted a gold-backed dinar for their oil. Both have been overthrown: Iraq and Libya. Iran is the only one left." Al-Diin spat on the floor by his feet and gestured with the pistol. "It may be about oil, but what it's really about is protecting American power, and its currency, at all costs. America can't invade Iran as things are. Claims about its nuclear development are too easily proved false by international inspections, which is what Iran is pushing for. American claims about it developing nuclear capability are viewed as more suspect than the claims about weapons of mass destruction in Iraq. But if there's an Iranian-sponsored terrorist attack... Iran falls, a puppet government is installed, and the demands for a gold-backed currency for oil stop."

"You're saying that all these people have to die..."

"So Iran can be attacked and the dollar continues to be oil's denominator. In..." al-Diin consulted his watch, "about four minutes. By which time I will be out of the building, and you'll be meeting your maker."

Alan processed the revelation. "You're a monster."

"No. I'm a pragmatist. And you're a dead man. Now turn around. Now!" al-Diin screamed. Alan pivoted, frantically looking for anything he could use as a weapon, but only saw his gun on the floor. Al-Diin raised the pistol, and then a series of pops echoed in the room, emanating from the doorway. The terrorist's head blew apart as three slugs tore into it and he dropped like a bag of rocks. Alan spun and found himself facing a thin blond man he'd never seen before.

"He's got the agent somewhere in here. We have to stop him," Alan exclaimed.

The man lowered his weapon. "Have you searched for it? Where is it?" he demanded. Alan registered a slight Russian accent. The man gestured with his gun at Alan's on the floor. "Pick up your weapon and let's find this damned thing before it's too late."

Alan turned and was approaching his pistol when the blow struck him on the back of the neck, and the room went dark as he slumped unconscious to the floor.

CHAPTER 36

The first thing he noticed was the pain, throbbing through his skull like he'd been hit by a truck. He reached and felt a bump on the back of his head the size of an egg, and he winced when he touched it.

Struggling, he pushed himself to his feet and swayed for a few seconds before remembering where he was and what he was doing. The biological weapon. Al-Diin dead.

The mystery Russian must have clocked him – but why? Why knock him out?

Alan glanced at his watch. He'd been out for almost four minutes.

That seemed significant for some reason, and then it hit him.

The agent.

He looked around frantically.

Where was the logical place to put it?

Fans.

He lurched towards the gargantuan spinning blades and heard a beep when he was still ten feet away. His eyes widened as a loud hiss came from the center fan, and he ran towards it unsteadily...and saw the canister emitting with a sigh the last of its contents as a fine mist into the air. The cloud was sucked instantly into the fan and disappeared. Alan swung back towards the door. There had to be an off switch of some sort. Had to be some way to kill the power and stop the ventilation from discharging death into the stadium – into the unsuspecting lungs of the innocents.

The room spun and he lost his footing, grabbing at one of the pumps for support as he fell, and then a blanket of tranquility descended upon him and everything faded.

❧

When Alan came to again, he remembered everything instantly. Reaching to his side, he groped at a nearby pipe to haul himself to his feet. Still dizzy, he moved slowly so he didn't pass out again. He checked his watch. He had been out for ten minutes.

Which meant that they were all dead. Everyone in the building. It was just a matter of time.

He pulled his cell phone from his jacket pocket and held it up, the screen blurry as he fought to focus.

No signal.

Of course not. They were underground in the sub-basement, high-density concrete enveloping them.

Alan staggered to the battered door and then out into the deserted corridor, the clamor of the generators and the music reverberating giddily in the background, a reminder that everyone in the building believed things were fine. He climbed the stairs slowly, each step an effort, and at the top used the wall for support as he edged towards the main area. He had no plan. Just get to the security team and warn them.

That they were all dead.

He pushed the service door open and stepped through, his footing unsteady from the effort, and then spotted two security guards by one of the oversized glass panels near the entrance.

"Hey. You two. Do you have a radio?" he called.

They exchanged glances and then one of them held his up.

"Why? Who are you, and what bus ran you over? You okay, man? What happened?"

"You need to call Homeland Security immediately. There's been a...there's been an incident. Something released into the ventilation system. It's not safe. Terrorist attack."

Their faces got wary, then fearful.

"Who are you? Is this some kind of a joke? Are you drunk or something?" the smaller of the two demanded. "This kind of shit will get you arrested and put away for a long time. You can't joke about—"

"It's no joke. There's a man, shot, downstairs in the ventilation room. A terrorist. The one on the videos. Something got released into the fans. I don't want to panic everyone, but you need to radio this in immediately." Alan pulled out his passport. "I'm with the Foreign Service. Make the call. Now."

The men's eyes widened and the one with the radio raised it to his lips with a trembling hand and spoke into it, his voice panicked.

Sixty seconds later Alan was surrounded by police, guns drawn.

He raised his hands over his head and waited patiently as they frisked him, then an older officer approached him, ready to begin with questions. Alan cut him off.

"You need to get Homeland Security. Now. You have a situation. This is not a joke. Notify them immediately, or you're going to have a riot on your hands and the city in chaos," Alan said, and then repeated his story about the ventilation system and the terrorist attack.

The officer moved away from the rest without speaking and then used his radio.

Ten minutes later Alan was cuffed in a holding area set up inside the building, as hazmat-suited figures ran chains through the doors so nobody could get out except through the main entrance. A gray-haired man in a rumpled suit with a grim expression approached him on the opposite side of the glass, standing on the sidewalk, and then one of the police inside the building un-cuffed Alan and handed him a cell phone. He held it to his ear, and the man outside introduced himself as Agent Ryker, with Homeland Security, and began peppering him with questions.

"We found the body downstairs, and the device. Who are you?" Ryker demanded.

"Check my ID. I'm with the Israeli consulate."

"I saw that. I'm guessing Mossad. Am I close?"

Alan didn't say anything.

"You know how bad this is, right?" Ryker asked.

"I'm completely aware. I was exposed. So I'm in the same boat as everyone else in here. You don't have to tell me how bad it is."

"What happened?"

Alan ran through the story again.

"This is going to be a nightmare. Trying to do crowd control on fourteen thousand people who will all want to get out at once. We don't know if this is contagious or not, so we can't allow anyone out..."

"May I make a suggestion?"

Ryker studied Alan's face. "Sure. What do I have to lose?" he responded glumly.

"The best way to ensure everyone doesn't try to exit at once would be to tell them that there's a hazard outside. A chemical spill or a bio-hazard on the street surrounding the coliseum that you're trying to clean up."

Ryker considered the suggestion, and then nodded slowly. "That's not bad. At least it'll buy us a little time to test the weapon canister and see what we're dealing with."

"The only way to keep everyone from trying to escape is to have them begging to stay safe inside."

Ryker nodded again. "You need to talk to anyone on your end?" he asked. "Technically you're not under arrest. You have diplomatic immunity. But I would appreciate some cooperation."

"I understand. I have a cell phone. It was confiscated along with the rest of my things. Please give me back my phone and my passport."

"All right." Ryker gave Alan a warning look. "I don't have to tell you to be discreet."

"No, I think by now I got that."

Twenty minutes later the ice show was interrupted by an announcement over the sound system about a hazard outside the stadium, warning everyone to stay seated while the authorities cleaned it up. The ice show then resumed for the final hour's performances. There were a few isolated outbursts of panic or outrage, but for the most part people were more annoyed at being delayed going home than anything. Crowd control was handled by the security forces that were already inside, while outside the National Guard was deployed, along with every hazardous materials team in the county and several thousand police and firefighters.

Alan got through to the director on his cell and explained the situation. There wasn't a lot either man could add to his dry report. The director sounded deflated when he wished Alan the best and hung up. It wasn't comforting.

Minutes ticked by, and then hours. After three had gone by, Ryker returned, bringing an entourage of serious-looking men inside the building, and confronted Alan. "Tell me what the hell is going on here."

"You seem upset that I, and a stadium full of women and children, aren't dead yet."

"The canister was clean. There was no agent," Ryker stated flatly.

Alan nodded. "I figured that out. I'm not dying. I'm pretty good at putting puzzle pieces together."

"What happened to it?"

Alan shook his head. "How would I know? Obviously something went very wrong for the bad guys. Crisis averted."

Ryker scowled at Alan, an angry tic twitching his left eye. "If there wasn't a dead terrorist downstairs with his prints all over the canister, I would arrest you, diplomatic immunity or not. You had a phony badge and were carrying a gun."

"But as you point out, there *is* diplomatic immunity, so it's a moot point. Look, we got lucky on the bio-agent. Sometimes that happens. You might want to say a little prayer of thanks tonight, because it doesn't happen often." Alan looked around at the crowd outside, finally being allowed to go home. "And this was a good place to get lucky, I hope you know."

Two men in their forties with a military bearing approached from down the hall and then stood silently in the corner of the room, arms folded, staring at Alan.

"What about this mystery man who shot Saif al-Diin? Can you describe him again?" Ryker ordered.

"I already told you. He was maybe five-eleven or so, thin, blondish, or maybe blond-gray hair. Wearing jeans and a brown leather jacket. No distinguishing features. And he struck me as Russian. That was the accent. It was subtle, but there."

"Russian. And he just walked in, blew al-Diin away, and clobbered you. Just like that," Ryker summarized skeptically.

Alan tentatively touched the bump on his head. "Pretty much just like that. And then I passed out."

The two new arrivals exchanged glances with Ryker.

"Tell me about your interaction with the terrorist again. What did he say?" Ryker asked.

"We've been through this. He said that he was going to kill everyone, that it was going to be the biggest event in the history of the country, that Allah was good...all the usual crap."

"And didn't you say something about Iran?"

"That was sort of confusing. He did mention Iran. But he wasn't very clear – at least not to me."

"Did he say that Iran was behind the attack?"

"No. That wasn't it. I...I'm sorry. The moments just before I blacked out are still kind of hazy. Like they're there, but when I try to focus on them, they sort of...flit away and go out of focus."

"So you don't know for sure whether he said that Iran was behind this?" one of the two new arrivals demanded from his position in the corner.

"I told you. I'm sorry. I thought I was clear. He in no way intimated that Iran was behind it. He just babbled something about Israel and Iran, and then the Russian came in and shot him. End of story."

Ryker's radio crackled, and he listened and then muttered into it. He looked up at Alan and shook his head. "I need to keep you a little longer. I hope that's not a problem."

"Well, actually, it is. I've sustained a blow to my head; I'm experiencing dizziness, memory loss, and disorientation; and I've said several times to your people that I need to get to a hospital. I think, almost three hours into this, I need to get a CT scan, not sit here so that I can be interrogated over and over – especially since I'm the one who spotted al-Diin in the first place. So I'm going to have to respectfully decline. I need medical attention, and you have no authority to hold me – isn't that correct? Am I missing anything?"

Ryker approached Alan until his nose was a foot away. "I can do anything I want. I can detain you without explanation for months. Do not screw with me. Your story about why you were here and how you spotted al-Diin is complete bullshit. I will hold you until I get straight answers, and that means the whole truth."

A frown flitted across Alan's face. "I spoke with the Israeli consulate a few minutes ago. They're sending people here. They know I'm here, and know that I've been cooperating, and also know I need urgent medical attention. So you have a choice. Either let me go when they arrive, or cause an international incident with severe diplomatic repercussions by bullying a friendly ally who just saved your ass. To me, the choice is clear, but if you want to play hardball, I'll request an attorney, clam up, and then sue everyone and everything for reckless endangerment, given my medical situation. And since I've told you, on the record, that I need medical attention, I presume if you continue to decline me access to it, I can sue you personally, because you're definitely not doing this by the book. I get the feeling it's because you don't like something about me. Maybe that I'm Israeli? I wonder how that will play in the press? 'U.S. Government violates diplomatic rights of Israeli hero.' I have a feeling it would be a career ender, Ryker. You sure you want to go out like that?"

Ryker's radio crackled with static, interrupting the stand-off, and he listened to a few sentences and then spoke softly into the device before moving back to Alan.

"There are two diplomats from the Israeli consulate here to take you to the hospital," Ryker fumed.

Alan nodded. "And my passport? I obviously have my phone…"

Ryker glared at the two men in the corner and then reached into the inside pocket of his jacket and retrieved Alan's passport. He handed it to him without saying a word.

Another officer by the door motioned to Alan, and he moved towards him, without looking back. They pushed through the door and then walked slowly down the long corridor to where the consular officials were waiting.

Ryker shook his head and sighed. "What do you think?" he asked the two men.

The taller scowled.

"He's lying."

CHAPTER 37

Washington D.C., United States of America

The club door swung open and the older man entered, then stalked to the usual room without saying a word. Inside, a pall of cigarette smoke drifted over the table, the air-conditioning struggling to clear the air. He sat down in his customary seat and exhaled noisily.

"This is a disaster," he said simply.

"We're still trying to get details, but it doesn't look good," a sweating, porcine bald man said from a corner, tapping furiously at a laptop computer.

"What happened?"

"It looks like the agent was deployed...but it was harmless. We don't know what to make of it."

"Well, I do. We got screwed. Why didn't we just get something from one of our own sources? Why again did we jeopardize this entire operation by buying it from this Russian?" the older man asked, his tone menacing.

Another man, youngish, in his late thirties, put his pen down and sighed.

"It was a good call. We couldn't have anything trace back to us. That would have been worse than what we're facing now. It had to come from a third party – one that would likely be perceived as an ally of Iran."

"That's always the problem with theory, isn't it? When it collides with fact?" the older man spat.

"Nobody's happy about this. But rather than recriminations, I would suggest we start thinking contingencies. This can still be used to further our purposes. A terrorist attempt – albeit unsuccessful due to the crack response of our intelligence apparatus – occurred, targeting innocent women and children. The public outrage will still be significant."

"But not nearly the same as if it had been successful. We all know that. And yes, we need to focus on making an omelet now that we have a bunch of broken eggs. But this could be the difference between success and failure. The international community isn't going to just step out of the way and let us invade Iran on a failed attempt, no matter how much spin we use. We've already been politely called liars by the atomic energy people when the intel we provided them on Iranian nuclear malfeasance turned out to be false. Gentlemen, after Iraq, we don't have the benefit of everyone believing us automatically. We played that card with the WMDs that never materialized. We don't get to double dip with another of the largest oil producers in the Middle East. No, we have a serious problem. I'm telling you that we're on perilously thin ice with this." The older man reached for a pitcher and poured himself a glass of water, ignoring the tumblers of scotch in front of several of the men. "So what have we got?"

"Reports are being disseminated calling this the largest attempted terrorist attack in history, outraged demands for action from all our usual suspects are pouring in, and the media is portraying it as 'suspected Iran-sponsored terrorist Saif al-Diin' on most channels. We're hoping that can create enough traction so that we—"

"The Russians, French, and Germans will say it's bullshit and speculation, and that nothing actually happened. And they'll be right. Sure, this will play well within our borders, but we won't get a get-out-of-jail card elsewhere." The older man shook his head.

"The President will be issuing a strongly worded statement within an hour."

"Big deal. Let me guess. 'Terrorism is bad. We will not rest until these bastards are all brought to justice. Those sponsoring it will be dragged kicking and screaming,' blah blah blah. All good, but we don't have any footage of babies lying in rubble. No corpses, no free lunch. Maybe we can make it work, but my gut says we blew this round. Not to mention blew half a billion dollars for nothing."

"Let's assume you're right. You have to agree that we're much closer now with the videos and this attack than we were. Maybe we're not in the end zone quite yet, but we're at the five yard line. So we plan something else that will tip the scales," the younger man said.

The older man rubbed his face and eased back in his chair, then leaned forward and placed both hands flat on the table, palms down.

"There's a lot at risk, gentlemen. We cannot afford to let this get away from us. And I get the sense it has. I hope nobody has any plans for the next few days, because we're going to be sitting in this room doing damage control. Now get the White House on the line and let me fine tune the speech. If we're going to turn a punt into a run, we're going to need to be all over the details on this one." The older man coughed. "And put the cigarettes out."

👁️

Moscow, Russian Federation

Jet took a final scan of the empty street before she ran headlong down the block and leapt at the side of the building, using the long stone planter as a launch pad as she vaulted up. Her hands found a hold on the decorative steel beams that stretched skyward above the eleven-foot-high concrete and glass wall of the ground floor, and she pushed up with her toes against the rough mortar, fighting for a grip. She inched up, little by little, and then her feet were pressed against either side of the steel girders, using the four-foot gap between the beams to create friction, stopping her from slipping down.

She took a deep breath and pulled herself up, and then began moving higher, climbing one story, then another, then another. As she passed the tenth story the breeze got stronger, tugging at her black top and pants, her backpack secure. Up she climbed, past the fifteenth, then the twentieth, then the twenty-fifth, a fly on the side of the post-modern tower, moving relentlessly heavenwards, invisible to anyone watching from below – not that there were many on the street in that district after it had gotten dark at seven.

At the top, she gripped the girder that ran around the lip and swung her torso up, seeming to defy gravity, then locked a leg around it and pulled, heaving her body over the edge. The motion sensors measured for movement in the air above the building, but not on the roof – the flaw in the ultra-expensive security precautions. She understood the reasoning: They wanted an early warning if something was dropping towards the roof; it would have to get through that invisible envelope to alight on the roof, by which time alarms would have already sounded, so roof sensors would – normally – be redundant.

She dropped three feet from the lip that encircled the edge to the hard, flat surface and took stock. Her watch said it was eight-ten. She didn't have

212

much time, although she was prepared to spend the night if Grigenko left early – but she was hoping to get this over with now.

Alan had called earlier to give her summary of the failed attack on the sports venue and had filled her in on the latest, including the terrorist's revelation about the false flag nature of the attack and the purported real reason behind it. Nothing surprised her anymore – she'd seen enough conniving and double-dealing to last her twenty lifetimes, so the idea that shadowy figures that were the real power in a government would contrive an attack on their own population in order to further their ends required no suspension of disbelief. It was an all-too-familiar pattern throughout human history, and there were no new ideas.

Jet scanned her surroundings and saw the helipad circle and next to it the access door to the lower floors. She knew better than to try to break in that way, though – she'd seen the blueprints and the electronics schematic, and knew there were both motion detectors and thermal sensors in the stairwell that led down to Grigenko's suite.

She crept to a ventilation duct, shrugged her backpack off, and removed a tool kit and a blow torch before cutting her way through the thin metal housing. Five minutes later she was in. She repacked the kit and slid it back into the sack, repositioning the ultra-compact Hechler & Koch MP7A1 submachine gun and silencer nearer the zippered opening for easy access.

Checking the time again, she removed a set of night vision goggles and pulled the strap over her head, adjusting it carefully, the thin coating of neoprene she'd affixed to the hardware to silence any inadvertent bumping spongy under her fingers. With a final glance around the roof, she flipped the goggles over her eyes and turned them on, then dropped headfirst into the shaft, using her hands to control her slide down the stainless steel chute.

CHAPTER 38

A tiny fiber optic camera on a telescoping rod slid through the grate that pumped fresh air into the gym and turned slowly, surveying the space, having done the same in the office area and come up blank before moving to the workout area. Movement caught its attention and after a few seconds of scanning, the camera snaked back up into the grate, soundless as smoke.

Grigenko stood in the center of his gymnasium, sweating and panting slightly, his nightly hour-long martial arts workout nearly concluded. He admired the sculpted shape of his arms and the steel ridges of his abdominal muscles in one of the floor-to-ceiling mirrors and then flung himself across the room in a series of flying kicks and flips. When he landed, he corrected his form automatically and made a mental note that he needed to work on those more. Something about the mid-air twist when spinning to the left was weak; he knew that most people favored either turning to the left or the right, and he automatically registered which in his adversaries – knowing which they would defer to could mean the difference between victory and defeat. He had worked sedulously to correct any preference and considered himself ambidextrous now, but the kicks were still a problem.

He steadied himself and then tried the entire sequence again, but reversing direction on each move, and when he landed he had a look of smug satisfaction on his face.

Better. Much better.

"Not bad for an amateur."

He spun and found himself face to face with Jet, who was glaring at him with luminescent green eyes, her finger on the trigger of the H&K MP7A1 submachine gun trained on his bare torso.

"How did you get in here?" he demanded, and then his expression changed as he recognized her. "Ah. Stupid question. I presume I have the dubious honor of meeting the infamous Jet? Mossad whore and serial killer?"

"You're not as stupid as you look. Of course, that would be hard, but it's still always entertaining when the walking dead speak. Your father cried like a blubbering baby when I killed him. Really an ugly display of character weakness. I see you take after him," she commented without emotion.

"Big talker when you have a gun on an unarmed man."

"Sort of like yours were when they came for me in Uruguay. I mopped the floor with them, by the way. I guess you heard. Never send boys to do a man's job."

Grigenko sneered but said nothing.

"I heard about the failure of the device you sold the terrorists. You couldn't even do that right, could you?" she taunted.

"Ha. I got half a billion dollars and gave them nothing but hope. The best transaction I've done yet. You think I'm stupid enough to sell them a weapon that would be inevitably traced back to me? The world isn't big enough to evade the heat that would bring. Who do you think called the Israelis, anyway? Are you really that dim?"

She nodded slowly. "Why the Mossad and not the CIA?"

"Because I knew there was a good chance the Americans would try to take him alive. The Mossad doesn't have those squeamish sentiments. But just in case, I also sent my own man to finish the job, which he ended up having to do, leaving the Mossad agent to pick up the pieces." He cracked a feral grin. "So what is it going to be? Shoot me in the head or the torso? Although with that little pop gun, you could probably cut me in two. Oh, and congratulations on getting past all the security. I guess it wasn't worth what I paid for it."

"Yet another stupid decision by a sub-par punk who inherited Daddy's money but can't fit into his shoes. Which is a joke, given what a pussy he was. A coward. Like his twin brother. Did you know I cut his brother's guts out and held his heart up for him to see with his last breath? Did Papa ever tell you? No? I see by your eyes that he didn't. Too bad. I know it was a big reason he was stupid enough to come after me in the first place, which resulted in him finishing up as an oily smudge on the runway in Nice. Lots of bad decision-making in your inbred family, I suppose."

He took a few steps back and held his arms out at his sides. "I wonder if your retarded daughter will live long enough to be trading blowjobs for a crack rock by the time she's twelve? I was considering leaving her alive and letting one of my South American contacts have her. Worse than just snuffing her. Then again, I've read your dossier, so I know you know what that's like. Foster dad and all. Must have been rough, but look at the bright side – you've probably got pretty good technique with all the practice." He leered at her. "So are you going to shoot me? I know you don't have the balls to fight me without a gun. Cowardly whores never do. I've met hundreds like you, and you're all the same. Weak. Pathetic."

Jet tried to force the rage and sting of his words away, but for a brief instance her anger got the better of her. She set the gun down and shrugged off the backpack, then stood and took three steps towards him.

"I really don't need a gun to take you down. I killed your father and his brother without breaking a sweat. I see no reason not to add you to the list." She raised her hands in a classic defensive position. "Come on, bitch boy, give it your best shot. Let's see what all your expensive lessons have taught you. You'll find taking on someone who knows what they're doing isn't as much fun as beating up people who are paid to lose."

Grigenko smirked – he'd gotten her to make her first bad decision by stoking her anger. She was making a classic mistake and allowing it to color her behavior.

"You should have shot me," he said as he approached. She took three more steps, closing the gap.

"Why waste the bullets on a nothing like you? I've taken down better before breakfast. Come on, pussy boy. Bring it," she snarled in Russian, then waited, bouncing on the balls of her feet.

When his offense came, it was better than she'd thought it would be, a combination of karate and her own specialty, Krav Maga – the Israeli martial art taught to members of the Mossad as one of their core disciplines.

She parried the blows and got in several brutal strikes, finishing with a flying roundhouse kick that nearly knocked his head off. Blood drooled from the corner of his mouth as he sized her up with new respect, and then he brushed it aside with his hand and licked it off his fingers. She had gotten a feel for him already, and he was strong – brutally strong – but he favored approaches that leveraged that strength, so his likely tactics were predictable.

"Looks like you got a booboo there, bitch boy," she taunted. Whenever possible, she wanted to keep him off-balance and operating from pride and rage – something she realized belatedly he had done masterfully with her.

Now she needed to keep him away from the gun. She had absolutely no doubt that he would try for it if he thought he could. "I thought you were going to bring shock and awe. You hit like a schoolgirl. Probably should have spent more time practicing and less time shaving your chest and admiring yourself in the mirror."

The next attack was sudden. She had barely spat out the final words of her taunt when he launched into the air, and she crouched and delivered a vicious strike to his groin with her right arm, then followed it up with a double blow to his kidneys. She had experienced that strike before, and the pain would be intense, blinding for a few seconds. Seizing the advantage, she spun and kicked him in the side of the head, his ear smashing against her Doc Martens boot. She was just preparing for the final blow in the series when he caught her by surprise with a spin and a lunging elbow strike, followed by a glancing punch to her jaw.

The sound of her ribs cracking was audible, and Grigenko smirked as he shook his head to clear it. The pain from Jet's fractured ribs was severe, but she had fought through worse. More alarming was that he had landed the devastating blow in the first place. Her jaw throbbed where he had clipped her, and she tasted the tell-tale saltiness of blood.

"I should have known not to go for the groin. I assumed you had balls." She spat a red stain onto the floor, and then launched her own attack as he was still recovering from the pain.

He parried her strikes, turned, and tried to land two of his own, but she dodged them and then pivoted and struck his chest full force with her knee, and heard ribs crack as well – but these were higher, potentially deadly if she could land another blow to make them compound, hopefully driving one through a lung. He delivered a powerful strike to her already-injured side, but she ignored the agony and drove her boot down hard onto the arch of his foot, snapping several of the bones and drawing a groan from him. His hands were swinging down to break her collarbone when she pounded the back of her head into his face with jarring force and felt a spray of warm blood on the back of her neck. She evaded the collarbone strike by dropping to the floor and then bashed his knee with a precisely targeted blow, as she had many times before, breaking boards and bricks in karate practice.

Grigenko was already falling to one knee, obviously severely incapacitated, the shattered foot and ribs dropping him. She leapt to her feet and stood over him, then backed up four strides and threw herself through a series of airborne flips and twists, finishing by slamming her boot into his chest with her full weight, driving the already splintered ribs through his lungs, and one through his heart. He toppled backwards, a crimson river streaming from his nose and mouth, gasping for breath through the gurgling blood, when a scream from behind Jet shattered the room's silence.

"Noooooooooooo!" Grigenko's mother stood twenty feet away, a Makarov pistol clenched in her shaking hand, pointed at Jet, who slowly turned to face her. Grigenko was drowning even as his heart pumped blood into his abdominal cavity, and he was barely able to raise his head for a final look at his mother before he collapsed and his head struck the floor with a *thunk*, the burbling of his labored breath increasing in volume.

"What have you done? You miserable bitch. I'll kill you, and I'll kill your whore daughter too. I'll make sure she's raped for weeks before—"

Grigenko's mother's vitriol was cut off as her son exhaled a groaning death rattle, his body violently convulsing behind Jet. Her pistol strayed as her attention was momentarily drawn to him, and when she looked back at Jet it was with puzzled surprise – the hilt of one of Jet's throwing knives quivering with her heart beat as it protruded from the base of her throat. Jet watched as she grabbed at the knife with a palsied hand, trying to pull it free, and then with the last of her energy brought the ugly little pistol up to shoot Jet.

Jet threw herself into the air in a flurry of forward somersaults, the final one converting into a scissor kick that knocked Grigenko's mother flat on her back, her weapon skittering harmlessly a few feet away. Jet stood, clutching her side, and then leaned over the dying woman and spat blood onto her hatred-contorted face.

"Rot in hell with your bastard son, and know that he failed. He was never good enough. Lousy genes."

The older woman's eyes fluttered and Jet saw the familiar fade in her focus as life fled her body; and then the crash of a door and running footsteps from the far end of the suite signaled that she only had seconds left to escape.

CHAPTER 39

The guards stopped at the gymnasium door, fumbling for the light switch in the now-darkened space. The overhead lamps flickered on a few seconds later, and the men stood gawping at the corpses on the floor, the blood pooling around their master stark evidence of their failure to protect him. They crept cautiously into the gym, weapons sweeping the cavernous empty room, and then the leader pointed at the door that led to the roof stairwell, warning the guards to silence with a curt gesture.

The men moved on stealthy feet towards the door. The leader's radio hissed static and a man's gruff baritone voice erupted from it.

"Dmitri. There's an alarm sounding down here from the roof door. It looks like someone's gotten in. Repeat. There's been a breach on the roof door. The motion detectors are going crazy. This is not a drill. Again, this is NOT a drill."

The leader turned the volume down, cursing the timing of the downstairs security man's alert, and then returned his attention to the door. His men looked at him, unsure of how to proceed, pistols searching for a non-existent threat.

His subordinate inched closer and leaned into him.

"What do we do? They're dead," he whispered, his eyes fearful – not of who might have killed Grigenko and his mother, but from the dawning realization that they had allowed one of the most high-profile oligarchs in Moscow to be slain on their watch.

"No shit. We go find whoever did this and return the favor. That's what we do. Now, you," he gestured to his second-in-command, "take Sasha, and on my signal, open the door and we'll rush it. One of you on either side, and then we'll go up the stairs," he motioned to the other four men.

They did as instructed, and on the count of three, flung the door wide, anticipating a rain of bullets or a grenade. They waited a few seconds, and when nothing materialized, Dmitri ran for the door, his men following him, their specialized Spetsnaz training kicking in as they prepared for a gun battle.

When they reached the roof exit, the leader listened intently, trying to get a sense of what awaited on the other side of the heavy steel door. Hearing nothing, he took a breath and then pushed it open and threw himself out onto the flat roof, rolling as he did to make a more difficult target in the gloom.

Two of his men followed him out and performed a methodical sector sweep, searching for the intruders.

After sixty seconds yielded nothing, Dmitri squinted in the dark, hunting for anything that would give them a clue. On the far edge he saw a glint on one of the steel girder lip edges. He ran towards it and peered over the side, looking down thirty stories at the empty street.

A black rappelling cord vibrated against the lip, and he could make out a figure far below, dropping at nearly the speed of gravity. With a wicked grin, he reached into his back pocket and withdrew a switchblade, then with a deft movement, snapped open the blade and sliced through the line.

❧◦❧

Jet saw the guard's head far above her, and against her best instincts, looked down. She was still six stories from the street – a deadly distance to fall. Knowing what would come next, she swung herself sideways just as the cord she'd been suspended from went slack.

She dropped a few feet when her hands and feet gripped a girder, and then the severed end of the rope fell past her to the street below. Jet relaxed her grip and began sliding down, controlling her drop speed with the soles of her feet so she wouldn't tear all the flesh from her hands. Ten seconds later she tumbled to the ground with a roll, simultaneously unclasping the rope from the web belt around her waist as she sprang to her feet.

Gunshots sounded from the corner of the building and ricochets whistled off the sidewalk as she sprinted down the block, reaching behind to her open backpack as she zigzagged away from the shooters. Slugs pounded against the cement as the men on the roof joined the lobby guards in shooting at her. She threw herself flat against the side of the building as she brought the MP7A1 up and sprayed three bursts at the pursuing gunmen, cutting them down before bolting again, running as fast as her legs would carry her.

She tore into the street at the end of the block and a Lexus struck her a glancing blow, knocking her off her feet, still clutching the submachine gun. The driver reflexively slammed on his brakes and pulled to a screeching stop, the car behind him almost flattening Jet as it swerved to avoid the Lexus, and then the driver opened his door to look back at her.

Jet raised her weapon and screamed at him in Russian. "Get out of the car. Now. Or I'll shoot."

The shocked driver raised his hands shakily over his head and stepped out and away from the vehicle, and then turned and ran when she came at him toting the gun. She slid behind the wheel, jammed the transmission into gear, and floored the gas, the wail of sirens now rapidly approaching. It sounded like they were coming straight at her down the street, so she spun the wheel hard left and did a sliding U-turn, the wheels fishtailing and burning rubber in protest as they fought for grip. An oncoming car stood on its horn as it narrowly missed colliding with her, and she stomped on the accelerator, urging the powerful motor to full throttle as she veered away from the near miss.

Two police cars with lights flashing appeared in the distance behind her, and she watched in her side mirror as they pulled to a stop at Grigenko's building. With any luck at all she'd be well clear of the area by the time the Lexus theft was reported, and she'd have ditched the car and would be in the Metro, anonymous among the millions of evening passengers.

She raised a hand and felt her jaw where Grigenko had clocked her – a couple of her teeth were loose, but the blood from the gash inside her mouth where her teeth had sliced her cheek had slowed, so all in all, she was in decent shape. Her ribs hurt, but she knew from experience that the only thing she could do was wrap them and wait for time to work its magic.

Another police car approached from the opposite direction, siren blaring, and then after it passed her it slowed and swung around – the Lexus driver must have grabbed one of the cops at the scene and they'd gotten on the radio. Glancing in the rearview mirror, she estimated that she had eight seconds of lead on it, so she dropped the shifter to low and gunned it, then took a hard right into an alley that ran parallel to a larger boulevard, the engine revving as she floored it.

A hobo jumped out of the way as she hit a garbage can trying to dodge him, and she almost lost control when the wheels hit a large puddle of water that had pooled in a low spot on the cobblestoned surface. Flashing blue lights told her the cop was still behind her, and she knew that trying to outrun him was a fool's errand. The Lexus bucked and she almost took the oil pan out as she flew over an uneven patch and then across a busy street, cars honking as she narrowly missed being T-boned by a delivery truck doing double the speed limit.

She doubted the cops would follow her through the intersection with such recklessness, but she underestimated their tenacity, and after a few moments the squad car re-appeared in her rearview mirror.

Making a split-second decision, she twisted the wheel at the end of the next block and took the car onto the sidewalk, then spun it and counted a few seconds in her head before stabbing the gas again, buckling her seatbelt as the car surged forward. She timed it correctly, and she slammed into the side of the police cruiser just as it emerged from the alley, a shower of glass and metal greeting her efforts as her air bag deployed, cushioning her from the worst of the collision.

Jet threw her door open, pulled herself out of the car, and was halfway down the block, moving at a run, when gunshots from the police vehicle echoed off the buildings and a chunk of brick tore out of the wall next to her.

She dropped to one knee and twisted, letting loose a one-second burst from the submachine gun, peppering the two cars with rounds, and then the weapon fell silent, its magazine empty. She automatically popped the spent one free and slapped a new thirty-round magazine home, and waited for another salvo from the police car.

A few seconds went by with no further shooting, so either one of her bullets had found home or the officers had decided that taking on a fully automatic weapon with pistols was a poor idea. She didn't stick around to find out which, and instead raced for the corner, glancing behind her to confirm that nobody was following her before she disappeared, heading for the Metro station two blocks away.

CHAPTER 40

Alan looked like he'd been dragged behind a tractor when he made it to the international terminal at Los Angeles International Airport, his flight for Buenos Aires via Mexico City ready for take-off in two hours. The harried ticket agent dutifully checked his passport and then issued him a boarding pass, tendering a thank you with a plastic smile that looked painted on. He strode through the departure ticketing area and took an escalator to the second level restaurants, where he opted for one of the nicer of the establishments and ordered a seven-dollar beer from a waitress who seemed annoyed that there were customers.

Once she brought his drink, he dialed Jet's cell phone. She picked up on the third ring.

"How are you?" he asked.

"Little sore. Took a few punches, but I've been through worse. Where are you? It sounds like a riot in the background."

"Close. I'm at the airport. How did it go?"

"No surprises. It's over. Now I just need to get out of here and back to Hannah as soon as possible."

He digested the news. "Any revelations?" he asked.

"He's the one that fingered al-Diin. Tipped off the Mossad because he knew they wouldn't screw around with trying to take the Arab alive," she reported.

"They got that right. But there may be another reason. He might have heard from al-Diin that there was U.S. involvement in the scheme, so he didn't want to chance giving them a nod. Who knows how much of the detail al-Diin passed on to his supporters?"

"Grigenko said he got paid a half billion."

Alan whistled. "That's a lot of shekels."

"I gather that price wasn't an issue. Have you thought about the director any?"

"You know, I have, but the only conclusion I can come to is that if he was somehow trading information to the Russians, that ended once he learned that Grigenko was a suspect in this terror scheme. Whether he's guilty or not we'll never know, and there's not a lot I can do about it either way. But I've rethought my future career plans, and I'm not going to be leading up his secret team anymore. He can find someone else. I've done my share, more than anyone..."

"I'd say you have, and I completely understand your decision. By the way, how's the head?"

"No concussion, thank God. Looks like my thick skull saved me again."

"That's good to hear. So where are you off to?"

"I heard somewhere around Buenos Aires might be nice this time of year."

She hesitated. "Really? What about going back home?"

"I've been doing a lot of thinking. I've been dead for a while, and it feels kind of good. Relaxing. I'm hoping that if I can find a nice girl who's also dead, it might not be such a bad deal..."

"You *have* been doing a lot of thinking. Probably not all of it G-rated, either."

"Guilty. But she also has to be rich, and extremely good-looking. And be able to kick my ass."

"I might know somebody. When will you be there?"

"I'll be on the ground in about eighteen hours. What time is it where you are? About ten o'clock at night? It's eleven a.m. here. When are you going to leave Moscow?"

"Tomorrow. I have a flight through Madrid. Leaves at eight tomorrow night. I'll be taking off about four hours after you touch down."

"You have any interest in hooking up for a glass of wine with a broken-down ex-agent with a bad attitude and sleep deprivation?" he asked playfully.

She paused. "You know what, Alan? There's nothing I would rather do. I'll call you tomorrow once you're on the ground, or you call me. Either way, I'll fill you in on my schedule."

"Sounds like a date. I'll talk to you tomorrow. Safe travels."

"Thanks. I'll have plenty of time to get some sleep. Maybe even dream a little."

"Dreaming is good."

He disconnected and smiled to himself. He had no idea what the future held, but the idea of meeting up with Jet in Buenos Aires felt like the right move. The Mossad could get along without him. The way he felt, it would have to.

The back of his neck prickled like someone was watching him. He turned and scanned the crowd of passengers, and then motion near the down escalator caught his eye. A woman with three unruly children was trying to get one to pick up her bag, and the toddler wasn't in the mood to listen. She was jerking her mother's arm, and then started bawling, crying so loud that it sounded like an air-raid siren. Just behind her, he caught a glimpse of a familiar profile that was hastily turning away from him.

The Russian.

He stood and grabbed his bag, but then a hand clutched his arm – the waitress, demanding payment for the beer. He felt in his pocket for a wad of dollars and threw a ten at her, then hoisted his duffle and looked for the Russian again. A sea of passengers moving up and down the escalators rippled like the surface of a lake in a high wind, and he looked vainly for the man, who had disappeared. Alan stood there, feeling sheepish, his beer half drunk, chasing phantoms in one of the busiest airports in North America, and then a tingle of anxiety hit.

Maybe he'd been seeing things. The doctor who'd examined him had expressed concern over the blow to his head and recommended a week's bed rest – which Alan had cheerfully ignored. Maybe the doctor knew a thing or two. Maybe Alan was hallucinating. Imagining things.

Or maybe the Russian had been there.

He spent the next five minutes scanning the crowd with no success, and then gave up and walked slowly towards the security check point. The line was long and the passengers oddly sheep-like as they were forced to take off their shoes. A seventy-year-old woman in front of him was having trouble with her sandals, and he held her elbow for her, supporting her as she slipped them off before putting them into a plastic crate and sending them through the scanner, manned by a bored three-hundred-pound man who looked ready to fall asleep.

Alan was singled out for an additional screening, no doubt because of his good looks, and submitted to a wand scan by a hirsute woman with an air of perpetual annoyance. Released from the inspection, he took another look behind him at the waiting travelers, but didn't see any Russian hit men.

The waiting area was only half full, the trip to Mexico City apparently not a wildly popular route for this airline, but his nerves were still on edge as he watched his fellow passengers trickle in. An hour later the first boarding call went out and everyone lined up, anxious to get preferential placement for their carry-on luggage in the overhead bins.

He settled into a seat towards the back of the plane and got a notebook-sized pillow from the weary stewardess, then tried to ease his racing thoughts as the plane taxied to the assigned runway and sat in a queue with six other jets.

Eventually it was their turn to take off, and as the g-force of rapid acceleration pushed him into his seat his thoughts were of a different kind of Jet — one that he was looking forward to seeing more than he would have thought possible.

Los Angeles disappeared below him and was replaced by the blue of the Pacific Ocean as they climbed and then gently banked south, and he was struck by the idea that today could be the beginning of a completely new life for him, if that was what he wanted. A life where his future was unknown, but that looked like it might involve another damaged spirit, both of them trying to make their way through a world that had used them and left their bodies washed up on the shore. Maybe that was all there was when you stripped away the veneer — just a brief time on the planet, a few experiences, and the company of those you loved. Maybe he could create something more meaningful than crisis after crisis, assignment after assignment, mission after mission. Maybe with Jet.

Maybe soon.

CHAPTER 41

Jet stood at the airport waiting to board her plane – a flight that would take her away from the madness that was Moscow and back to Uruguay, and to Hannah...and Alan. She had been trying to reach Magdalena on her cell phone for the last two hours, but there was no answer. The woman had probably let the phone run out of charge, or had left it somewhere in the house while she went out with Hannah. Jet tried not to conjure up nightmare scenarios in her head, and instead repeated calming thoughts. There was no more danger. There were no more threats. The world was safe for them again. Life would return to being simple and good.

But a part of her felt a buzz of apprehension. Something seemed wrong. She had no reason to think so, but she felt it in her gut.

She checked the number and called Alan, but there was no answer on his phone, either. Strange. He would have landed three hours ago. At least.

Jet tried Magdalena one more time, but the call simply timed out after six rings. There was no doubt a benign explanation – she needed to stop spinning doomsday visions and take her mind off of her fixation. She would be in Argentina in twenty more hours, and then would be in Uruguay shortly thereafter, reunited with her daughter, ready to slip off to a new beginning somewhere else.

With the Russian dead, the final threat to her existence had been neutralized, and she knew that in order to stay sane she would need to drop out of operational mode and allow her civilian side to take over again. Seeing danger behind every rock and assuming the absolute worst was a viable survival strategy when in the field on a mission, but it was unsuitable for every-day life. What was a boon in an operational environment could quickly become paranoia once back at home, and she made a mental commitment to herself to find that tranquility, that peace, that she'd had before this whole new nightmare had started. For a little while, at least, she'd managed to be calm and happy, her universe limited to caring for her daughter and being normal. Whatever that meant, she knew the difference between the way she reacted under pressure and the easy, relatively carefree outlook she'd had only a few short weeks before.

She fingered the leather pouch around her neck absently as she pulled up the web browser on her phone and scanned the news, trying to distract herself, and read all about the terrorist strike that had resulted in a near miss. It was the lead topic on all the online sites, and she couldn't escape it, along with the strangely similar message that the terrorist had been somehow connected with Iran. Alan's words came back to haunt her, and she remembered his account of what al-Diin had told him.

But that was finished. It wasn't Alan's problem anymore, and it certainly wasn't hers. Her duty was to care for Hannah and keep her safe, see to it that she grew up strong, adjusted, and healthy, not to rid the world of injustice or fight impossible battles with unbeatable foes. She'd leave that to others from here on out. She'd done her duty, and it was questionable that the world was any better for it, but no matter. Jet was going into permanent retirement, once and for all. That was all there was to it.

A voice came over the loudspeaker announcing the commencement of boarding, and the departure lounge roiled with sudden motion as the passengers queued up for the Air France flight. She listened as two French businessmen bickered in front of her, their handmade silk suits gleaming in the artificial light, and felt a pang of envy. Their universe involved jockeying for advantage, negotiating the next deal, counting their profits and bemoaning their losses, insulated from the world she inhabited by the invisible shield of ignorance and privilege. If only she could live in their reality and forget what she knew.

The problem being, of course, that she couldn't purge her memory of the things she'd seen and the deeds she'd done. They would always be there, coloring things, whispering warnings even when there were no more wars left to fight, her enemies vanquished, the menace an illusory phantom, an artifact not based in anything but her imagination.

It was time to put down the sword and walk off the battlefield. She'd put in her time. Now she was flying to a new beginning, filled with possibility, with a chance to start over.

Standing in line, she tried Alan's phone one more time, with no answer, and then dialed Magdalena again with identical results as she moved with the other passengers. The queue inched forward towards the attendant at the gate taking the boarding passes, gifting each new arrival with a plastic smile and a blank stare. Once past the officious woman and in the jetway, heavy rain blew against the steel siding as she walked towards the plane, matching her mood. In spite of her calming mantra, the fact was that she had talked to Magdalena yesterday with no problem. And now, suddenly, both Alan's phone and hers were out of commission? At the same time? Her field instincts screamed in her head that there was no such thing as coincidence, even as her civilian logic argued that of course there was – random, odd events happened all the time, and correlation did not imply causation.

Her heart beat so hard it felt like it would burst out of her chest, and once she'd taken her seat she had to force herself to relax, to lose the tension and the seed of anxiety that threatened to burgeon into full-scale panic. It was over. There was no more danger. Alan's flight had probably been delayed, or his battery had run out of juice. It happened. There were myriad innocent explanations she could think of. Just as there were countless to explain why Magdalena wasn't answering. None of them requiring a belief that something bad had happened, or that the boogeyman was alive and well and coming for her.

The jet backed out of the gate with a creak from the landing gear as the stewardess gave a dispirited safety presentation in French, and Jet pretended interest in her magazine as her mind whirred at ten thousand RPM. There were a million reasons for her not to be worried, and yet all she could think of as the plane leapt into the gray drizzle was that it might not be coincidence that the only two people on the planet she cared about had gone dark while she was poised in the sky like the mythical son of Daedalus, hurtling through space at over five hundred miles per hour towards a destiny that now seemed as tentative as a first kiss.

JET IV – Reckoning pits Jet against the deadliest threat yet – an enemy with endless resources who will stop at nothing to destroy her. From the mountains of Indonesia to the streets of Washington, Jet discovers in a breakneck-paced roller-coaster of action that danger lurks in the unlikeliest of places and nothing is as it seems.

For preview and purchase details visit: RussellBlake.com

AFTERWORD

Parkour is a popular combination of gymnastics, martial arts, and sport practiced by "traceurs." Perhaps its most impressive characteristic is its practitioners' ability to do the seemingly impossible and defy gravity. Some incredible videos of parkour and free running are available for consideration on YouTube. My favorites are Oleg Vorslav, this variety of traceurs, and one of the sports' stars, David Belle.

Anyone who imagines that I stretch the limits of what is physically possible in my JET series might want to watch these clips in their entirety before arriving at a final conclusion.

The conspiracy that acts as the basis for JET III is based on a number of disturbing reports, one of the most accessible being this one.

While not all conspiracy theories hold water, not all are gibberish, either. I would advise interested readers to spend some time researching so they can draw their own conclusions.

ABOUT THE AUTHOR

Russell Blake lives full time on the Pacific coast of Mexico. He is the acclaimed author of the thrillers: *Fatal Exchange*, *The Geronimo Breach*, *Zero Sum*, *The Delphi Chronicle* trilogy (*The Manuscript*, *The Tortoise and the Hare*, and *Phoenix Rising*), *King of Swords*, *Night of the Assassin*, *The Voynich Cypher*, *Revenge of the Assassin*, *Return of the Assassin*, *Blood of the Assassin*, *Silver Justice*, *JET*, *JET II – Betrayal*, *JET III – Vengeance*, *JET IV – Reckoning*, *JET V - Legacy*, *Upon a Pale Horse*, *BLACK*, and *BLACK is Back*.

Non-fiction novels include the international bestseller *An Angel With Fur* (animal biography) and *How To Sell A Gazillion eBooks (while drunk, high or incarcerated)* – a joyfully vicious parody of all things writing and self-publishing related.

"Capt." Russell enjoys writing, fishing, playing with his dogs, collecting and sampling tequila, and waging an ongoing battle against world domination by clowns.

Sign up for e-mail updates about new Russell Blake releases

http://russellblake.com/contact/mailing-list

Made in the USA
Middletown, DE
28 November 2020

25487878R00142